Until Nico

Aurora Rose Reynolds

Contents

This book is dedicated to my brothers from another mother. We may not share the same blood, but I love you both S & W.

They say a man's eyes are a direct link to his soul. When I looked in his
eyes, all I saw was his love for me.

Chapter 1

Sophie

I JUMP WHEN the desk phone starts going off; it never rings, so I'm caught off guard by the shrill sound inside the quiet library. "Middle School Library, Ms. Grates speaking. How can I help you?" I answer on the second ring.

"I found a phone, and this is the number that comes up on the screen when I turn it on," a deep male voice answers. His smooth Southern drawl makes the hairs on my arms stand on end. I pull my handbag out from under the desk and dig through it, looking for my phone. "Hello, did you hear me?" the guy on the other end says more impatiently. I forgot he was even on the line during my search.

"Yes, I'm here. Sorry. It's my cell," I tell him, holding the desk phone between my shoulder and ear.

"Look, I gotta get out of town and won't be back for a week, so can you meet me somewhere?"

"Um, I'm not sure that's a good idea," I reply, worrying my bottom lip.

"Do you want your phone or not?"

"Yes, of course I want my phone," I say, becoming annoyed. What kind of stupid question is that?

"Then you need to meet me so I can give it to you."

"I don't get off work for another hour. Can you meet me after that?" I cross my fingers, hoping he can. I don't know what I would do without my phone for a week—not that I want to call or text anyone, but I was kicking ass in Candy Crush and wanted to beat my last score.

"Jesus, where the fuck do you wanna meet?" he grumbles, making me smile. I don't know why, but it kind of makes me happy I am annoying him.

"Can you meet me out front of Jack's Bar-B-Que in an hour and a half?"

"Sure, fine." I can tell by his tone that he's completely irritated, and I smile even bigger.

"Thanks a lot," I mummer.

"What are you wearing?" he asks, making the grin slide off my face.

"What the hell does that matter?"

"Look," he huffs out, "I have your phone, which means you don't have a phone, right?"

"Right," I repeat like an idiot.

"That means I can't call to tell you when I get there. Therefore, I need to know what you're wearing so I can spot you on the street, right?" I can hear the smile in his voice now.

"I guess that makes sense," I say, and he chuckles, the deepness of his laughter making my belly flutter.

"So, let's try this again. What are you wearing?"

"Oh." I look down at myself, feeling stupid about what I'm going to say to him. "Um...a grey skirt, a white silk blouse... Oh! And I have brown hair," I add at the end, since I don't know how many women might be wearing the same kind of thing I am.

"All right, sweetheart. I'll see you in an hour and a half," he says, and before I have a chance to say anything else, the line goes dead.

I hang up the receiver and toss my bag back under the desk before putting all the books that have been checked in throughout the day back on the shelves.

I started working at the school library a year ago when I moved to Nashville from Seattle. I work here three days a week, and the rest of the time, I work from home as a medical insurance specialist. I like working here; it's quiet, and the pay is good—and it doesn't hurt that I spend most of my day alone.

I finish out my shift by updating the computer system, and after making sure that no one is still browsing the shelves, I lock up. When I leave the building, I notice that most of the staff has left for the day. The parking lot is empty except for my red Audi. I get in my car, turn it on, and flip the button for the convertible top, which takes a second to go back accordion-style and lock into place. The sound of Addicted to Love by Florence and the Machine starts playing as I head downtown.

When I reach the area I'm supposed to meet the guy with my phone, it takes a few minutes to find parking. This part of town is always crazy around this time of day. By the time I reach Jake's, I'm about ten minutes later than I planned on being. I look around, wondering what this guy might look like. There are so many people walking around, so I feel like an idiot for not having asked him what he was wearing too. I pick a spot next to the building and cross my arms over my chest. I want to sit down so badly; my feet are killing me. I have a sick love for heels, and the ones I wore today are paying me back for wearing them for more than a few hours.

I look around and see a guy staring at me. He's about my age, not much taller than my five feet five inches, cute, and wearing a suit and tie. I start to wave to see if he's the one I'm meeting, but then another guy catches my attention. He's about six three and huge, and I don't mean just in height; his body looks like it's been chiseled from stone. He's wearing black boots, washed-out blue jeans, and a white t-shirt, and every piece of skin exposed is covered with tattoos. His ears have those gauge thingies in them. His dark blond hair is cut low on the sides, and the top is in a fauxhawk. His jaw is strong, with a few days of stubble, and his eyes are so blue that they almost look like contacts. He is beautiful in a way that is unusual but no less gorgeous.

His eyes come to me before looking away quickly, and the next second, they come back to me and do a head-to-toe sweep. I gulp at the intense expression on his face. I glance past him to the other guy—or at least try to—but Mr. Tattoo starts towards me, blocking my view. I want to take a step back, but I can't go anywhere. Then I see my phone in his hand.

"This yours?" he asks.

I nod like an idiot. He shakes his head, running his free hand down his face, and then his eyes sweep over me again.

"You have got to be fucking kidding me," he says, seeming upset.

I look down at myself, wondering how I could've offended him. I look normal—or my working-outside-the-house normal. When I'm at home working, I wear baggy sweats I cut off to make shorts or pajama pants that hang off of me along with tank tops or T-shirts. The few days a week I get out of the house, I like to dress up or at least wear heels.

"This cannot be fucking happening," he growls, and I wonder if he is completely crazy.

"What?" I ask, finally finding my voice. I have to tilt my head way back; even in my four-inch heels, he still towers over me.

"You."

"Me, what?" I ask, confused.

"Never mind. Who is this?" He presses the button on my phone, the screen lights up, and a picture of Jamie Dornan wearing nothing but a pair of jeans takes up the screen.

"Um…that's Jamie," I reply, wondering why he is asking but too afraid to ask him; the look on his face isn't very inviting for conversation.

"He your man?"

"I wish," I mumble under my breath and hear him growl.

My head flies back as I search his face; his jaw is ticking, and his knuckles of the hand holding my phone are turning white.

"What does that mean?" he asks.

"That's Jamie Dornan. He's playing Fifty. I don't know him." I feel my cheeks heat up and look down at my feet.

What the hell's wrong with me? Why am I not afraid right now? I have been scared of virtually everything my whole life, and now, when I should be running for cover, I'm not scared at all. Just a little embarrassed.

"I don't have time for this," he says, and I don't know what he's talking about, but I all of a sudden really want my phone out of his hand before he crushes it to smithereens.

When I look up again, I see that he is walking away. My eyebrows come together, and I wonder what he is doing. Then I realize he still has my cell.

"Hey! You can't steal my phone!" I run after him, grabbing his arm.

He looks down at me then stops short. I'm completely caught off guard when he wraps an arm around my waist, pulling me flush against him. His free hand goes into my hair and pulls my head back, and then he kisses me. No, not kisses—he consumes me. My body starts to buzz like someone just plugged me into an electrical outlet, and I start to feel lightheaded. When he pulls his mouth from mine, I gasp, my fingers going to my lips.

"What was that?" I whisper, looking into his eyes.

"What's your name?" he asks, still holding me close.

"Sophie," I tell him, my answer spoken behind my fingers.

His body is as hard as a rock against mine; I can feel every muscle, every contour, and it takes everything in me to keep breathing. I realize this is the first time in my life I have ever felt small, my curvy figure never having allowed it before.

"Sophie," he repeats, standing up to his full height and pulling me with him. I look around and wonder if time has stopped for anyone else. "My name is Nico."

"Of course it is," I say, staring into his amazing eyes, thinking that a guy who looks like him would have a name like that—cool and hot, something that rolls easily off your tongue but is hard to forget.

"I'll see you when I get back into town, Sophie," he says as he lets me go, making sure I'm steady on my feet.

"What?" I ask, looking around again.

"Here's your phone." He hands me my cell, and I'm still a little lightheaded when he starts to walk off again. I watch in a daze as he leaves, but then he turns around to face me from a few yards away. "Sophie?"

"Yeah?"

"Change the picture on your phone," he demands before he turns and disappears into the crowd.

I stand there for a few seconds wondering what just happened. Eventually, I pull myself together enough to make it to my car. When I get there, I realize that I didn't even put the top up or take my bag with me because I had been in such a hurry. I turn quickly to look in my backseat, seeing that my bag is still there. I breathe out a sigh of relief, start my car, and head home.

I live in a small, two-bedroom house just outside of Nashville. I bought it cash with the money I got from my mom's life insurance policy after she passed away. It's not much, but it's home. I pull into my garage and hop out, dragging my bag with me. I need a beer...or a shot of something. I unlock my door, and as I step inside, I kick my shoes off so they go flying down the hall towards my room.

After dropping my bag by the door and the infamous phone on the table, I head to my kitchen, open my freezer, and pull out the bottle of vodka I keep there in case of emergencies. I don't have time to find a shot glass, so I pull a coffee mug down from the cupboard, fill it half full, and shoot it back. Practically coughing up a lung as I try to catch my breath, I fill the glass up again and shakily take another shot. This time, I'm prepared for it, so I hold my breath as the burn fills my chest. I put the bottle away, feeling more relaxed already.

I head to my room, strip off my clothes, and put on a T-shirt. It's early, so I head to the living room, grabbing my phone along the way. I plop down on my couch, put my feet up on the coffee table, turn the TV on, start up the DVR, and press play on The Big Bang Theory. I sit there for a few minutes in a daze, not absorbing even a single second of my favorite show. I look at my cell in my hand, and clicking on the screen, I look at the picture of Jamie. I don't know why, but I can't help but smile as I think of Nico's reaction to it. The tattooed stranger is hot, slightly scary, but definitely interesting.

Nico

I AM HAPPY to be home. I have been gone for four days chasing a skip, and I thought it would have taken me a little longer to catch up with the guy, but luckily for me, he was half moron. I'm shutting off my car in front of my townhouse when my phone rings. I look at the caller ID hopefully; I know it's not going to be sweet Sophie, but that doesn't mean I don't want it to be. Kenton's number flashes on the screen. I'm sure he has another case for me, but right now, that's not happening. I'm going to have a beer and go to bed, and then tomorrow, I'm going over to the local middle school.

"Yeah," I answer, pulling my bag out of the backseat.

"Didn't take you long to catch Johnson."

"That's because he's an idiot," I tell him. "He hid out at his mom's house. You would think he would've learned his lesson after the last two times I've gone after him. Most of the time I was gone was spent on the road getting there and then getting home. When are you going to get a private jet so I don't have to put miles on my car?"

"Stop bitching. You made fifteen hundred dollars in two days."

He isn't wrong. Between selling my part of the construction business back to my brothers and chasing after skips, I am sitting on a nice stack of cash.

"So why are you calling?"

"What? I can't just call to see how my cousin's doing?"

"Do I sound stupid to you?"

"All right, all right… The thing is, I need you to help me out with something."

"What?" I shake my head, making my way up to my door.

"A friend of mine from Vegas called. He has a girl that needs a place to crash for a little while."

"And what does that have to do with me?"

"Can she stay with you until Cassie gets the rest of her shit out of my house?"

"Hell no!" I bellow as I shove my keys into the lock.

The second the door opens, Daisy starts going wild. I scoop her up in one hand as she begins licking my chin and any other piece of me she can get to.

"You still have that dog?" He laughs, hearing Daisy through the phone.

"Yes," I growl. All the fuckers in my life think it's funny I own a little fur-ball for a dog. I rescued Daisy from a flophouse. She was so small at the time that she could fit in the palm of my hand. I was going to give her to one of my family members, but I couldn't do it. After a week of having her with me, I grew attached to her.

"Look, man, I just need your help this one time."

"No, you should have put that bitch's shit out months ago," I remind him. I hated his ex; she was one of those women who tried to lead you around by your dick.

"Don't make it seem like I haven't wanted to. She swore she was coming this weekend to get all her stuff, but until then, I don't have room for this chick who's coming."

"Who is she?" I ask curiously.

"You know my friend Link who works as a bouncer in Vegas?"

"Yeah. He works at a strip club, right?"

"Yeah. Well, I guess this stripper saw some shit go down. He called and asked me to keep an eye out for her until it's safe for her to go home."

"Wow, your own personal stripper living with you."

"She could live with you first."

"I'm seeing someone, so you're gonna have to find something else to do with this chick or toss your ex's shit outside. Or burn it behind your house for all I care."

"You're seeing someone?" I can hear the disbelief in his voice. I'm not surprised—I don't date; I hook up and go home.

"I just got home. I don't have time for this right now. Call your ex and tell her she needs to come get her stuff tomorrow or you're burning it. And honestly, if she doesn't show up, I say we have a bonfire with that shit."

"Look, you and I both know she isn't gonna come get her crap. She thinks, if it's here, she has a reason to come back."

"So put it in your car, take it to her house, and put it on her lawn."

"I would have done that, but I need a truck and haven't had time."

"She's been out for almost a year. How the hell haven't you had time?"

"Okay, I've had time. I just haven't wanted to deal with all the crying that comes along with seeing her."

"Aw, you cry when you see her?"

"Tears of joy that she's out of my life, fucker."

I laugh along with him as I set Daisy on the ground and grab a beer out of the fridge, popping the top and taking a swig. "If she doesn't come by this weekend to get her stuff, let me know and I'll go with you to take it to her. I'm sure we can borrow Cash's truck."

"Sounds good. So who's this chick you're seeing? Is it the redhead you were talking to at the bar the other night?"

"No, and you don't know her." Shit, I don't even know her.

All I know about her is that she smells like apples and cinnamon and she has the softest brown hair I've ever seen or felt, brown eyes that darken to almost black when she's kissed, and skin the color of milk that turns pink when she's nervous or embarrassed.

"Did you hear me?"

"What?" I growl, annoyed that he interrupted my daydream of beautiful Sophie.

"I asked if you were up for another job this week?"

"I'm not sure right now."

"All right. Just let me know."

"Yeah, sure. Later, cous'."

"Later."

I clicked off the phone before tossing it onto the counter. I glance down at Daisy, who is sitting at my feet looking up at me. I open up her treat jar, and her eyes follow my every move. I hold the treat a few inches above her head as she stands up on her hind legs to dance around before I drop it to her. I wander from the kitchen into my room, pull off my shirt, and toss it onto the floor, followed by my jeans and boxers.

After going into the bathroom, I start up the shower and let the glass stall steam up before stepping inside. I let the hot water run over me. My head tilts back as I think about Sophie and her big brown eyes looking up at me with nervousness and hunger but without even a hint of real fear—something I have never seen on a woman's face before but will forever be etched into my brain. I knew the minute I saw her that she was it. How I knew? I don't know, but it was like my soul lit up—cheesy as fuck, but also true. I don't really have time for her right now, and she is not a woman who looks like she would ever be interested in someone like me, but that doesn't mean I'm not going to try.

She has a look of innocence about her; I guess it could be a front, but something tells me it's not. I feel myself getting hard thinking about those fucking heels she had on; they should be illegal. She looked like every man's naughty secretary fantasy, or maybe a dirty librarian. I palm myself, moving in long, steady strokes. I wouldn't mind seeing her on her knees in front of me, her skirt up around her waist, her legs spread out to show off her pussy, her top open with her breasts hanging over the top of her bra, and her nipples hard and dark pink from being sucked, licked, and bitten. I would stand in front of her, feeding her my cock. My hands would fist her hair, dictating her pace. I feel my balls draw up, my strokes moving faster. One of her hands would cup them gently while her other hand would grip the base of my cock as I fucked into her mouth.

"Shit," I groan, echoing into the empty shower as long jets of cum hit the wall in front of me. I haven't jacked off to the thought of a woman I know since I was thirteen, when Margret Jenkins showed me her tits in the boys' bathroom on a dare. I catch my breath before I wash up and head to bed. Tomorrow is going to be a busy day.

When I walk into the middle school, I'm not surprised when the security guard asks who I am and what I'm doing here. I explain to him that I'm looking for a librarian by the name of Sophie. He doesn't know who she is, so he sends me to the principal's office so someone there can help me out. I'm used to being judged by my appearance. I'm covered in tattoos, and I have a fauxhawk and gauges in my ears. Basically, I look like a person you should run from.

"Can I help you?"

I look down at an older woman with light-purple hair and a large smile. "I'm looking for Sophie."

"The Sophie who works in the library?" she questions, her smile becoming wider.

"Yes. Can you point me in her direction?"

"Oh! She's not here today."

"Why are you looking for Sophie?" a male voice asks, and I turn my head to look over my shoulder.

"She's a friend," I tell him, turning back around.

"Sophie doesn't have friends," he says in a way that makes it sound like he has tried to be her frien, but she wasn't interested.

I turn to face him, looking him over. He's dressed like he works here—most likely a teacher—his khaki pants and button-down shirt giving him away.

"She has me," I tell him.

His eyes look me over before he speaks again. "I find that hard to believe."

"Is that so?" I raise a brow.

"Honey, she will be here tomorrow," the lady says. I look at her and smile, and she beams back at me.

"Thanks," I reply, tapping on the top of her desk before walking past the guy, out the door, down the hall, and out to my car. I have to wait another day, but I know it'll be worth it when I see her again.

When I get to the school the next day, I go directly to the office.

"You came back," the same lady as before greets me. "I'm Sue, by the way." She leans forward then, like she is going to tell me a secret.

"Mr. Rasmussen was not happy yesterday." She wags her finger at me then smiles like the cat that got the canary before sitting back in her chair and clapping her hands together once. "So I guess you need directions to the library."

"That would be helpful." I smile.

"You sure are pretty." She laughs. "If I was a few years younger, I'd be a jaguar for you."

"A jaguar?" I ask on a chuckle.

"You know, an older lady with a younger man."

"A cougar, you mean," I correct her with a grin.

"Sure. Whatever you say, honey. All I know is I would have given Ms. Grates a run for her money."

"Sue, if you want me, you've got me," I tell her, leaning in the way she did before.

"Oh no, honey. I wouldn't even know what to do with you." She smiles, her eyes sparkling. I shrug and she laughs. "All right, mister. I gotta hang on to your ID while you're on school property, but just sign in here and you can go to the library. Take a right out the door, walk until you get to the end of the hall, and take a left. It's the last door on the left."

"Thanks, doll," I reply, smiling as I hand her my driver's license, sign the visitor's sheet, and walk out of the office. I have to say, that's the first time I've ever been hit on by a woman my grandmother's age.

When I get to the library's doors, I look through the small window and spot Sophie right away as she stands on her tiptoes to put away books. Today, she is wearing navy-blue slacks with wide legs and a high waist that ends just under her breasts, which are covered in a bright red, short-sleeved, button-down top that matches her heels.

Jesus. Sophie is in heels and looking like she does is going to be the death of me. I push open the door and am bombarded by the smell of books. Sophie turns her head to look at who has come in, and when she sees that it's me, her eyes go wide and her mouth opens and closes a couple of times.

"What are you doing here?" she finally asks before looking around like she is waiting for someone to jump out at her.

"I told you I would see you when I got back to town. I'm back in town," I state the obvious.

"Um...okay, but what are you doing here?" she repeats, pointing to the floor.

"I don't have your number, and I want to take you out to dinner."

"Dinner?"

"Yes, a meal you eat at the end of the day."

"I know what dinner is. I just don't do that," she mumbles, looking adorable.

"You don't eat dinner?" I ask, confused.

"No, I don't do dinner with other people," she replies.

"You don't do dinner with other people?" I tilt my head to the side, watching her.

"Like...date—I don't date," she huffs out, crossing her arms over her chest, which only accentuates it. My eyes are drawn there, and she immediately lowers her arms to her sides.

"It's not a date. It's dinner."

"I know...you said that."

"So what would you like to eat on our non-date dinner?" I ask, taking a step towards her, the smell of apples and cinnamon growing stronger the closer I get.

"Nothing. We're not having dinner together."

"What time do you get off work?"

"Six—I mean, I don't know." She chews her lower lip, her cheeks turning a pretty shade of pink.

"All right, so no dinner then." I shrug. "Can I get your number?"

She shakes her head no, her cheeks growing even darker. Fuck me, she's cute. "Sorry," she whispers, looking away.

For some reason, alarm bells start going off in my head. "It's all good." I beat back the urge to touch her, my mind warring with my body. I watch her for a second and then start to come up with a plan.

"I have to get back to work," she says, looking at the floor.

"All right, sweet Sophie. I'll see you around."

"Bye, Nico," she says softly.

I turn after giving her a chin lift, my chest feeling tight at the sound of my name leaving her mouth. After getting my ID back from Sue and signing out, I leave the school knowing that this isn't over. Not by a long shot.

Chapter 2

FOR THE SECOND day in a row, I'm waiting outside the school. It's 6:02 when the door opens and Sophie comes walking out. Each time I see her, she looks even more beautiful than before. I watch her expression go from surprise to shy happiness as she spots me standing next to my car…just like yesterday.

Yesterday when I left her in the library, I went to the grocery store, bought a pint of Phish Food ice cream and a set of plastic spoons, and took it back to the school, where I waited for her to get off work. She said she didn't do dinner; she never said anything about dessert. When she saw me standing there with the frozen treat, she said that she really shouldn't, but I told her that it wasn't a date and I was just meeting her after school for ice cream. Then I explained how my fragile ego couldn't bear her denying me her company, making her laugh lightly and give in. We stood outside her car for an hour with a pint of ice cream between us. She was shy but also cute and funny.

Now, I watch as she gets closer and closer, her eyes looking me over then landing on my hand. Today, I stopped at the gas station and got two ice cream cookies. She told me yesterday these are her favorite. I hold one out to her, and she smiles as she shakes her head, making my heart beat a little faster. Yes, I know I'm a fucking pussy, but I couldn't give a fuck.

"What are you doing here"—she pauses—"again?" she asks, taking the ice cream from my hand and unwrapping it.

"Someone told me you like these."

"Someone has a big mouth," she says, taking a bite out of the giant frozen cookie.

"She does," I agree, looking at her mouth.

She laughs and smacks me on the chest. She covers her mouth with her hand, chewing while holding up one finger. "What are you really doing here?" she asks after she swallows.

"Just in the neighborhood." I shrug and take a bite of my cookie before immediately spitting it on the ground.

"Hey! What the hell?" she asks, offended, grabbing the rest of the cookie out of my hand.

"That tastes like shit." I wipe my mouth before reaching into my car for a bottle of water.

"No, it doesn't," she defends with an exasperated look on her face.

"Baby, it tastes like cardboard," I tell her, watching as her face goes soft at my endearment.

"Well, I guess I like eating cardboard then."

I shake my head, looking at her smile. "So are you working tomorrow?" I ask her, leaning against my car.

She finishes off her cookie, and mine is halfway to her mouth when she answers, "Yes, but tomorrow I work from home." She puts her bag on top of my car, leans her side against the door, and takes another bite of her ice cream.

I watch her movements, noticing that everything is so fluid and graceful. The urge to touch her is so overwhelming I have to cross my arms over my chest to keep myself in check.

"What about you? Do you work tomorrow?"

"Nah. I have some time off," I reply, watching her closely.

She nods her head and looks around. "I never asked you—what kind of work do you do?"

"I'm a bounty hunter," I answer smoothly.

"Wow," she says, her eyes getting big. "Like Dog?"

"You mean the TV show Dog the Bounty Hunter?" I ask, laughing.

"Yeah! I used to love that show!" She smiles and her cheeks turn pink. She lowers her head so her hair falls in front of her face.

"It's nothing like that, but yeah, that's what I do."

"Isn't that dangerous?" she asks, her eyes meeting mine and her face losing some of the color.

"It can be if you're not smart," I confirm with a nod.

"Are you smart?" Her words are quietly spoken.

"Always." I watch in fascination as her eyes go from worried to respect.

"How often do you work?" she asks while taking another bite of the cookie.

"It depends. Sometimes once a month, and others, three times a week." I shrug.

"That's cool. I mean, it's cool if you like doing it."

"I do. I used to work construction with my brothers, but then I got into this by helping my cousin. I found I had a knack for it and haven't been able to stop. And you, do you like what you do?"

"Yes. It's not exciting, but I like it, and it pays the bills, so that's a plus."

I nod in understanding. "What about here? Do you like working at the school?" I ask curiously.

"This is what I love doing." Her face lights up, her voice becoming animated. "I love books. Have since I was a little girl. I used to go to the toy store with my mom and walk out with a book. I guess I'm still like that to this day. I can't go to the store without buying one."

"It's a good feeling, doing something you love," I tell her, knowing how important it is to do things that make you happy.

"Yeah, it is," she says and licks her fingers, and it's in this moment that I know how unaware of herself she really is. She did that not knowing the effect she's having on me. I doubt she even understands the way she affects men in general. It could be an act, but I seriously doubt it. She doesn't seem like she's trying to be seductive; she's just being herself.

"Where are you from? You have an accent I can't place," I say, trying to clear the image in my head of her licking something else.

"I have an accent?" she asks, pointing to herself and laughing. Then she shakes her head and replies, "No, you have an accent. I sound normal."

"You may sound normal to yourself, but to me—and I'm sure to a lot of other people around here—you have an accent."

"I never thought of that." Her head tilts to the side, her smile getting bigger. "I feel kinda cool. I always wanted an accent, though I wished it was a European one, but hey, I'll settle for this." She giggles, and my head goes back and I laugh harder than I have in a long time. When I lift my head and our eyes meet, hers are soft and her smile is gentle. "You have a really great laugh," she says almost to herself.

Words are caught in my throat. I don't know what it is she's doing to me, but I feel completely off-kilter. I'm not used to the feelings I'm having. That's why I tried to walk away from her the first time I saw her, but then she grabbed my arm and I looked down at her, and something in me shifted. I knew if I walked away I would regret it for the rest of my life.

"So I should probably go," she tells me, looking away quickly.

My chest tightens in response. I don't want her to leave, but I don't want to scare her off either. "Can I get your number?"

"Um, I…" She studies me, her eyes searching my face. "Yeah, okay. Sure."

"Here. Just program it into my phone." I pull my phone out of my back pocket and hand it to her.

"Oh…okay." She presses the button on my phone, and in her concentration, her bottom lip gets a workout from her teeth.

My fingers automatically curve under her chin, pulling her lip down with my thumb so she releases it. Her head lifts and her lips part. Our eyes lock, and I fight the urge to lean forward and press my mouth to hers.

"Don't do that, baby," I say quietly before cupping my hand around hers, pulling her concentration back to my phone in her hand.

"Sorry," she whispers, the pink tip of her tongue coming out to lick her lip, making me groan.

When she is done plugging in her number, I take the phone from her and press the call button. Her phone starts ringing and she pulls it from her bag. I slip it from her hand to look at the picture on the screen, and this time, it's a picture of the ocean at sunset.

"Good girl," I tell her, and I smile when her eyes narrow.

"I didn't change it because of you. I just got tired of looking at that picture," she says defensively, pulling the phone from my hand. I smile bigger, and I know it's cocky, but I can't bring myself to care. She slaps my chest with the back of her hand again, but I catch it before she can pull it away. "I'm serious!" she cries, making me laugh.

I tug her hand and she steps towards me. "I know you are."

She's standing so close that her apple-cinnamon smell floods my system. This close, I can see a small scattering of freckles along the ridge of her nose, and I also notice that her eyes have small golden flecks near the center but are almost black around the edges.

"You have a lot of tattoos." Her softly spoken words pull my attention from her face to where she's touching me.

"I do."

I watch as her finger traces a few of the tattoos on my hand that's holding hers. Her skin is completely unmarked. She's so pure I don't even want to touch her; something about her is too sweet for someone like me.

"I use to want a tattoo," she says, sounding far away. Her face is still bent down, watching as her fingers wander over my skin. I'm so hard I'm surprised my dick doesn't bust through my jeans to get to her.

"You don't anymore?" I ask her.

Her head comes up, and she swallows, shrugs, and shakes her head.

Those alarm bells are going off again, but I don't understand why. "So you never told me where you're from," I say, wanting to know as much as I can about her from just talking to her. I can have her background checked, and I will, but I still want her to open up to me.

"I'm from Seattle," she answers quietly.

"What brought you here?"

"I was just ready for a change." She shrugs and steps back. Someone who isn't used to reading people may not have noticed the wobble of her chin or the way her little fist clenched at her side, but I did. "I really need to go. Thanks for the ice cream." She pulls her bag closer to her body, almost as if she's trying to protect herself.

I don't move; I know she's running, but I just don't know what from. I definitely don't want her to run from me.

"Any time, sweet Sophie," I tell her gently. "Send me a text when you get home."

She nods and opens her door. When it's shut, she rolls down the window. "Bye, Nico."

I lift my chin and watch her take off. I'm still standing there watching when she pulls out of the parking lot.

"She doesn't date." Fuck. My head drops, and I know exactly who's speaking. "I tried, and a few other guys have tried, so don't waste your time."

"Did you ever think maybe she just doesn't want to date you?" I turn around to face the guy from the office.

"Did you not hear me? I said she didn't want to date me or anyone else that's asked her."

"Yeah? All that means to me is she's got taste," I tell him with a shrug.

"Whatever," he says, walking off.

I shake my head in revulsion. I have known guys like him my whole life; they think if a woman doesn't want them, then there must be something wrong with her, when in reality, it's them.

I get in my car and watch as he gets in his. He puts on a pair of sunglasses and looks at himself in the mirror before taking off. I pull out my cell and dial Justin, our computer guru. He knows how to find information on anyone and anything.

"Hey, man. How's it hanging?" I ask him.

"A little to the left," he says, laughing at his own joke. I smile but don't laugh along with him. "So, I guess your calling for a reason."

"Yeah, I have a phone number I need you to run for me." I give him the number, listening as he plugs it in on his keyboard.

"Is this about the girl you're seeing?" he asks with a grin in his voice.

"Jesus, you fuckers need a fucking life." I lay my head back against my headrest.

"Hey, I just know because Kenton said you turned down the chance for a stripper to stay with you. I offered him my place and told him she could share my bed with me too."

"Man, shut up and run the number. You wouldn't even know what to do with a woman if she sat on your face."

"That's not true. I've watched plenty of educational material."

"I'm sure you have." I can't help but smile.

"All right, so on a soft run, it says her name is Sophie Grates. She's twenty-three, owns her house, which she paid in full, and has a credit score of seven twenty. She drives an Audi and owes six thousand on it. She has two credit cards in her name—one American Express and one Victoria's Secret—both paid on time. Her mom passed away in a car accident when Sophie was fifteen. She got emancipated when she was sixteen and went into Job Corps." My stomach is in knots. Her mom passed away when she was so young, and not long after that, she moved out on her own. "Did you hear me, man?"

"What?"

"I asked if you wanted me to do a hard run on her."

"Nah. Thanks, man. I'll talk to you tomorrow."

"Sure," he says and hangs up.

I pull out of the parking lot thinking about sweet Sophie being on her own for so long. When I reach my house, my phone buzzes, and I pull it out after shutting off my car.

Sophie: *Home :)*

I feel my heart thud in my chest when I see it's her.

Me: *Where's home?*
Sophie: *Nice try.*

I grin when she doesn't give in so easily.

Me: *If I don't know, how can I bring you ice cream?*
Sophie: *You can't.*

My eyebrows pull together as I try again.

Me: *What about taking you out?*
Sophie: *I don't really think that's a good idea.*

She clearly doesn't like the idea of going out anywhere, so I try a different tactic.

Me: *What about dinner at my place? Or yours?*
Sophie: *How do I know you're not a serial killer?*

I laugh aloud as I type out my response.

Me: *I'm not. You can even call my mom ;)*
Sophie: *LOL! I don't know what's wrong with me, but okay. Dinner at my place. Is tomorrow okay?*
Me: *I wouldn't miss it. What's your address?*
Sophie: *Um, I'm going to give it to you tomorrow, if that's okay?*

She's catching on, I think with a grin. I probably wouldn't be able to wait until tomorrow to go see her if I knew where she lives.

Me: *Good girl.*
Sophie: *You should probably be running as fast as you can. I could be a crazy person.*

I don't want to scare her away, but I give her a little taste of the intensity I feel when it comes to her.

Me: *I never run, Sophie. NEVER.*
Sophie: *Oh.*
Me: *All right, sweet Sophie. Get some sleep and message me tomorrow.*

Sophie: *Night, Nico.*

I swear I can hear her whisper those words to me, and I let out a deep breath I didn't realize I was holding and finally make my way inside my townhouse.

Sophie

OH GOD, WHAT was I thinking? I put down my phone and look around my bedroom and then at my bed. I doubt Nico could even fit on the thing. Wait, why the hell am I thinking about him fitting in my bed? We're not going to be in bed; we're going to be eating in the kitchen. An image of me sitting on the counter and Nico in front of me with his head between my legs has me groaning and covering my face. Dinner… Think about dinner. What could I make him to eat? I don't think he would be impressed with a meal consisting of Lean Cuisine.

I pull out my laptop and type in 'food that men like to eat.' Half the things on the list of guy-food has me gagging, like lamb. There was no way I could make lamb without thinking of a cute little lamb face. Other things on the list—like calf liver and hog trotters—just leave me feeling nauseated and wondering if men really eat that kind of stuff. After thirty minutes of searching, I decide to just make pasta with meat sauce, which seems to be a common ingredient in all the meals I've looked through. Meat, meat, and more meat. I lie down on my bed and start giggling. Men with meat like meat. Okay, I need help. I'm definitely nervous about tomorrow.

I haven't dated; I have always been too scared. My mom passed away when I was fifteen, leaving only my dad to raise me. Not long after her passing, my dad started drinking. At first, it was a beer here and there, but then it turned into an every-night thing. When I was sixteen, he started going out nightly to a local bar. The bar closed at one, and thirty minutes later, my dad would come home, bringing the party with him. I never felt safe; I was constantly on edge, never knowing if someone would stumble into my room drunk or high. I told my dad that I didn't feel safe, but he just waved it off as me being a dramatic teenager.

Then one night, I was sick—like really sick. I had a fever and needed water and Tylenol. I got up and made my way into the kitchen, and once I was there, a guy who often attended my dad's parties cornered me in the kitchen. I remember the fear I felt when he shoved me into the corner near the fridge, away from the view of all the others. I tried to get free from his hold, but he only held me tighter, and when I attempted to scream, he covered my mouth with his as he tried to force me to kiss him. I fought back as much as I could, and when another man showed up, I felt relief—until he started helping the guy who was holding me. They were both mocking me, telling me all the horribly disgusting things they were going to do to me.

I can still remember seeing people coming in and out of the kitchen, either oblivious to what was going on or not caring. When one of them stuck their hand between my legs, I reared my head back, busting the guy who first cornered me in the nose. Blood went everywhere. His hands let me go, as did his friend's, and I ran out of the kitchen to my room, locking the door behind me. I hid in my closet with my phone and called the police. Not long after that, my dad came into my room and found me in the closet. He looked distraught, apologizing for everything that happened, but I couldn't care anymore. I was done making excuses for him.

Two weeks later, I got emancipated from my father and joined Job Corps. It's what I needed at the time, the environment almost military. We had schedules we had to keep, things we were responsible for, and school, which I excelled at. I've never regretted what I did. The only thing I have ever regretted is losing contact with my father, but part of me felt like if I were important to him, he would have gotten into contact with me.

My phone rings, bringing me out of my thoughts. I look at the name and roll my eyes, smiling.

"Hello, Maggie," I answer my phone, exaggerating a put-out voice. She's always teasing me that I lead the most boring life ever, so I play it up for fun.

"Hey, bitch. What are you up to?" she asks.

We were roommates in Job Corps and have been the closest friends ever since. She still lives in Seattle and is getting married in a couple months to her longtime fiancé, Devon, who was also in JC with us.

"Nothing much."

"Geez, girl. It's always 'nothing much' with you. When the hell are you going to have some good gossip for me?"

"Not everyone is a gossip slut like you," I tell her, laughing.

"Hey, now. I'm not a gossip."

"Sure you aren't." Maggie knows everything about everyone, and because of her, I know things about people I have never even met in my life—and a lot of those things are details I wish I never, ever knew.

"I can't help it if people want to open up to me. I'm like Dr. Phil or Oprah."

"This is true," I say as I lie down on the couch, and I can't help but laugh when I think about the position I'm in.

"What's so funny?"

"Well, Dr. Phil, I met someone, and I'm now sprawled on my couch, so you wanna shrink me?"

"What?!" I hear the shock in her voice. Maggie has been trying to get me to date for years, but I have never felt comfortable with anyone before. That's why it surprises me that Nico—Mr. Tattoo—is the one to make me feel this way. "Well, spill it, girl. Who is he? Tell me every-thing!"

"His name is Nico, and he is gorgeous, funny, and sweet. He asked me out and I turned him down, but then the last two days, he's been waiting for me by my car with ice cream when I got out of work."

"But you turned him down?"

"Yes."

"And you're going out with him?"

"Well, tomorrow he's coming over for dinner," I clarify.

"Holy shit," she whispers, knowing how big this is for me.

"I know," I whisper back, smiling.

"Girl, I'm so happy for you. Even if things don't work out with him, I'm glad you're at least going to get out of that bubble you've placed yourself in and try to live a little."

"Well, I don't even know what I'm doing, and I doubt he will stick around for long after he realizes I'm a crazy, but I want to see what happens," I tell her, meaning it from the bottom of my soul.

"You're not crazy, Sophie. You had a traumatic experience. You just need to realize you're not broken and that the past has made you a stronger person. I love you, and Devon loves you. You deserve to be happy."

"I'm happy," I say, feeling a little defensive.

"I know you think you're happy, honey, but you've been locking yourself up for way too long. Living a life in solitude is not happiness."

"I've gotten better," I whine.

"You have. I agree," she concedes.

"I just need time," I add quietly.

"You've had plenty of time, girl," she says, sounding frustrated.

"What do you want me to do?" I ask exasperatedly.

"I want you to talk to someone about what happened."

"I talk to you."

"I know you've told me everything, but this is something I can't help you with. You need to talk to someone who deals with this kind of thing," she says gently.

"Maybe I shouldn't go out with him until I figure things out for myself," I say, my stomach pitching. The feeling surprises me, making me realize I how much I do want to see him again.

"Do not use your past as an excuse to not live your life. This guy is the first one you have been interested in. To me, that says it all. Date him and see what happens. Maybe you can open up to him about your past, but while you're doing that, find a professional to talk to as well."

"I know you're right, but I'm afraid," I admit.

"Which tells me you're still living in that moment. Honey, that was years ago. Yes, it was a horrible thing that happened to you, but luckily it wasn't as bad as it could have been."

Her words make me shudder, but I know she's right. I think my mom's death and the events that happened after I lost her are still plaguing me. It's hard to get close to people when you realize how quickly they can be taken away.

"I know it could have been a lot worse, and I need to start living again… I just don't know how."

"One day at a time. Every day, push yourself to do something you're afraid of. And find a group or a counselor to talk to!" She practically yells the last part.

"I'll try," I promise.

"Don't try. Do."

"Okay." I sigh.

"So, are you still coming home for your fitting?" she asks, changing the subject.

"Yes." I smile. "And my dress better not be ugly."

"Girl, you should know by now your dress is going to be hideous. I do not want you to outshine me at my own wedding."

"Like that could ever happen." I laugh.

Maggie is one of the most beautiful people I know. Her long, lean body with skin the color of dark chocolate makes her honey-colored eyes pop; that, along with her long reddish-brown hair she has kept in thin dreadlocks since she was little, makes her even more exotic-looking.

"Oh please, girl. You know you're hot," she says, growling the end.

"I love you," I tell her, feeling tears sting my eyes.

"You know I love you too, girl. Okay, enough of this mushy shit. Tomorrow, when this guy leaves, I expect you to call me and tell me every detail."

"Promise. Talk to you then," I say, listening to her goodbye before hanging up.

I close my eyes and then open them up, looking at the ceiling feeling a sense of hope when I say aloud to myself, "Don't try. Do."

Chapter 3

Nico

I PULL UP in front of Sophie's house and look around the neighborhood. It's a quiet area where the people—mostly middle class—who work in downtown Nashville live. I pick up the flowers I bought for her off the passenger's seat and make my way up to her front porch, noticing the flowers that line the walkway and the hanging plants along the front of her house. I stretch my neck before knocking once. I can hear music playing on the other side of the door and then some kind of banging. After a few seconds, I hear a couple of locks turn. Then the door is opened and Sophie is standing there. Her hair is up on top of her head, her cheeks are flushed, and my eyes travel down her body to see that she's wearing a plain black tank top and jeans with bare feet, her toes painted a deep purple.

"Hi," she says softly, and my eyes leisurely come back up her body to meet hers.

"Hey," I greet as she opens the door farther, stepping back for me to enter.

"Did you find it okay?" she asks.

My brain takes a second to process her words; I'm still stuck on her bare feet and how sexy she looks dressed in jeans. "Yeah. I don't live far from here." I watch as her eyes look me over, and I see nervousness, but also hunger. We both stand there staring at each other, but then her eyes travel down to my hand and get humorously big. "These are for you." I lift my hand, righting the flowers and awkwardly holding them out to her.

"Oh, wow. Thank you," she says breathily, taking the flowers from my hand and bringing them to her face to smell them. After a few moments of just watching her appreciate my simple gift, my dick is already trying to inch closer to her through the roughness of my jeans. She seems to shake herself and tells me, "Um…dinner is cooking. I hope you don't mind pasta."

"It smells great," I say, breathing in through my nose, the smell of garlic and freshly baked bread assaulting me.

"I didn't even think to ask you if you could eat carbs."

"What?" I ask, confused.

"Well, you're all muscles. I know that a lot of weight trainers don't eat pasta," she says matter-of-factly.

"I'm not a weight trainer," I tell her, laughing.

"You're not?"

"No. I work out because my job requires me to stay in shape, but I eat whatever the hell I want."

"Okay, good." She smiles.

Once again, we're both just standing here watching each other. I run a hand through my hair and laugh when I see her eyes drop to my waist. She jumps, her head flying up. "Um…I-I'm just going to put these in some water. Do you want a beer or something?" she rushes out.

"Sure," I say, taking a quick look around her house.

It's small, maybe two bedrooms, and the living room is comfortably snug, with a TV, a small loveseat, and a matching chair. I follow her into the kitchen, my eyes watching her hips and ass as she walks. The kitchen is a decent size, with a small dining area attached.

I study her as she pulls a chair from the table, carrying it over to the fridge. "What are you doing?" I ask, seeing the unstable chair wobble as she begins to climb up on top of it.

"My vases are up here," she says distractedly as she tries to keep her balance on the chair. I walk over to her and pick her up with my hands around her waist. "What are you doing?!" she screeches, her fingers digging into my arms.

"Saving you from breaking your neck," I tell her, setting her down and squeezing her waist once before placing my hand on her belly to push her back a step. I move the chair out of the way and open the cupboard. "Which one do you want?" I look down at her.

"You just picked me up," she mumbles almost to herself.

"Yes, so you wouldn't accidentally off yourself."

"You just picked me up like I weighed nothing," she says in disbelief.

"You don't weigh much," I inform her. "So, which one do you want?" I repeat my question, watching her face.

"It doesn't matter," she replies, and I pull down the first one I touch. "Not that one," she says, so I put it back in the cupboard and grab another. "Not that one either," she states, making me smile.

"Babe, this will go a lot faster if you just tell me which one you want."

"The tall, clear pink one," she answers then bites her lip, and I know she just changed her mind again.

"You sure?" I ask teasingly.

She shakes her head. "The blue one."

"You sure?" My hand hovering over the blue vase.

"I'm sure." She nods.

I pull it down halfway and she reaches up, taking it from me. I close the cupboard and put the chair back.

"The beer is in the fridge. There is also tea, juice, and pop. Just help yourself," she says, picking up the flowers from the counter.

I grab a beer and lean against the counter to watch her as she measures the flowers, pulls a knife out of the butcher block, lays the flowers over the sink, and then starts to saw the ends off. It takes everything in me not to snatch it away from her and do it myself to make sure she doesn't cut herself. Once she's done, she fills the vase with water from the sink's faucet, drops the flowers in and arranges them, and then sets the bouquet on her table. When she turns around, she jumps like she's startled.

"You okay?"

"Yeah," she says, pressing her hand to her chest.

"You forgot I was here, didn't you?" I smile.

"Maybe," she says, looking sheepish. She walks over to the stove and checks the water in the big stainless-steel pot.

"Not used to having people in your house?" I question, taking another sip of beer.

"I don't really know too many people around here."

I watch as she measures out some pasta before dropping it into the boiling water. "How long have you been in Nashville?"

"Six months. I wanted to buy a house, and I couldn't do that in Seattle, so I decided to move down here." She pulls the lid off another pot, grabbing the long-handled wooden spoon from the spoon rest sitting between the burners and starts stirring whatever it is inside.

"You moved by yourself?"

"Yeah." She shrugs her shoulders and lets out a long breath.

"It must have been hard to leave your friends and family behind to move to another state where you didn't know anyone," I say gently, not knowing if this topic of conversation will send her shutting down.

"Not really. I have always kinda been a loner."

"What about your family?" Even though I already know some about her past, I want her to open up to me.

"My mom died when I was fifteen," she whispers, "and my dad isn't in my life. My mom and dad were only children, my grandparents are all dead, and I don't have any siblings." She bites her lip and continues to stir the pasta sauce.

"I'm sorry." I take a step towards her, running my hand down her back trying to comfort her. Her body stiffens under my touch, and I watch as she forces herself to relax. "Are you okay?" I ask softly, feeling like I need to treat her like a skittish cat I really want to pet.

"Yeah, I just... I'm not used to people touching me," she says, making my heart squeeze. I don't move away from her. She never said she didn't like or want people to touch her, just that she's not used to it. I want her to get used to me touching her.

"So what are you making?" I change the subject, using the excuse of seeing what she's stirring in the pot to move closer to her.

"Spaghetti with meat sauce," she replies with a small laugh.

"What's funny?" I smile automatically.

"Nothing." She looks at me over her shoulder, her eyes widening when she sees how close I am to her. "Wh—" She clears her throat. "What about you? Does your family live around here?"

"They live about forty-five minutes away. I drive to see them every few days." I lean back against the counter so I can see her face.

"Are you close to them?"

"I am. My mom and dad are still married and still very much in love. I have three brothers—Asher, Trevor, and Cash. Asher is married and has four girls, Trevor is married and has both a daughter and a son on the way, and Cash has one of each too."

"Cash isn't married?"

"He was, and I'm sure he'll be getting married again soon. His story is long and contains a lot of drama. His ex-wife is certifiably insane. Now he's back with his first love, and they have their daughter and my nephew."

"And you? You've never been married?"

"No. Have you?"

"No." She looks at me, and I can see that she wants to say more. "I've never been married."

All I can think is, Thank fuck. Her eyes get big, like she's read my mind, and I smile as I watch her cheeks turn pink.

"Do you want me to help you with anything?"

"If you can strain the pasta, that would help."

She walks to the sink and puts the colander down inside it before going to the fridge, where she pulls out a salad. Then she walks over to put it on the table. She makes her way back to the stove to turn off all the burners, and as I finish straining all the water from the noodles, I watch her, mesmerized, as she leans close to the sauce, inhales deeply, and lets out a soft moan. Again, she's completely unaware of how fucking sexy she is.

I have to force myself to unlock the death grip I've unintentionally clamped onto her plastic colander. Luckily, I haven't snapped it yet. When we have everything ready, we both sit at the table, where she starts putting the pasta on each of our plates.

"This is awkward," she says, catching me off guard.

"Really? You think so?" I ask, not feeling the least bit out of place.

"You don't?" she asks in response, her eyes meeting mine.

"No. Do you feel uncomfortable around me?"

"No, I guess not," she says, taking a deep breath.

"As long as you don't feel uncomfortable, awkward is okay." I run my fingers over the top of her hand.

"I guess you're right," she concedes with a little shiver.

I unwillingly force my hand away from hers to pick up my fork, and while we eat, the conversation is light and easy. After we finish the simple but delicious dinner she cooked, we both stand in the kitchen, me with my hip to the counter, and her sitting across from me next to the sink after we finished washing the dishes.

"So, your dog is named Daisy?" She laughs as I pull out my phone to scroll through my pictures so I can show her some of Daisy.

"Here she is." I hold my cell out to her.

She looks at the screen and her eyebrows rise. Then she brings her focus back to me with a curious look on her face. "She's adorable. And so not the kind of dog I would expect you to have."

"Why's that?" I ask with a straight face, knowing the reason. Daisy is a cream-colored miniature Pomeranian who weighed about four pounds the last time I took her to the vet. She looks like she should be some blond-haired, blue-eyed valley girl's lapdog.

"You just seem like you would own a Rottweiler or Doberman," she says with a shrug.

"Is that so?" I raise an eyebrow.

"I'm sorry. that was rude." She looks back down at the phone.

I put a finger under her chin, bringing her eyes back to me. "I'm just kidding. I know she doesn't fit my image, but she's mine. I rescued her while I was on a job when she was just a pup, and I had to bottle-feed her. She was so small she fit right in the palm of my hand," I tell her, holding up my hand and smiling.

"Aww...you're a proud papa." The smile she gives me has me wanting to lean in and taste it.

"I guess I am."

She goes back to looking at my phone, and I go back to watching her. She is beautiful in a way that is completely natural; none of it is fake or for show. It's just her—who she is. She hands me my phone back, looking around before putting her eyes back on mine. "So, um...do you want to watch a movie or something?"

"Sure, if you're up to it."

"Yeah. I have Netflix and On-Demand, so you can pretty much pick whatever."

I follow her into the living room and sit down on the sofa to watch as she sets up the TV before coming back to sit next to me. Her couch is small, so it forces her to sit close.

"What would you like to watch?" she asks, turning her head to me.

"Doesn't matter." I twirl a small piece of her hair that has fallen out of her messy bun around my finger.

"How about The Breakfast Club? I haven't seen it in a long time," she suggests, unconsciously tilting her head towards me.

"Sounds good."

I want to kiss her. My brain is battling against my body, wanting to get closer to her, wanting to taste her mouth again; it's taking everything in me not to close the small gap between us. I watch her eyes flare slightly, and then she licks her bottom lip, making me wonder if she is thinking the same thing.

Sophie

I TAKE A deep breath, trying to calm myself. Looking away from Nico takes all my power; I'm so drawn to him that I wonder if it's normal or healthy, and it makes me second-guess things. I don't want someone just so they'll fill the hollow places inside of me.

"So, The Breakfast Club it is, then," I say, trying to be casual about it in an attempt to cover how nervous I'm feeling.

"Sounds good," he replies, sitting back against the couch and getting comfortable. Now I'm wishing I would have paid the extra one hundred dollars and gotten a bigger couch instead of the loveseat.

I start the movie and sit back against the cushion, and I'm so close to him that I can feel the heat from his body. I don't know how to sit, so I move my legs under me and start to lean against the armrest.

"Come 'ere," he says with a smile teasing his lips as he pulls me by the arm.

My body moves into his, his arm sliding around me and holding me to him. He smells like leather and musk, and I want to explore him to find out where the smell is coming from. I bite the tip of my tongue hard, trying to find something else to think about other than how hard his body feels against mine.

"Relax," he whispers, running his hand down my arm. I shiver against him—not from cold, but from the way it feels when he touches me. "You warm enough?"

"Yeah," I whisper, taking another breath as my belly goes crazy with butterflies. I feel his chest moving and I think he's laughing, so I turn my head to look up at him.

"You know, you're really adorable," he says when our eyes meet. I scrunch up my face at him. I don't want to be adorable; I want to be beautiful or sexy, not adorable.

"Relax, sweet Sophie. We're just watching a movie." His hand cups my cheek, his thumb sliding over my lower lip as his eyes follow.

My breath catches and I nod. His hand drops and slides around my shoulder, pulling me snug against him. I can't help but to relax as he slides it gently up and down my arm. We watch the movie in comfortable silence, and at some point, I fall asleep.

I wake to the room being cast in a blue glow. It takes a second to remember where I am and who I'm lying on. I put my hand to my mouth, knowing that I probably just drooled all over his shirt, and when I turn my head to apologize, I see that he's asleep. His arm tightens around me like he doesn't want me to move. I watch him closely, taking in every contour of his face and the slight stubble along his jaw. Even in sleep, he looks dangerous, but then I think about how gentle he is with me and I wonder how it's possible for someone to be so complicatedly beautiful.

When he showed up tonight, I wanted to fall into his arms. He looked hot standing there, wearing a plaid shirt with the sleeves rolled up, showing off his tattoos and his black jeans hugging his thighs. Then I saw the flowers. They were such a complete contrast to the way he looks, and I almost laughed when he held them out to me, looking unsure about them.

My fingers twitch; I want to trace the outline of his lips with my fingers. I lift my hand slowly; my finger touching his bottom lip causes him to jerk his head away. My hand freezes then moves on its own accord when he stills. His lip is smooth and warm, and I can still remember how it felt against my own when he kissed me. My finger moves slowly as I watch its trail, mesmerized, captivated... Then I scream when his mouth clamps down around my finger, his teeth biting down, not hard, but enough so that I can't pull away.

My eyes jump up to meet his as his hands go under my arms, his mouth not releasing my finger, and he pulls me on top of him. He runs his tongue over my fingertip behind his teeth as he situates himself underneath me.

"What are you doing?" I breathe.

"I think I should be asking you that," he says, smiling, and I can feel a large bulge against my belly.

"Sorry. I just..." I try to get away, but he holds me a little tighter, making my pulse spike.

"You're safe with me," he says, reading my face.

I force myself to relax, reminding myself that he has been nothing but kind to me.

"I like that you want to touch me." He gently pushes my hair away from my face. My eyes close at the contact then open to see him smiling. "We both fell asleep?" he asks as his hand continues to run over my hair and down my back.

"I didn't realize how tired I was," I say with a nod. My eyes start to feel heavy as he strokes me, so I lay my head against his chest, wondering not for the first time why I feel so safe with someone I don't know all that well.

"I like this," he whispers, pressing his lips to the top of my head.

I snuggle closer, enjoying his warmth and the way he smells. In the back of my head, I keep thinking about the things Maggie said along with the way Nico makes me feel and how much I want to explore things with him, but I wonder if I should wait until I'm in a better place mentally.

I must have fallen asleep again, because I'm suddenly aware that I'm being carried into my room. Nico lays me on the bed then pulls a blanket up over me.

"I'm the worst date ever," I say tiredly as I snuggle down into my bed.

"This wasn't a date, remember?" he says quietly.

"Oh yeah. I don't do that." I smile.

"If this was a date, it was the best one I've ever had." His hand slides gently down the side of my face. I think he is going to kiss me—I want him to kiss me—so I turn my head slightly, but his nose skims my cheek, and his lips go to my forehead. "Sleep, baby. I'm going to head home. I'll call you tomorrow," he tells me, kissing me once more; this time, his lips touch the corner of mine. I watch his shadow leaving the room.

I can hear the doors close, and I know I need to get up and lock my deadbolt and set the alarm, but it takes a minute for me to get out of bed. I pull off my jeans and bra before wandering into the living room to make sure everything is off. I turn on the hall light and start setting the deadbolt when there is a knock on the door. I look through the peephole, seeing Nico standing on the other side, which makes my belly flutter once again.

"Hey. Did you forget something?" I ask when the door is open.

"Yes," he replies, his body suddenly pressing me against the wall. "Jesus," he groans, looking down my body.

I forgot I'm almost naked, wearing nothing but a tank top and a pair of boy shorts. When his hand grabs my ass and his mouth lands on mine, I'm instantly reminded of my state of undress. My mouth opens under his, my tongue following what his is doing. My fingers fist into his T-shirt to hold him to me. His hand on my ass squeezes, making me moan into his mouth. He presses me harder into the wall, and I can feel his excitement through his jeans and my thin tank top.

I don't really know what I'm doing, so I follow his lead and give up everything I have to that kiss. He rips his mouth away before placing his forehead to mine. We're both breathing heavily, and it takes a second to come back to myself. I slowly loosen my hands, which have wrapped around his shirt so tightly that my fingers now have impressions on them. He tightens his hand on my ass, his fingers digging into my skin. When I open my eyes, his eyes are on my mouth.

"I knew I wouldn't be able to sleep tonight if I didn't come back and do that." He presses his lips to mine again, this time just a touch before moving away.

"I'm glad you came back for that." I feel my cheeks heat up, and I start to look away, but his fingers go under my chin. His eyes roam my face, and I don't know what he sees, but I feel exposed and want to pull away.

"All right, sweet Sophie. Get some sleep." His hand drops from my ass, and as his body pulls away from mine, he takes his warmth with him. He kisses my forehead and then tilts my head back to kiss my mouth once more before heading out the door he just barged through. "Lock up, babe," he says over his shoulder.

"'Night, Nico," I say softly, closing the door behind him. My fingers touch my mouth and I smile as I lean back against the door. I could definitely get used to him kissing me.

Chapter 4

Nico

I PULL UP to the front of my house, exhausted. It's been four days since I've seen Sophie. I got a call for a run I couldn't pass up not long after I left her standing inside her house wearing nothing but a tank top and panties, her mouth still swollen from what mine did to it. My phone buzzes, and thinking that it's her, I look at the screen, but instead, I see that it's a text from Asher. I groan, opening the message; all I want to do is take a shower and sleep before I see Sophie.

Asher: *You busy?*

Yes, busily about to pass out, I think.

Me: *Why?*

Don't say you need me; don't say you need me… I chant to myself with my fingers crossed as I wait for his reply.

Asher: *I need your help setting up the pool fence.*

"Shiiit," I groan out loud. I scrub my eyes with my fists and let out a sigh before I respond.

Me: *On my way.*

When I pull out onto the highway and hit dial on my phone, the loud ringing fills my car.

"Hey. Did you make it home already?" Sophie answers, making me smile.

"I did, but then my brother messaged me, so I'm heading to his house."

"You haven't slept. Are you going to be okay?" The concern in her voice only solidifies why she is the one.

"I'll be okay. I was hoping I could see you at some point tonight."

"Oh," she replies quietly, making my eyes draw together.

"Oh? Baby, you know you're a killer on a man's ego, right?"

"Sorry, it's just…"

I listen as she takes a breath, but when she doesn't continue, I ask, "Haven't you ever dated anyone?"

"Um…"

"What are you, a virgin?" I joke, expecting her to laugh.

"I should let you go while you're driving," she says quickly.

"No, you shouldn't." I grip my steering wheel tighter.

"I really should," she argues.

"No, you're going to tell me exactly what's wrong with you," I growl.

"Actually, I'm getting off the phone," she snaps, and the phone goes dead.

"What the fuck?" I press dial on the phone again, and this time, it goes right to voicemail.

She's lucky I have to meet my brother; otherwise, I would be at her house dealing with this shit face to face. I drive the rest of the way to Asher's with my music on full blast, thinking over our conversation. I have never let a woman affect me, never given a fuck what they think, say, or do. I have been told the same shit my whole life about the boom and used to think it was a bunch of bullshit. That is, until Asher met November, Trevor pulled his head out of his ass and claimed Liz, and now Cash with Lilly. Then I felt it for myself when I saw Sophie.

"I'm such an asshole," I say aloud as everything clicks into place. Her shyness, the way she carries herself, how her body reacts when I touch her—either she's had very little experience or is a virgin, and I just threw that shit in her face. "Fuck me," I whisper into my empty car. I shake my head and drive the rest of the way, coming up with a plan. No way am I letting her push me away.

I pull up to Asher's house twenty minutes later, shut off my car, and hop out.

"Uncle Nico's here!" July yells over her shoulder before running down the steps straight into me.

"Hey, kiddo." I swing her up into my arms.

"You didn't bring Daisy," she pouts, looking over my shoulder and into my car.

"Nope. She's at home."

"Awww! But I wanted to see her," she whines.

"How about the next time I go out of town, you babysit her for me?"

"Really?!" she squeals.

"Really," I say, kissing her head before setting her down once we get into the house.

"Thank God you're here," November says as soon as she sees me. I raise an eyebrow, and she shakes her head as she gives me a hug. "Those three"—she points out the glass backdoors towards the pool where Asher, Trevor, and Cash are all standing—"have been trying to get the kid gate put up around the pool for the last three hours. I tried to help them, but they refused to listen. Hopefully, now that you're here, they will stop arguing like a bunch of old ladies and just get it done already."

"I'll see what I can do." I laugh when she rolls her eyes. Then I walk out to the back patio and down to the pool area where—just like November said—Asher, Trevor, and Cash are all arguing.

"You do know that, if you guys stopped bitching for a few minutes, you would probably already be done, right?" I ask, walking up to join the circle.

"You think this shit's easy? There aren't even instructions in English! All this shit is in Chinese," Cash complains, shoving the piece of paper at me.

I don't even bother looking for English directions; I just look at the picture, glance at the pieces, and immediately start to assemble the fence.

"You have always been a fucking show-off," Trevor says in disgust, making me laugh.

"You're just mad I'm smarter than you."

"You wish, motherfucker," he replies, helping me put pieces together.

"You girls going to stand there and watch, or are you going to help us out?" I ask Asher and Cash, who are both just standing over us in identical poses with their arms crossed over their chests.

Realizing they've been called out, they immediate jump into action. It takes thirty minutes to get the last piece attached, but once we're done, we all stand back to appreciate our hard work.

"That didn't take long to do once y'all stopped bitching," I pointed out, just to rub it in their faces.

"We would have figured it out…eventually," Cash says, smiling—something he does a lot more these days.

"How are Lilly and Ashlyn doing living with you?" I ask him.

"Good. They're settling in. Never thought I'd be thankful to Jules for anything in my life besides Jax, but she proved to be useful getting Lilly to live with me, even if the situation was fucked up."

"True," I agree; Lilly is the best thing to happen to Jax and Cash. Every time I'm around them as a family, I see the love she has for my brother. In the beginning, I was worried about her intentions, but now, I know she is exactly what Cash said she is—a good woman.

"How's work been?" Trevor asks. He always asks me the same thing, and I know they all want me to go back to working with them, but I can't; I love what I do.

"Good. Busy." I give him the same vague answer I always do.

"Guess there's never a short supply of criminals. At least you have job security," Asher says, laughing.

I look at my brothers and chuckle. I'm blessed to have such an awesome family, and I can't wait for everyone to meet Sophie.

I PULL UP in front of Sophie's house a little after ten; all of her lights are out, but that's not going to stop me from seeing her right now. I'm about to get out of the car when I see movement. It's dark out, but I can see someone in all black walking around the side of her house. I reach over and open my glove box, grabbing my Glock. I get out of my car and put the gun in the waistband of my jeans at my back. I pull my hoodie down over it before heading towards her house.

I stay in the shadows, watching as the guy walks around to her backyard. I follow but then stop long enough to send a quick text to Kenton with the address, along with a code telling him that I need backup.

I watch the person as they walk from window to window, and I can tell that whoever it is is trying to find a way inside. He tries the last window at the back of the house, and when I see this one open, I pull out my gun and walk up behind the person. Just as they are getting ready to climb inside, I put my hand to the back of their sweatshirt and yank them back.

"What the fuck?" a male's voice cries as I place my gun to his head.

Rage like I have never felt in my life consumes me. I feel out of control and know I could kill this guy without a second thought.

"I was just going to ask you the same question, motherfucker," I say near his ear. I start to pull his hoodie off, but he turns slightly and I feel a sharp pain in my side.

In sudden shock, I drop to my knees and watch as the guy takes off running. I fight to take back control of the muscles in my body that have been seized by the voltage from the Taser.

"Nico?" I hear Sophie's voice behind me. I look over my shoulder and our gazes meet before she looks down at my side, her eyes going wide. "What happened?"

"Sophie, go back inside," I tell her through gritted teeth. I don't want her out here if the guy is still around.

"But—"

"Sophie, go back inside. Now," I say, watching as she does what she's told before I pull out my phone to call Kenton to let him know what just happened.

After I finally get control back, I check around the house to see if I can catch the guy's trail, but there is no sign of him. I've circled the house three times when Kenton pulls up and parks behind my car.

"Cops are on the way," he says as soon as he gets out.

"Good." I run my hands down my face.

"How the hell did he get the drop on you?" he asks.

"I wasn't expecting him to have a Taser," I admit.

"You know the rules, man. Expect the unexpected."

"You don't need to tell me that shit," I growl, already completely pissed off at myself. Thinking that something could've happened to Sophie when I was right here because I wasn't on my game has me mad as fuck.

"Is that her?" Kenton asks, looking over at the house.

I turn to see Sophie standing just inside her open front door. "It is." I take a deep breath as I look at her.

"Where the fuck did you find her?"

My head turns to him, and I can see the appreciation on his face. "Cousin or not, I will fuck you up," I tell him.

"Just a question," he says, smiling.

I shake my head, not in the mood for bullshit right now.

It takes a few minutes for the cops to show. Luckily for us, we're in good with the local precinct and know most of the men who show up. As soon as I've told them what went down, I head up to the house where Sophie is standing on the front porch, her face free of makeup, her hair down around her shoulders, her legs covered in pajama bottoms with cupcakes all over them. She has a sweatshirt pulled tight around her middle.

"What happened?"

"When I pulled up, I saw someone walking around the back of your house. I followed him and watched as he tried to open a few windows until he got to the last one—"

She cuts me off. "Oh my God! What was he going to do?"

"I don't know, but you're safe, baby," I tell her, closing the distance between us. I pull her into my chest, not giving her a choice but to take comfort from me. "You're going to have to make a statement to the police about what happened."

"I don't even understand what happened," she whispers, and I can hear the fear in her voice, which only serves to make me angrier. I squeeze her a little tighter, reminding myself that she is here and safe, but my mind knows what could have happened. "How did you know to come?" she asks into my chest.

"I didn't. I just wasn't going to let you push me away," I tell her.

Her body goes tight, and then I hear the faint whisper of her words spoken against my T-shirt as her body relaxes against mine. "Thank you."

I don't reply; I don't need to. She couldn't have kept me away if she'd tried.

It's almost midnight by the time the police leave. Sophie is a mess after learning that the person who tried to break into her house had gotten away without anyone having a clue about who he was. I close the door behind the cops and turn to see Sophie biting her lip and looking around her living room.

"You should pack a bag."

"Pack a bag for what?" she asks, taking off her hoodie, leaving her in nothing but a light-blue tank top. My eyes drop to her breasts, seeing her nipples through the thin material.

"You're going to stay with me for the night," I say, watching as she paces around the living room. My eyes and dick follow her every move.

"Yeah, that's not happening. I appreciate you being here for me, but I'll be okay," she says, and I can tell she's still worried, even though she's trying to cover it up.

"If you're not staying at my house with me, then I'm staying here with you," I tell her firmly.

"Um...no," she replies, turning a little pink.

"Sophie, I don't have time to argue with you about this shit. I'm fucking tired. I just got off the road, dealt with family shit, and then showed up here to talk to you, only to have to deal with some crazy-ass motherfucker trying to break into your house," I growl, losing patience.

She looks at me and her eyes go soft, and she takes a breath before looking around her small living space. "What are we doing, Nico? We don't even know each other."

"That's why we're doing what we're doing. This is part of dating. We're going to get to know each other."

"Nico, this is just..." She pauses, lifting her hands. "It's just... I've never done this before."

"What part of it haven't you done, baby?" I question while taking a step towards her.

"I have never done any of this." She motions between us with a flick of her wrist.

"I have never done this before either," I say softly, approaching my skittish kitten.

"I'm sure." She lets out a long breath.

"Have I fucked women before? Yes, I have. I'm not going to lie and say I've saved myself, but this—me pursuing you, wanting to spend time with you in and out of bed, getting to know you and your likes and dislikes? All of this shit is new to me, sweet Sophie."

"You might regret trying to get to know me," she mumbles, looking down at her feet.

"I can tell you with one hundred percent certainty that the only thing I would regret is not trying," I tell her with a finger under her chin as I force her eyes up to meet mine. "Now, are we staying here, or at my house?"

"Nico—"

"Sophie, if we stay here, I need to go get Daisy. I've been gone. She doesn't like to be alone all the time, and I told my neighbor she didn't need to go over there tonight because I would be home."

"Fine, but I'm sleeping on the couch." She breathes out a whoosh of air, blowing some hair out of her face. I smile, and her eyes narrow. "Why do I feel like I just got screwed?"

"Baby, when you get screwed, you'll know it," I smirk.

"Nico." She glares as she says my name, sounding like a warning. I smile, making her growl.

"Sophie, relax," I say soothingly.

"How can I relax when you say things like that?"

I walk over to the couch, sit down, and then grab her hand, forcing her into my lap.

"What are you doing?!" she cries, trying to get up.

"We're going to talk," I say, squeezing her hips.

"I don't need to sit on your lap in order for us to talk," she complains, squirming and trying to get away.

"I want you here. Stop wiggling your hot little ass around on my lap or we're going to end up doing something else."

Her body stills immediately and she crosses her arms over her chest. "Fine. Talk."

"Look at me," I tell her. She doesn't, so I turn her face with my fingers. "You said you haven't done this before, right?"

"Yes," she growls, and I catch myself before I laugh.

"All right, baby. I want you to be honest with me. Are you a virgin?" I ask gently.

"That is none of your business!" she snaps as she tries to get up again.

"I plan on being well-acquainted with your body, so yes, it is my business."

"See? That's what I'm talking about! Why do you say things like that?" She wiggles on my lap again, causing my already-hard cock to turn steel under her.

"Because it's the truth. I want to know you, Sophie, but I need to know what I'm dealing with so I don't go too fast for you," I say, looking into her eyes.

"This is too fast," she mumbles, making me smile again.

"I will never force you to do something you don't want to do, but I will always encourage you when I know you're just afraid to try. You can't let your fears hold you back."

"What are you talking about?" she whispers, her eyes getting big, making me feel like I just hit the nail on the head.

"I don't know what happened to you that made you lock yourself away, but I know that's what you've done. I hope you can open up to me about it someday, but until you can talk to me about whatever it was, I need you to be open with me about other things. I don't want you to be afraid of me, and I'm not going to know if it's just nerves or something else unless you're honest."

"Yes, I'm a virgin." She pulls her face away from my hand. "Are you happy now?"

"There is nothing wrong with that, baby."

"Oh, please. What other twenty-three-year-old woman do you know who is a virgin?"

"None, but I'm not going to complain that you are. The thought of another man touching you makes me wanna fuck something up." My grip around her hips tightens slightly.

"You're scaring me."

"Don't be scared." I pull her face towards me and then tilt it down so I can kiss her forehead. "Now go pack a bag."

"Geez, you're bossy," she grumbles, getting off my lap.

I sit in the living room, waiting on her for a while. I'm not really sure how long it's been, because I start to doze, and my eyes are closed when I hear her enter. I open one eye to see her standing across the room, watching me.

"You ready?"

"Yeah," she says, walking into the kitchen to grab her keys and purse off the counter. We head out the front door. "I'm going to follow you in my car so I'll have it there in the morning when I go to work."

"That's fine. Now let's go. I'm ready for bed."

"I'm not sleeping with you," she says from beside me as I tug her keys out of her hand and lock the door.

"Not yet, sweet Sophie," I tell her, leading her to her car and not saying anything else about it. I make sure she's in before I make my way across the street to my own.

Once we pull up to my house, I pull into the right side of my drive-way so she can fit her car next to mine. I hop out, meeting her at the front of her car, where I take her bag from her and then put my hand on her lower back to guide her up to the front porch.

"This is your house?" she asks in awe.

"Yeah," I tell her, trying to see what she sees.

I live in a 2,2,000-square-foot two-story brick townhouse with a two-car garage at the end of a cul-de-sac. My brothers hate where I live, preferring to have lots of land, but for me, I don't need all that. I like having neighbors and a sense of community.

"It's really nice."

"Thanks," I say, opening the door, and immediately, Daisy starts jumping around at our feet.

"Oh my God!" Sophie squeals as she bends down, plucking Daisy, who is all too happy to have someone to lick and pay attention to her, off the floor.

I set Sophie's bag down on the couch before walking into the kitch-en to grab a bottle of water out of the fridge. "You want something to drink?" I ask, watching her as her eyes move around the house to take everything in.

"No, thanks. I'm just ready for bed." She yawns, and Daisy takes the opportunity to lick into her mouth. "Ewww." She laughs, kissing Daisy's head before setting her on the ground.

"You finally see me, huh?" I ask, scooping up my dog. I pet her for a minute before grabbing her a treat and setting her down again. "I'll show you to your room if you're ready to sleep."

"Yes, please. I'm exhausted." She yawns again, covering her mouth.

I walk to the couch, getting her bag before heading to one of my spare bedrooms. I want her to sleep in my room, but I know without even trying that it would be pushing it. "I'm right across the hall if you need me."

"Thanks," she says, looking around, seeming a little unsure of herself.

"This is the bathroom," I tell her, tapping my knuckles on one of the doors. I go to the closet to get down an extra blanket and set it on the bed. Daisy runs in excitedly and jumps up on the bed, looking between us for a second before curling up and lying down. "I don't think so, girl." I pick her up, bringing her to my chest.

"She can stay in here with me if she wants," Sophie says, looking at Daisy with a small smile.

I unconsciously give the pup a peck on top of her head, eliciting wet licks under my chin when I look up and ask, "You sure?"

"Yeah, I don't mind," she says, looking at me with soft eyes.

I set Daisy back on the bed, and then pull Sophie into me. "Remember, I'm across the hall if you need me."

"I remember," she whispers.

"All right, baby. Get some sleep." I bend down, kissing her forehead and then her mouth before heading out of the room.

I walk across the hall, take off my clothes, and get into bed. I lie there, hands under my pillow, looking at the ceiling, thinking about my life and what I do for a living, and wondering how that could affect the girl across the hall. It takes a while for sleep to take me even though I am completely exhausted, but when it does, I dream about a brown-eyed girl.

What I didn't know was that, for the first time ever, the girl across the hall felt something other than fear when she went to sleep.

Chapter 5

Sophie

"HEY, YOU NEED to wake up."

The voice close to my ear makes me scream out, and I roll away and sit up, looking around and not recognizing where I am. Then my eyes land on Nico, and last night comes back to me. I flop back down on the bed and cover my face with my hands while trying to get my heart back under control.

"I didn't mean to scare you, but your alarm has been going off for the last twenty minutes."

I uncover my face, look over at Nico, and inhale deeply. He's only wearing a pair of loose basketball shorts. His whole body is perfect—from his defined arms, the expanse of his wide chest, his abs, and the deep V leading into his shorts.

"You were working out?" I ask like an idiot, seeing sweat covering his entire torso.

He smirks, running a hand over his head. "Yeah. I needed to burn off some pent-up energy," he says, and I see his eyes drop to my breasts, watching as they heat before meeting mine again. "Looks like I'm going to be working out a lot," he mumbles.

I bite my lip to keep from laughing. Daisy decides then to crawl out from under the covers, where she slept the whole night. When she finally wiggles free, she runs back and forth between the two of us before deciding that she wants Nico. I watch as he lifts her to his face just far enough away that she can't reach him with her tongue, and then he flips her to her back and holds her against his chest like a baby so he can rub her belly. I swear I can hear music playing and see little hearts dancing

53

around my head with how swoon-worthy he is standing there with his tiny dog who, I can tell without a doubt, he adores. I never thought I would be jealous of a dog, but what I wouldn't give to have him pet me like that.

"You hungry?"

"A little. What time is it?" I mumble, distracted by his abs.

"Just after seven."

"Oh, shit!" I yell, throwing back the covers and hopping out of bed. "I have to get ready for work or I'm going to be late." I run to the end of the bed to grab my bag and make a run for the bathroom when I'm tugged backwards. I look back and see Nico with his hand around the strap of my bag.

"You can get ready as soon as you tell me good morning."

"Oh, sorry. Morning," I say in a rush, trying to tug free.

"Tell me good morning with your mouth, Sophie." The command in his voice has a tingle building between my legs, and I watch nervously as he puts Daisy down on the ground.

"What?" I breathe, and he laughs, pulling me closer with his hand on my bag.

"Kiss me, Sophie."

"Oh. I need to brush my teeth," I say, looking at his lips.

"No, you need to kiss me," he says, tugging until I'm standing in front of him.

I fidget there for a second, just looking at him, not really sure how to do this but surprisingly wanting to. Then I remember that movie with Will Smith, when he tells the guy that, if he's going to kiss someone, he should only lean in halfway and make the other person close the distance. I drop my bag, stand on my tiptoes, lean in my half, and close my eyes. When nothing happens, I open one eye and then the other.

"Good girl," he says before his mouth comes down on mine in a light kiss that makes my insides flutter. "I always want you to know it's me kissing you," he says against my mouth.

"How could I not?" I say without thinking.

I groan and start to look at the ground when his hands circle my neck, his thumbs going under my chin to tilt my head back. His face lowers to mine, his tongue touches my bottom lip, and I lean closer, my hands landing on his chest, feeling the heat of his skin under my palms. My mouth opens, and he groans when my tongue touches his. I'm so lost in the kiss that I whimper when he pulls his mouth from mine.

"That's how I want you to say good morning." His hands travel down to mine, which are still on his chest, and he grabs them to pull them back behind his neck. Then his hands travel down along my sides and to my waist, pulling my hips closer to his.

"I have to get ready for work," I say softly, my hands running up the back of his longer hair to run it through my fingers.

His hands palm my ass, pulling me even closer to him. "I like you here," he says as his fingers travel up the back of my tank and run along my back. I like it here too. I don't know what this is, but I like it, and I want more. "You get off at six, right?" he asks. It takes a second for me to answer; the warmth of his skin, his scent, and the way his hands feel on me all have my body buzzing with something I've never felt before. "You wanna have dinner at your house or mine?"

"Are you going to cook?" I ask, tilting my head to the side studying his face.

"Of course," he says, nipping my neck and making my breath hitch.

"I really need to get ready for work," I say again, my hands going down the back of his neck from his shoulders to his chest.

"I really don't want to let you go, but I know you need to get ready," he says, bringing his face to mine and kissing me once more on the mouth before turning me around to face the bathroom; he pats my ass, sending me on my way.

I walk into the bathroom before remembering I left my bag. I go back out to grab it, and he has it in his hand, holding it out to me with a smirk on his face.

"Thanks," I say, reaching out to take it. I squeak out when he drops the bag, grabs my hand, and pulls me back to him, hearing the thud at the same time his mouth lands on mine. His hands go to my ass, lifting me closer to him, and this time, the kiss is a lot deeper and rougher than the ones before.

I'm panting and trying to crawl up his body when he pulls his mouth away from mine, muttering a quiet, "Fuck."

"Wow," I say, bringing my fingers to my lips.

"I'm going to need to work out a lot," he growls, making me smile at his words. "All right, now," he says, picking up my bag. "Go get ready for work."

I look into his eyes, seeing that they're heavy with lust. My heart skips a beat as I take my bag from him and stumble into the bathroom, shutting the door behind me. I lean back against the cool wood and take a few deep breaths. Once my heartbeat calms, I look into the mirror; my lips are dark pink and swollen, my cheeks are flushed an attractive shade of pink, and I see a happiness in my eyes that looks foreign to me.

After I finish getting ready in the bathroom, I slip on my heels—four-inch cream-lace peep-toe booties with bows going up the center. I straighten out my navy-blue pencil skirt and make sure my top is tucked in before heading into the kitchen. I walk across the living room carpet, watching as Nico types away on the laptop in front of him at the counter. He's still shirtless; his golden skin covered with tattoos is so gorgeous that I really want to trace every single one with my tongue and fingers as he tells me the history behind each of them.

As soon as my feet hit the tile floor, his head comes up and turns towards me. I watch him shake his head when his eyes travel down my body to my feet. When our gazes meet again, my step falters at his heated look.

"I don't know how I'm going to be able to cope knowing that men are looking at you when you're out. I don't even want to think about the times I'm out of town, leaving you alone."

"Men don't look at me." I scrunch up my eyebrows and shake my head.

"Fuck yes, they do! You just don't notice, and they're too chickenshit to talk to you. No man wants to give a woman the power to crush his ego, and baby, I hate to tell you this, because I like that you don't realize how beautiful you are, but you are the kind of woman that could make a man feel like he has it all or make him feel like he has absolutely nothing."

I've been holding my breath; I can't believe he just said that. I'm not stupid. I know I'm considered attractive, but I've never had anyone make me feel like he just did with those few words.

"Do you want some coffee?" he asks like he didn't just turn my world upside down. I look at the clock, seeing that I have time, so I nod once, walking the rest of the way into the kitchen. "How about some toast?"

"Yes, thank you."

I sit on one of his barstools and watch as he moves around the kitchen, first putting bread in the toaster then pulling out a coffee cup and pouring me some. He pulls the milk out of the fridge and holds it up in question; when I nod, he pours some in the mug and then does the same with the sugar. When he's done, he places the cup in front of me. Then he gets the toast, spreads butter on it, and places it in front of me, where I'm sitting at the island.

"Do you have any honey?" I ask, picking up a piece of toast.

"Sure, babe," he says, handing me a bear-shaped bottle of honey from one of his cupboards before coming back to sit next to me.

"Did you decorate?" I ask, squeezing a giant glob of honey onto one of the pieces of toast.

I love his house; I'm surprised at how well it's decorated. All of his furniture is modern and edgy. In the living room, he has low black carpet and a dark-grey suede couch with black and red pillows, and the entertainment center, coffee tables, and side tables are all the same black-lacquered finish. The kitchen is all dark wood and black granite, with gleaming stainless-steel appliances. Even in his guest room, the furniture was well put together. I could see him in everything, but have a hard time believing he decorated it on his own.

"No, Liz did," he says so affectionately that my stomach drops.

I watch as he takes a drink of coffee; I never even thought that he might have a girlfriend. Oh, shit—what if he still has a girlfriend? My stomach rolls, and I drop my piece of toast to my plate.

"Liz is my sister-in-law," he says, catching me off guard. I turn to look at him. He has a look on his face that makes me feel like an idiot. "I like that look on you though."

"What?" I look away, trying to hide my face with my hair.

"You, looking like you lost something…but only because it was me you were thinking about."

"You're full of yourself," I say, trying to cover how I really feel.

"Nope. I know I want you. Now, seeing that look, I know you feel the same," he says in a tone that is so serious I hold my breath for a second before recovering.

"I may not have any experience dating, but I'm pretty sure that this," I say, pointing between the two of us, "isn't normal." I shake my head.

"Baby, if I was normal, you wouldn't be sitting here right now. You would be at work or at home doing what you do every single day after you pushed me away the first time," he says, taking another drink of coffee.

He is right. I hate that he is right. I hate that I am so transparent to someone who is a virtual stranger. Everything Maggie said keeps running through my mind—which reminds me that I never called her after our dinner the other night. I look over at Nico and my stomach drops. I don't think it's fair to explore this thing with him when I'm not even sure who I really am.

His eyes meet mine, and he shakes his head. "I don't know what's going on in that pretty little head of yours, but know this—you run and I will find you."

"What are you talking about?" I ask nervously.

"Tell me something," he says, turning towards me, his knees caging me in. "What do you feel when we're together?"

I want to say, "Safe," but know that sounds stupid, so I keep my mouth closed.

"Tell me," he urges, leaning towards me.

"I…I don't know." I look down at my hands.

"You do know. Say it," he demands.

"Safe," I whisper, still looking at my hands. I feel his fingers at my chin as he lifts my face so our eyes meet.

"You are safe with me, Sophie." His fingers run along my jaw. "We are going to explore this thing between us. We are going to take it as slowly as you need, but you are not going to push me away. It's not going to work. You push me, and I will push back."

"There's a lot you don't know," I tell him, looking over his shoulder before meeting his eyes again.

"Yeah." He nods, his thumb running over my bottom lip. "But we have time. Tonight, I'll make dinner here and we can work on getting to know each other."

"Sure." I sigh, starting to understand something about him—he is relentless.

"Finish your toast," he says, picking his coffee back up and turning slightly away from me, his legs still boxing me in.

I start eating again, trying not to think about the way it feels every time his hand rubs along my arm or back like he can't stop touching me. I finish my toast then stick my finger into my mouth to suck the honey off. I start to put my thumb in my mouth when he grabs my wrist, bringing my hand to his mouth, and his eyes meet mine as his lips close around my thumb.

I'm paralyzed. The space between my thighs starts to tingle. I bite my lip to avoid the moan I feel in my throat. I watch in fascination as he pulls my thumb out of his mouth, placing a light kiss on the tip, and I swear I feel it on my clit.

"Sweet." He leans in, placing a kiss on my lips before picking up my plate and walking into the kitchen, leaving me in a gooey mess sitting on the barstool.

I stand on shaky legs, taking a breath before walking over to my bag to pick it up off the couch.

"Do you have everything?"

I nod; I can't seem to talk anymore.

"I'll walk you out." He places his hand on the small of my back, leading me to the front door.

He opens it, and I stop to look up at him. "Thank you for...you know...last night...and this morning," I say, my cheeks heating up, making me feel like a dork.

"You're welcome." He smiles before lowering his head to kiss me.

I lean into him, loving the way it feels when he is so close to me. He pulls his mouth away after just a small touch of his lips, leaving me feeling disappointed. "Baby, as much as I want to really kiss you, I can't. I'm hanging on by a very short thread and know that, if I kiss you like I want, you won't be going to work, and we will be doing a whole lot of stuff you're not ready for."

"Oh," I whisper, reading his face.

"Now, come on before all my good intentions go out the window," he says with one more small kiss.

"Okay." I bite my lip to keep from grinning, liking that I affect him so deeply. I turn and walk out the door and down the steps, and make my way to my car. I start to turn around to give him a wave, but I'm startled when I bump into his solid, still-naked chest. "You don't have a shirt on," I tell him shakily, looking around and wondering how many women are peeking through their blinds trying to get a glimpse of him.

"And?" he prompts, sliding my car key from my hand and opening my door.

"People can see you."

"Babe?" His eyebrows draw together in confusion.

"Nico?" I hear a feminine voice call, and I turn my head and watch as a woman with black hair pulled up into a high ponytail, pink shorts, and a pink hoodie unzipped to show off her tits runs across the lawn to Nico's driveway. "Oh God, I'm so glad I caught you!" she cries, her long, fake nails digging into his arm. "Henry left this morning and the darn sink in our bathroom won't shut off. Can you come over and look at it?"

I can't help but glare at her. Is she serious? I watch as her eyes travel over his body and she licks her lips. That's when I've had enough.

"I'm sorry, but can you give us a second please?" I ask with my sweetest smile before grabbing Nico's hand so I can drag him back into the house without giving him a choice.

"What are you doing?" he asks as I open the front door.

Daisy starts going crazy like she's been alone for a year instead of just a few minutes. I don't even stop to explain myself. I go to the room across from the one I slept in last night, knowing that it's Nico's. Then I open the door and look around. Spotting his dresser, I walk to it and start opening drawers.

"Sophie?"

"Just a second," I say, finally finding a drawer with shirts and pulling out the first one my hand lands on. "Here. Put this on," I demand, shoving the shirt at him. When I hear his laugh, I turn around to see him smiling, and it's not a normal smile. That's when I realize what I just did.

"You done?" he asks, his fingers running along the underside of my jaw. I can't speak; I can't even look at him. It's official—I'm crazy.

"Um…" I mumble, looking over his shoulder. His hand on my cheek brings my eyes back to him.

"You're really fucking beautiful when you get all territorial."

I can't believe I just dragged him inside to get a shirt. I didn't even think—I just hated that that woman was looking at him like he was her next meal. "Um…" I mumble again.

"You're making it really fucking hard for me to not kiss you," he groans before taking a step back and pulling the shirt over his head. "All right, let's try this again," he says, taking my hand and leading me back outside to my car.

The woman, Deb, is still here; her eyes go to our hands and narrow before she lifts them and plasters a smile on her face.

"Deb, this is my girlfriend, Sophie." My stomach flips over at the word 'girlfriend.' I'm not going to correct him in front of Deb though. "Sophie, this is Deb. She lives next door and watches Daisy when I'm out of town."

"Oh, that's so nice of you, Deb," I say, my smile matching hers in fakeness.

"I didn't know you have a girlfriend." She takes her eyes off me, looking at Nico.

"I don't have time to look at your sink today, Deb," he says, ignoring her comment.

"Sophie's going to work and I have some stuff to do. You should call George and see if he can come by." He opens my car door, waiting while I get in. It's already eighty degrees out, so I start my car and flip the switch for my top to roll back.

"George always takes forever to get here. Are you sure you can't come over and have a quick look?" she pouts.

"Desperate much?" I mumble to myself while tying my hair up into a ponytail. I look up at Nico, who is watching me closely with a small smirk on his face.

"I'll see you tonight for dinner, baby. Just come here when you get off," he says, leaning his body into my car.

"Okay," I whisper, mesmerized by the flecks of gold in his eyes, the way he's looking at me, and the way my chest feels every time he calls me baby in that sexy, deep voice of his.

He leans in more, his mouth touching mine. When he goes to pull away, I capture his head with my hands in his hair, holding him to me and taking the kiss I wanted earlier. He growls into my mouth, his hand on the door going to my knee then up my thigh under my skirt. My skin tingles where he touches. I feel one finger slide across the seam of my panties, causing me to gasp and pull my mouth from his. Our eyes meet, and his finger travels over the seam again, this time with a little more pressure.

"This is going to be mine, sweet Sophie." I lick my bottom lip, and his mouth comes back down on mine in a soft, teasing touch before pulling away. He looks at me before standing to his full height. "See you later, baby." He smiles and taps the door of my car before taking a step back.

"Have a good day. Bye, Deb," I say cheerfully and smile. He shakes his head and grins bigger.

I back out of the driveway before putting my car in drive and taking off, watching in the rearview mirror as he says something to Deb, who looks like she's begging him. I shake my head. I can't blame her; I would beg him too.

I turn my gaze in the mirror to myself and smile. Luckily for me, I don't need to beg. Then I think about everything I have been through and how much help I need, and I decide that today is the day. I can't put it off any longer. If I want to be with Nico—and I definitely want to be with Nico—I need to try to fix myself.

I PUSH NICO to his back and climb on top of him, my mouth going to his neck and my hands going up his shirt. I love everything he's been showing me about making out. I feel the smoothness of his skin under my palms and want more, so I tug his shirt over his head before pressing my hips down, feeling his erection hit perfectly every time I move my hips. He groans, and his hands slide up my sides under my shirt, dragging it up and over my head. I sit back so he can unhook my bra. His mouth moves to my neck, nipping and licking as his hand unclasps my bra.

"You have the most beautiful tits."

His words cause a moan to climb up my throat as his lips lock around one nipple, his free hand pulling on the other one. My head drops forward to watch him. His hand travels down my back and into my jeans, grabbing my ass and pressing me harder into him, causing me to whimper again.

"Please," I moan, tossing my head back.

He rolls us over so I'm under him. His hand moves to the front of my jeans. The sound of my zipper being lowered fills my ears. Then his fingers press into me, causing me to lift my head and latch on to his bottom lip with my teeth.

"You're so wet—so fucking wet. I can't wait to sink into your tight little pussy and have you dripping around me, gripping me tight while I fuck you hard." This is something else I've learned about myself—the dirtier he talks, the hotter I get. "I want you to come for me, Sophie. I want to feel your tight, hot little pussy pull my fingers deep inside of you."

"Nico! Oh…God…" I whimper, my fingers digging into his arm.

"Come for me, sweet girl," his lips whisper across my ear.

My hips lift higher; my heels dig into the bed as I shatter, my orgasm taking me into another world before sending me back to earth. When I come back to myself, I'm wrapped tight in his arms with my head pressed into his chest.

"You okay?"

I nod, listening to his heart beat rapidly against my ear. "Are you okay?"

"Never better," he tells me sincerely.

"But you—" I start to tell him that he hasn't gotten off. Actually, since he started introducing me to sex, he has never even taken off his pants.

"We will get to that, baby. But for now, it's about you."

"I want to make you feel good too," I tell him, burying my face into his chest.

"Watching you get off makes me feel good," he says while stroking my hair.

"I want to touch you. You never let me touch you," I whine.

"You will one day, but right now, I need to keep my boy away from you. It's important I take my time with you. I want you to be ready when we finally go there. If you touch me, all my good intensions will go out the window," he explains.

"Fine," I pout. I am happy he is giving me time to get used to fore-play and building up to sex, but I still want to touch him like he touches me.

"You're adorable when you pout." He smiles before kissing me. "So how was your day? Did you go to your meeting?" he asks, running his hand along my back.

"Yes." I hold my breath.

He doesn't know the kind of meetings I am going to. I never told him what happened to me; I don't want him to think I'm tainted or something, even though I know it's stupid to feel that way. I just told him that I'm going to meetings to help with the loss of my mom. I feel bad about lying, but I don't know how to tell him what the meetings are really for.

I started going to meetings two months ago, gathering all the infor-mation that first day he called me his girlfriend, and have gone once a week since then. I like having a group of women to talk to who understand what I'm feeling, even though I kind of feel like an imposter sitting with them. The things most of them have been through make me feel weak.

"You know, if you ever want to talk to me about how you're dealing with the loss of your mom, I'm here for you." He hugs me closer, the ball of guilt in my stomach getting heavier by the second.

"I know. Thank you," I choke out. "I'm so sleepy," I whisper, want-ing to get away from talking. "I'm gonna head home."

"Stay with me." He hugs me again, making me feel sick. "You don't work at the school tomorrow. We can sleep in."

I want that. I want to sleep next to him, to have him hold me and make me feel better, but I just can't. "I think I should go home," I repeat more softly this time.

"All right, sweet Sophie," he whispers, making me feel worse. He always does exactly what I want; he never pushes me.

"Thank you."

I get off the bed and put on my bra and shirt before watching him pull his shirt back over his head. He follows me out into the living room, grabbing his keys. He always follows me home when I'm over here late. He walks me into my house to check everything out and then kisses me before leaving for the night, telling me to lock up after him while reminding me to set the alarm.

"I really wish you would stay," he says gently.

"I just need time," I tell him. Seeing the look on his face has me wanting to kick my own ass, but I don't know what to do; I feel stuck.

"As long as you need, Sophie." He hands me my keys.

I hope he's not lying and doesn't give up on me. I want to be better; I hate that I'm hurting him. I walk to him, wrapping my arms around his waist before lifting up on my toes while pulling his mouth down to mine for a kiss. I try to tell him everything with that one kiss. When I pull away, he looks at me and I can see that he's searching my eyes, trying to understand. I wish I understood myself.

"All right. Let's get you home." He kisses my forehead before leading me out to my car.

I bite my cheek the whole way home, and I bite it harder as he kisses me goodnight. When the door finally closes behind him, I let the tears I've been holding in fall.

Chapter 6

Nico

I QUIETLY OPEN the door to my house, not wanting to wake Sophie, who stayed over to watch Daisy. We have been seeing each other for a few months now. I'm head over fucking heels in love with her crazy ass, yet only Kenton and Asher know about her. This is not by choice; I want my family to get to know her. The day Asher found out about Sophie, he, Kenton, and I had spent the morning moving Kenton's ex's shit to her house. As soon as we got back to my place, Kenton and Asher pulled a bottle of Jack out of my cabinet, claiming they were toasting to crazy bitches. Kenton looked at me and smiled right then, and I knew he was going to start some shit.

"How are things going with Sophie?" he asked, and Asher looked at me with a what-the-fuck-is-he-talking-about expression on his face.

"Things are fine," I gritted out. Kenton knew I had my reasons for not telling my family about Sophie yet.

"Who's Sophie?" Asher asked Kenton, completely cutting me out of the conversation.

"Who's Sophie? Now isn't that the million-dollar question?" Kenton asked, tapping his chin.

"Who's Sophie?" Asher turned his attention to me, and I glared at Kenton, who shrugged before I looked at Asher.

"Sophie is—"

"Sophie is his boom," Kenton said, cutting me off and laughing like this was the funniest shit in the whole world.

"What?" Asher asked in disbelief.

"It's true. Why do you think he has been taking jobs that are closer to home and hasn't been going to see y'all as often?"

"Jesus, do we need to go to the store so I can buy you some fucking tampons?" I growled at Kenton.

"At some point, you need to tell people what's going on," he said, making my temper flare.

"And I will when I'm fucking ready."

"Why didn't you say something?" Asher asked, and I could see him slipping into big-brother mode. I shook my head before looking at him again.

"Things with Sophie aren't easy, and I need time before I bring her around everyone."

"We're your family."

"Yes, and I will bring her around. Just not yet," I told him firmly.

"Mom's going to flip the fuck out," Asher said, smiling.

I smiled back. He is right; my mom is going to be happy as hell I am settling down, but she is going to flip because I haven't told her anything. I know my mom will love Sophie, and it kills me every time I have to go to my parents' without her.

I'm brought back to the present by Daisy, who's jumping around at my feet. "Hey, girl." I drop my bag to the floor before crouching down to scoop her up. "Were you a good girl while I was gone?" I ask, flipping her onto her back so she can get a tummy rub.

When I walk into the kitchen, I see the note Sophie left on the counter. Like always, if she knew I was coming home late, she would leave a note letting me know where I could find dinner.

"You're home."

I turn at the sound of her voice to see her standing at the opening of the kitchen. She's wearing one of my shirts, her hair is up, and her face is makeup-free. I love that she stays here when I'm out of town. I love even more that she wears my tees to bed when I'm gone.

"I am." I turn away from her and start the microwave.

"Are you okay?" she asks softly.

I take a second, trying to think of a way to answer that question. Am

I okay? Fuck no. Do I want to talk to her about why I'm not okay? Again, fuck no.

I turn to look at her. Jesus, she is so fucking beautiful that just looking at her makes my gut get tight. I want to do what she needs. I always want her to be happy. She told me she needs time, that she's trying to work through some things from her past. I understand that. I know her mom died when she was young, and I know it had to have left a scar on her. She opened up to me about some things, but a lot of information she shared about her past is either from before her mother's death or after she left home and went to Job Corps. There's a huge chunk of time she always skims over. I know that whatever it is she's holding in is the thing keeping us at a standstill.

I want to be with her; I want a future with her, but I need her to want it too. That's why last night, after getting off the phone with her, I called Justin and had him do a hard run—also known as an extensive background check—on her. What I never expected was for him to tell me about a police report from right before she was emancipated from her father shortly after her mother's death.

"Come here," I tell her, setting Daisy on the ground.

"What's wrong?" She shuffles her feet, not looking at me.

"Come here, Sophie," I repeat more firmly this time. I hold out my hand, and she finally walks to me, her steps slow and unsure.

"I feel like something's wrong," she whispers, searching my face when my hand wraps around hers pulls her to me.

"We need to talk."

"Oh no," she whispers.

I pick her up, placing her on the counter, where I stand between her legs, not giving her any room to run when I say what I have to say. "I need to tell you something."

"Okay." She nods, her hands balling into fists on her thighs.

"I had your background ran a few months ago. And again yesterday."

"What?" she breathes, her eyes widening.

"You won't open up to me, Sophie."

"I cannot believe you did that!"

"You didn't give me much choice," I say calmly.

"I didn't?" she asks, narrowing her eyes.

"No, you didn't," I growl.

"You can't just force me to talk to you." She pushes my chest.

"I'm not forcing you," I argue, not budging.

"You had my background ran, you jerk. What do you call that?"

"I needed to know what I'm dealing with," I explain.

"Don't worry about it. You don't need to deal with it anymore!" she yells, shoving my chest, trying to get off the counter.

"Stop." I grab her wrists, bringing them around her back and caging her in. "No more bullshit, Sophie. Talk to me. I need you to tell me what happened," I say, softening my voice.

"I think it's stupid," she says quietly, her body finally sagging against mine.

"What?" I ask surprised.

"Now that I've been going to my group and hearing stories from other women who have really been hurt, my story seems stupid," she says quietly.

"It's not stupid." I pick her up off the counter, and her legs wrap around my hips as I carry her down the hall to my room.

"What are you doing?" she asks as I lay her on the bed then climb in next to her.

"We're going to talk. You're going to tell me what happened," I state.

"You know, I really don't like it when you completely ignore what I tell you."

"Okay, baby. Talk to me," I tell her, adjusting her so that we're face to face.

"Gahhhh, you're so annoying," she whines.

"Talk, Soph."

"Fine." She sighs, closing her eyes.

I listen quietly, running my hand through her hair as she tells me everything I already learned from her police report. Hearing it from her mouth has me ready to kill someone, and by the time she's done talking, I have mentally planned my trip to Seattle.

"So, you see, it's really not that bad," she says, looking up at me.

I know it could have been much worse, but I also know that what happened to her changed the course of her life even more than it had already when she lost her mother. And even if she doesn't want to admit it, I know that the loss of her mom when she was so young has a lot to do with her avoiding any type of relationship with people.

"Sophie, what happened to you was bad," I confirm.

"Not as bad as it could have been," she says softly. "I always knew it could have been worse, but I never understood to what extreme. After hearing what happened to some of the women in my group, I understand now, and I'm even more thankful. I hate that I've been so weak."

"You did what you had to do to protect yourself."

"I didn't though. I hid out in my house, afraid to meet new people or even date."

"You moved to another state all alone," I remind her.

"Only because I wanted to buy a house."

"You can say you did it because you wanted to buy a house, but I think you did it because you were ready to change your life. You're a lot stronger than you give yourself credit for."

"I don't know," she mumbles, nervously playing with the pocket of my T-shirt.

"I do. Look at how you are with me."

"You're sweet." She smiles, running her fingers along my jaw.

I'm glad she sees me that way; I never want her to be afraid of me "You tryin' to ruin my street cred?"

She doesn't answer. She just looks down at Daisy, who's now cuddled up between us. When her eyes come up, mine narrow on her.

"What?" She smiles.

"You tryin' to say my dog isn't badass?"

"Um…" She starts to laugh, "I never said anything like that."

"You said it all with your eyes."

"I didn't. I swear!" She laughs, and I run a finger down the center of her face, feeling my eyes go soft before leaning in to kiss her.

"You are a lot stronger than you think, and that's why, tomorrow, we're going to my parents' house."

"I can't," she says, and I'm done talking about this.

I roll her to her back, pinning her underneath me. Her chest begins rising and falling rapidly, and I slide to the side, keeping her hands where they are with one on mine. My eyes stay locked on hers as I slowly slide my T-shirt she's wearing up until her tits are exposed. I have been gradually teaching her about sex. When I take her for the first time, I want her to know what to expect. I never want her to be afraid of me for any reason.

"Jesus," I whisper, looking at her tits—large, over a handful, nipples firm and dark pink. I lean forward, pulling first one then the other into my mouth, licking and biting. Her body starts wiggling under mine, her moans becoming louder, her nails digging into my scalp. "You want me to make you come?" I ask, biting down on her nipple while pinching her other one.

"Yes," she moans, her head pressing back into the pillow, her body arching.

I squeeze her breast before running my palm down her stomach along the edge of her shorts and dipping under, my fingers meeting smooth skin the whole way. Knowing she is completely bare has me gritting my teeth. I slide one finger over her clit, circling as I watch her face; her eyes pop open and meet mine. She looks gorgeous like this— her face flushed, her bottom lip tucked between her teeth, her breasts quickly rising and falling. Sliding one finger lower, I enter her slowly, studying her expression. She's so tight and wet that my already-hard dick jumps, wanting to see for itself what she would feel like wrapped around it.

"Oh God, Nico," she moans, her eyes closing again.

I start to move my finger a little quicker, and then I add another one, using my thumb to press and roll her clit. When I suck her nipple into my mouth, she cries out as her pussy pulls my fingers deeper, her body grinding down on my hand before shaking and going limp.

"Holy cow," she breathes, opening her eyes.

I lean forward to kiss her, my fingers still between her legs moving in slow stokes. I gently pull my fingers out before bringing them to my mouth, licking them clean and kissing her once again.

"You're fucking beautiful, baby, but watching you get off is mind-blowing."

Her head comes forward, her face going into my neck. I hold her for a few minutes, just enjoying her smell and the way she feels tucked next to me.

"I need to eat." I watch her eyes heat. "Food, baby," I tell her, smiling before fixing her shirt and pulling her out of bed.

"But...I want to touch you," she says, tugging against my hand that's pulling her towards the kitchen.

"You will, just not tonight," I tell her, fighting my body for control.

"Why not?"

"I need to eat, and then tomorrow, we're gonna have a busy day when I introduce you to my family, so we'll need a good night's sleep."

"I'm not ready," she whimpers, and I just shake my head, guiding her down the hall.

"I'm done talking about this. You're going to meet my family," I state.

"But—"

"No buts, baby. It's past time." I lead her into the kitchen, where I heat the food she left out for me for the second time. She watches quietly; I can see the wheels in her head spinning. "What's going on in that head of yours?"

"I can't meet your family," she says quietly.

"Yes, you can, and you are going to."

"What if I have a breakdown or something?"

"I'll be there with you," I say, looking her straight in the eyes.

"Your family will think I'm nuts." She shakes her head.

"They're nuts, so they won't even notice that you're nuts."

"I'm not nuts. Don't say that." She smacks my arm.

I grab her hand, bringing it to my mouth and kissing it. "Sophie, relax. They will love you," I say soothingly.

"How do you know that?"

"I just do."

We sit in the kitchen while I eat and she watches me closely. When I finish, we go back to my room. She gets into bed, while I make quick work in the shower before pulling on a pair of sweats and climbing into bed with her.

"It will be okay," I reassure her, kissing the top of her head and pulling her closer to me.

"Okay," she says quietly.

I listen to her breathing even out before I follow her to sleep.

When I wake up, the sun is just starting to shine through the window. I look around, seeing that Sophie isn't in bed; I listen, trying to see if I can hear her somewhere in the house.

"Soph?" I call, and nothing. I feel my eyebrows draw together, and I sit up in bed. "Soph?" I call again, and this time, Daisy comes into the room. That's when I know she took off.

Getting out of bed, I walk into the kitchen. The house is quiet; her bag, which was on the bar last night, is now gone, along with her keys.

"Fuck," I whisper, running my hands down my face. I can't believe I slept through her leaving. I have always been a light sleeper, and the one time that shit would have come in handy, I fucking slept like the dead.

I walk back to the room, pick up my phone, and hit dial on her number. When it goes right to voicemail, my blood pressure starts to rise. "Call me back," I demand then toss my phone on the bed before pulling a pair of jeans, a shirt, and boots on. Once dressed, I head to the kitchen, feed Daisy and grab the keys for my bike, go to my garage and pull the tarp off my Harley, and hop on before using my feet to back it out of the driveway.

I stop at her house first, knowing full-well she won't be here. I get off my bike and let myself inside using the key she gave me a few weeks ago. She's had a key to my place almost from the start. After our first run-in with my neighbor, Sophie decided she should be the one watching Daisy when I go out of town. I'm cool with that; Deb is harmless, but still. If it makes Sophie feel more secure, I am down with it.

I walk into her house, seeing that everything's the same as it always is. She keeps her place in order, except for her bedroom, which, as usual, has clothes and shoes scattered all over the place. I look around, trying to gauge if she's been back here since leaving my house. Her overnight bag is on the bed, and I take a few steps and open it up. The first thing I see is my shirt. I shake my head, digging around for a few more seconds. Not finding anything helpful, I shove everything back inside before heading out to search around town.

The longer I look, the more pissed I become. I have called her on and off all day, and she hasn't answered or returned my calls. The more hours that pass without hearing from her, the more tightly wound and worried I become. When I left her place this morning, I placed a piece of tape on the edge of the door to let me know if she returned home, and so far, she hasn't. I decide to go home and feed Daisy before going back to Sophie's to camp out until she gets there.

I look at the clock on the wall when the front door opens. It's after three in the morning. I sit forward on the couch, watching as she puts her bag down near the door then kicks off her shoes so they go flying towards her room. When she finally sees me, she screams out and backs up into her closed door, holding her chest. I notice that her eyes are red and puffy. Knowing that she has been crying all day about some dumb shit she talked herself into only pisses me off more.

"What are you doing here?" she asks, pushing a hand through her hair.

"What am I doing here? Is that really the question you want to fucking ask me right now?" My eyebrows come together.

"Look, I'm sorry, but I don't think we should see each other any-more," she says as I stand.

"You don't think we should see each other anymore," I repeat, walk-ing towards her in measured steps.

"That's what I just said. I just... I just don't think this is working out," she stutters, looking past me, probably wondering if she could make it if she bolts.

My eyes narrow on her before I reply. "You're mine, Sophie. I don't give a fuck what you think or what the excuse is you try to give me, but you are mine." I let out a growl as I press her into the wall. I'm so pissed I can't even see straight. "You snuck out of my bed then out of the house. Do you know how worried I've been?"

"You shouldn't have been," she says shakily.

"I shouldn't be worried about my woman when she sneaks out of my bed and is gone until three in the morning?"

"Well...I—" She tries to look away, so I force her face back towards mine with my hand on her jaw.

"That was fucked up," I tell her, pronouncing the last two words clearly and slowly.

"I'm sorry. I just don't think this is working out," she tries again.

"You said that already, and it's bullshit. You're just afraid and using it as an excuse to push me away. I told you before. You run, I chase."

"You're insane," she says, trying to wiggle free.

"Probably, but that doesn't change the fact you're mine. I'm done with the bullshit, Sophie," I growl in her ear, my grip on her tightening.

"It's not bullshit."

"Baby, you're not listening to me."

"I am! You just said the way I feel is bullshit," she argues.

"No, you pushing me and anyone else who tries to get close to you away is bullshit."

"You can't say that."

"Fuck if I can't. You have been doing it from the start, pushing me away while holding on tight. I told you yesterday. I'm done with it."

"I'm not ready!" she yells in my face, catching me off guard.

"When, huh?" I ask, pressing her deeper into the wall. "What do you need? Ten more years? In ten years, will you be ready to try to live again? Or will you find some other excuse?" I roar my questions.

"Stop it," she says softly, tears filling her eyes.

"No, Sophie, I'm not going to stop. I need you with me, but in order for that to happen, I need you to want us as much as I do. I need you to stop letting your fears run you."

"I'm afraid!" she cries.

"You think I don't know that? I won't let anything happen to you," I tell her gently, pulling her body against mine.

"What if I lose you too?" She whispers the words, and my heart cracks open. I knew that this was one of the things holding her back, and I am fucking happy that she is finally realizing it.

"You won't." I hold her tight as her body sags against mine, and I say a silent prayer that she is finally getting it. "No more running, Sophie," I say, running my hand down her back. "From now on, we figure this out together."

"I'm sorry I ran and that you were worried," she apologizes quietly.

"It's fine." I hold her a little tighter, breathing in her smell. "You need to pack some shit so we can go home," I tell her after a few minutes.

"I'm home."

"We're going to my house, where you will be staying more often than not from now on," I state.

"You can't just decide that," she says, shaking her head.

"I didn't just decide that. I decided it a long time ago." I step away from her, turning her towards her room. "Now, go pack so we can go home. I'm fucking exhausted after searching for your ass all over the city today."

"You're very annoying," she says, walking to her bedroom.

I follow behind her, watching as she dumps the stuff in her overnight bag onto the bed. "You stole my shirt."

"What?" she asks, looking over her shoulder.

"You stole my shirt," I repeat, picking up my shirt off the bed and showing it to her.

"I must have forgotten about it." She looks away quickly, making me smile.

"Admit it, baby. You were taking a piece of me with you."

"You are so full of yourself," she says with fake exasperation.

"Whatever you say." I laugh when her cheeks turn pink. I watch her put some stuff in the bag and notice how little she's bringing. "That's not enough," I tell her when she starts to zip it up.

"It's plenty."

"No, pack more."

I walk to her closet, grabbing another bag down from a high shelf. As I'm pulling it down, something hits me on top of my head before bouncing off and hitting the floor with a rubbery thud. Sophie squeaks before running towards me, grabbing whatever it is that hit me and putting it behind her back.

"What is that?"

"Nothing," she answers, walking backwards.

"Really?" I place the bag on the bed before slowly following her.

"Nico, stop right there," she says, her face becoming bright red.

"What's behind your back, baby?"

"It's nothing," she says, her eyes growing bigger the closer I get to her. She starts to turn, and that's when a big purple dildo fumbles out of her hands, bouncing once before rolling under the bed. "It's not mine, I swear!" she says, looking distraught, holding up both her hands in front of her.

"It's not your dildo?" I ask, trying not to laugh.

"No, it's my friend's."

"You have your friend's dildo?" I cock my head to the side.

"Yes," she says, her shoulders slumping.

"So you're telling me you keep a dildo...for your friend...in your closet?" I start to laugh.

"Oh God, that sounds really stupid." She covers her face. "I mean, my friend got it for me."

I bend down, picking it up from underneath the bed. The thing is not only bright purple with sparkles, but it has to be at least a foot long and three inches across.

"I'm going to kill Maggie," she whispers with her eyes closed.

"Babe, I seriously hope you never tried to use this," I say, turning it over in my hand.

"Oh. My. God. Kill me now," she groans, her eyes still closed.

"Baby." I laugh so hard that tears start to fall from my eyes.

"No, I'm pretending that if I can't see you, then this isn't really happening," she says, making me laugh harder than I have in my entire life.

"Look at me," I finally wheeze out.

"Nuh-uh…" she mumbles, eyes still closed.

I drop the dildo to the bed before I put my hands in her hair and stop laughing. "Open your eyes, Sophie."

"No."

"Baby, please open your eyes." I push her hair away from her face. "Hey," I say when she finally opens them. "You know, with me, you never have to be embarrassed, right?"

"You say that, but a giant purple dildo just fell out of my closet and hit you on the head. That is the definition of a reason to be embarrassed."

"You have to admit it's pretty damn funny." I chuckle, and her eyes narrow.

"I'm really going to kill Maggie," she growls.

"Is that the only toy you have?" I ask, watching her eyes get wide.

"I don't have toys."

"Guess we'll have to change that."

"What?" she breathes, searching my face.

"Finish packing," I tell her without saying anything else. My dick's hard as fuck thinking about the things I'm going to show her. The image of fucking her with her wrists bound to my bed and clamps attached to her nipples has me groaning and shoving my face into her neck. "Please just finish packing." I kiss her once on the side of her neck before stepping back.

"Okay," she whispers shakily before going back to her bed to finish packing.

IT'S AFTER FIVE in the morning by the time we reach my house. I park my bike back in the garage before helping Sophie carry her bags inside.

"Hey, girl." Sophie stops to pick up Daisy, who is bouncing around at our feet. She follows me down the hall to my bedroom, talking to Daisy in a baby voice the whole way. I drop her bags into my closet, walk to Sophie to take Daisy from her hands, and set her outside the bedroom door before closing it. "What are you doing? She always sleeps with me when I'm here," she says, her eyebrows drawing together.

"You're right, but we're not going to sleep right now," I tell her, walking her backwards towards the bed.

My mouth drops to hers and I lick the seam of her mouth before pulling her bottom lip between my teeth and biting it. I feel her fingers digging into my chest as my hands slide her shirt up and over her head. I'm done holding myself back. I pull away from her long enough to drag my shirt over my head. I can hear her breathing increase as my hands go to the button of her jeans, unsnapping it before dragging her zipper down.

Our eyes are locked; her hands go to my shoulders, her nails digging into my skin. I shove her jeans down her hips before pushing her back to the bed, grabbing them by the ankles, and pulling them off completely. I toss them to the side, running my hands up her calves to her thighs before taking her mouth in another deep kiss. I move between her legs, spreading them wider with mine. I slide my hand around her back, flicking the clasp of her bra and popping it open.

"Oh," she whispers, her eyes widening as I slowly drag her straps down her shoulders, exposing her tits.

"Jesus, you're beautiful." I drop to my knees on the floor so her breasts are level with my face. Keeping our eyes locked, I pull one nipple into my mouth. Hers opens on a silent moan, her head falling back. "Watch me, baby," I demand. My hands run up her thighs and my thumbs trail over her pussy on the outside of her panties before traveling up to her hips. "Lift."

She does as she's told, her hips lifting slightly off the bed enough for me to pull them down. I lean back to drag them down her legs. Once off, I go back to my original position between her legs. Our eyes meet again, and hers look nervous.

"Trust me to take care of you."

She nods, and I pull her mouth up to mine, my fingers fisting in her hair as I kiss her once more before dragging my mouth away to kissing a trail down her neck, cupping both breasts. Then I lick and bite both nipples before kissing down her stomach. I nip the skin above her pubic bone and see the muscles of her abdomen tighten.

"Sit up and watch me."

Her arms go behind her to prop herself up on her elbows, pushing her breasts out. I spread her thighs farther apart before licking her pussy from bottom to top.

"Oh God!" she cries out, one of her arms coming out from behind her. Her hand grabs my hair.

I keep at her, licking her, fucking her with my mouth. I put one finger inside her then add another, her hips lifting as she screams my name. I feel her pussy already clamping down hard on my fingers.

"Fuck, baby, you're so hot." I pull her limp body up the bed before leaning back to pull off my jeans and positioning myself between her legs. Leaning forward, I kiss her deeply as her fingers dig into the muscles of my ass, trying to pull me inside. "You want my cock?" I ask against her mouth, biting her bottom lip. My dick is throbbing, my balls pulling up tight, ready to explode.

"Yes, please," she begs, her hands moving up to claw my back. Her nails burrowing into my skin causes me to shift my hips forward, the head of my cock rubbing against her wetness.

"I'm gonna give it to you, but I gotta go slow. I don't want to hurt you."

She nods, her eyes widening when she looks down between our bodies. I can see fear on her face now. I'm not a small guy to begin with, and having a Prince Albert piercing makes look that much more intimidating, which is why I didn't show her before.

"What is that?" she asks. If it weren't for the scared sound of her voice, I would have laughed.

"It's just a piercing, baby. Look at me." I hold her face; her eyes lock on mine. "I promise it will feel good."

She nods, and I hold my cock in one hand, sliding through her folds before pressing myself slowly inside her. Her wet, tight heat wrapping around me has my head dropping forward, my teeth gritting.

"You feel so good." I lift my head so I can watch her face; her eyes close, and I can feel the barrier proving that she is mine and only mine. I run my finger along her cheek, and her eyes open at my touch. "You know, the moment I saw you, I knew you were the one for me," I say gently, watching her eyes get big. "You're mine, Sophie. Every beautiful inch of you is mine."

I thrust completely inside her, wanting to get it over with. She cries out, and I stop moving, just watching her face as she adjusts to me. She feels so good that it's taking everything in me not to slam into her like a madman.

"I gotta move, baby. Are you okay?"

"Yes." She brings her fingers up to my face, running them down my jaw. The look on her face is so gentle, and it holds so much emotion that I know she feels it too.

I start to move slowly at first, my hand traveling down her side to lift her thigh around my waist. Our mouths meet again in a slow kiss. My strokes are slow and gentle, not wanting to hurt her. Her pussy starts to pull me deeper, and I'm so close that my balls start to pull up tight from the way her walls are squeezing me.

"I need you to come," I tell her.

"I can't," she pants.

I circle my hips, hitting her g-spot. Her head falls back, and a loud moan leaves her mouth.

"You can. I can feel it. I need you to let go, baby." I pull back, rolling my thumb over her clit before pinching it, causing her to clamp down harder. "Shit," I breathe, trying to hold off my own orgasm.

"Nico!" she cries, rolling her hips up to meet mine.

"Let go."

I lean forward, pulling her nipple into my mouth before biting down. Our bodies are both slick with sweat, our breathing heavy. She cries out, her head lifting and her mouth locking down on my shoulder, causing my own orgasm. I can feel my release all the way to my toes. With her pussy squeezing my cock, I slow my strokes, taking her mouth in another deep kiss before laying my forehead against hers as I try to catch my breath.

"I love you," she whispers, her eyes closing. I know she's half asleep and probably won't remember saying it, but I will. I feel the same. I knew from the moment I saw her that she's it—my boom.

I slide out of her, hating to lose that connection. My head falls forward when I realize I didn't wear a condom. "Shit."

"What's wrong?" she asks, running a hand through my hair, down the back of my neck.

"Nothing, baby. Stay here; I'll be right back." I slide down the bed, kissing her stomach before going into the bathroom.

I turn on the hot water in the sink, grabbing a couple of washcloths and cleaning myself up quickly before walking back into the room. I take a second to appreciate her—her hair spread out across my pillow, her body glistening with sweat, her legs still slightly parted, showing off her pussy.

I walk to the side of the bed, trying to figure out exactly what I want to say to her. I fucked up. She was a virgin, and chances are she's not on the pill, but I can't bring myself to be disappointed if she got pregnant. I want that. I know I'm clean; I get tested every couple of months. I got checked right after I met her.

Her eyes slightly open as I bend, placing the warm cloth between her legs.

"How you feeling?"

"Fine. Sleepy," she replies with a small smile, her eyes heavy with sleep.

"You want a shirt?" I ask, knowing that she always sleeps in something. Someday, I will get her used to sleeping naked, but not now.

"Yes, please." She sits up, watching as I grab a shirt from the dresser for her, and a pair of boxers for myself, pulling them up on the way to the bed.

"I really hate covering you up," I tell her, helping her into the shirt.

She laughs, flopping back onto the bed. "I'm so tired." She yawns through her words.

"Well, sneaking out of the bed this morning before spending the day hiding from your man will do that to you."

"I'm really sorry about that," she says, her voice quiet and her eyes soft. "I hate that you were worried. I just didn't know what to do. I feel like ever since I met you, I have wanted something I've never wanted before, and that scares me. I don't know what I'm doing, and my head is all messed up. I just want to make sure I'm good enough for you."

I know I'm looking at her like she's crazy. Sophie's not being good enough for me is laughable, but I can tell by the look on her face that she's serious. I sit down on the side of the bed before pulling her around into my lap.

"You're crazy, you know that?" I push the hair out of her face.

"Stop calling me that," she snaps, slapping my arm.

"No, baby. If you think for one second that what you just said isn't completely whacked, then you're crazy."

"I'm not. It's true."

"No, first of all, you're way too good for someone like me, but I'm way too fucking selfish to let you go."

"I'm not too good for you." She shakes her head. "You're too good for me. You make me feel safe, and that makes me worry. I don't want to use you as a crutch."

"Baby, when you're in a relationship, it's give and take. It's only right that I make you feel safe, because you make me feel whole."

"This seems like it's moving really fast," she whispers, laying her head on my shoulder.

"You have no idea what fast is. We have been together for a few months, and I've been going slow, wanting you to be comfortable. But like I told you yesterday, I'm done. I will make sure you're happy, but I won't let you continue to put things on hold just because you're afraid." I run my hand down her back and kiss the top of her head. "I need to tell you something."

"Oh God." She buries her face into my chest. "The last time you said that you needed to tell me something, you told me you had my background ran."

"Are you on birth control?" I ask, ignoring her last remark.

"No," she says quietly.

"I forgot the condom. I'm clean. I got checked right after we met."

"I could still get pregnant," she whispers.

"You could." I pull her tighter against me. "I wouldn't mind that."

"I'm starting to think you're the crazy one." She looks up at me, shaking her head.

"I know what I want. I keep telling you this, baby, but you're just not getting it. You are it for me." I lean forward, kissing her forehead.

"How is it possible that you can scare me and make me feel safe at the same time?" she asks, looking up at me, her finger running across my bottom lip.

"I don't know, Sophie, but I do know that what we have is good. No more running." I run a finger down the center of her face.

"I won't run again." She yawns, cuddling closer to me. I bite back a smile, wondering how one chick can make me crazy happy then make me just plain crazy.

"All right. Let's go to sleep."

I settle her back on the bed before letting Daisy into the room. I climb in next to her, and Sophie shifts, her head going to my chest, her arm around my waist, and her leg over mine. I hear her light snore a few minutes after she relaxes. Daisy jumps up on the bed, pushing her way under the covers before settling in. I close my eyes and smile as an image of Sophie, round with my child, flashes through my head.

I know what I want. I always get what I want. And that's the last thought in my head before I fall asleep.

Chapter 7

Sophie

I WAKE UP when I hear a loud ringing. I'm so comfortable that I don't want to open my eyes. I pull my leg higher over Nico's hip, trying to let sleep take me away again. I can feel the slight ache between my thighs, and last night comes back to me, making me smile.

"What's up, bro?" I hear Nico say right before I feel his lips at the top of my head and he slides out from under me. "Yeah, I was up late," he tells the person on the phone. My eyes open, and I see that he's leaving the room.

"Nico?"

"Just a second, baby. My brother's on the phone," he says, walking out of the room.

I get up and swing my legs over the side of the bed. "I'm going to get some water if that's okay?" I say when I see him standing in the hall when I open the door.

"I'll get you some. Go lay back down, baby. I'll be right there," he says, pulling my chin up and kissing me softly on the mouth before turning me back towards the bedroom. After a few minutes, he comes back in the room smiling at me. "Soon. She's just starting to accept that she's mine." He laughs, handing me a glass of water.

"Maybe," I say, smiling into the cup.

"You are. Do you need me to prove it again?" he asks.

I feel my face heat up, but between my legs starts to throb.

"Sure, man. I'll call you soon," he says into the phone before hanging up and tossing it on the nightstand. "Do we need to have another talk?" he asks, crawling across the bed to where I'm lying.

"No. No more talking." I rub my legs together; the look on his face has my whole body primed.

I can't believe I hadn't had sex before. Sex is awesome, something I definitely want to do a lot more of. Then I remember his piercing and how it felt when he was inside me. I want to get a good look at it. I have never even seen anything like that before; it is strangely beautiful on his cock, and it fits him perfectly.

"You're right. We don't need to talk to have this conversation," he states, his body coming over mine, caging me in.

His mouth takes mine in a deep kiss, and before I know it, my shirt is off and his mouth is on my breast, tugging at one of my nipples. I arch into him, dragging my nails down his back.

"Are you sore?" he asks, looking at me, his eyes dark.

"No." I tell him a half-truth. I am a little tender, but nothing will stop me from wanting him again.

"Who does this beautiful body belong to, Sophie?" he asks, clamping down on my other nipple.

"Me," I say with a smile.

"Wrong," he growls, biting down on my nipple, causing me to cry out. "This is all mine." His hand runs from my neck, down between by breasts, over the roundness of my stomach, to between my legs, cupping me there. "You see this?" His fingers wiggle between my legs then up and around my clit. "This is all mine." His mouth opens on my neck before kissing up to my ear. "You're mine, sweet Sophie."

Two fingers plunge into me, causing my head to bend back and my hips to lift up. I don't argue with him; it's pointless. I'm his, just like he says I am. I love this man. As crazy as it is, I'm in love with him.

"That's it. Come for me," he says, his fingers moving more rapidly.

I do as he says and come with a cry, clinging to him as his hips move to between my legs, and with one thrust, he is inside me, making me yell out.

"Fuck, yes. This is mine," he groans, pulling out before sinking back in.

My legs wrap around him, his mouth comes back down on mine, his tongue sweeps into my mouth, and then his teeth bite my bottom then top lip. It's all too much. My body is overwhelmed by the feelings he's causing. His hips roll again, his hands going under my ass and lifting it higher.

"I'm going to come," I breathe into his mouth.

His breaths mix with mine as I feel myself clamp down around him. This time, the feelings consume me before we roll and I'm on top, looking down at him. His hands go to my hips, rocking me back and forth. I sit up, my hands going to his chest and our eyes locking.

"Fuck," he groans. His head falls back as my hips roll and lift, hitting my g-spot every time I slide down.

I have no idea what I'm doing, but judging by the look on his face, I don't think I'm doing it wrong. I sit back, my hands going to my breasts, trying to recreate the feeling he gives me when he sucks on my nipples. My eyes close, and I bite my lip, tugging hard.

"Jesus, baby." My eyes open at the sound of his rough voice; I look down to see his eyes darken, his bottom lip between his teeth, and his muscles flexing. His hips start lifting up to meet mine. "Shit." His thumb goes to my clit, sending me over the edge. I fall forward, my breathing erratic. I can feel him pulsing inside me, and I remember that we didn't use a condom again.

"We didn't use a condom," I say, panting.

"Good," he says, running his hand down my back.

"You can't be serious," I groan, rubbing my face against his chest.

"Deadly." He holds me tighter. "You're stuck with me." I lift my head to look into his eyes. "I'm going to get you pregnant within the next couple of months. Hell, you could be pregnant right now."

"You can't just plan that. And I'm not pregnant." I roll my eyes.

"Just did, and you never know. You could be carrying my son right now," he mumbles against my mouth before kissing me again.

I know this isn't normal, but it feels right. The image of a sweet baby boy goes through my head, and I can imagine Nico and his hard exterior being so gentle and sweet with a tiny baby. Knowing how he is with Daisy only makes me want to see the vision come to life. I pull my mouth away from his and lay my head against his chest. I must've fallen asleep, because the next thing I know, the doorbell is going off, causing me to jump.

"Someone's at the door," I mumble sleepily.

"I know. Let me up, baby," Nico says, rolling us to the side.

I feel him slide out and can't believe I slept with him inside me. Pulling the covers up over my shoulder, I watch as he goes to the dresser, pulls out a pair of sweats, and puts them on before leaving the room. Daisy makes her way out of the covers, scaring me half to death before she jumps off the bed to follow Nico. I roll to my back and lie there for a second. Then I remember that Nico left the room without a shirt and wonder if it's Deb stopping by. Since I've been seeing Nico, that woman has stopped by at least three times under the ruse of needing something. I know that Nico isn't interested in her, but for me, I can't help but feel a little territorial where he's concerned.

I get out of bed, find a shirt for him, and pull another one on over my head. It's so long that it hits me just above my knees, so I figure I'm covered enough. I walk into the living room and see Nico in the kitchen with his hip against the counter and a cup of coffee in his hand. Another guy is there with him; his back is to me, but he's big—even a little bigger than Nico. I pause where the hardwood floors start when Nico's head turns my way and our eyes lock. I feel nervous seeing this other guy in the kitchen, and not knowing who he is makes my hands begin to sweat and the need to run take over.

"Come here, Sophie," Nico says, his eyes watching me closely.

I swallow hard, trying to fight my own fears, trusting Nico to take care of me. The guy in the kitchen has turned his head and is now watching me, and I tug at the bottom of Nico's shirt I put on.

"Sophie," Nico repeats, and I look at him and see that he has stepped away from the counter. "This is my cousin, Kenton. Remember you saw him with me when the guy was trying to break into your house?"

His cousin. This guy is part of his family. I take a breath then let it out. "Yeah, hi. Nice to meet you," I say, smiling shyly at him as I wipe my sweaty palms off on the shirt.

His eyes look me over then go soft. "You too, doll," he says gently.

What is with these big scary guys and their gentle souls? I wonder.

"You want some coffee, babe?" Nico asks.

My eyes go to him and I nod. "Yes, please. I'll be right back," I say, walking quickly back to the room; I need to put some pants on. I already feel uncomfortable being around people, and being half dressed won't work in my favor.

When I get back to the kitchen, Nico has a cup of coffee and toast with honey waiting for me. I hand him a shirt, and he smiles, kissing my forehead before setting the shirt on the counter. Suddenly, he lifts me at my waist and sets me on the counter near the corner so that he is between me and Kenton. I'm not sure if he knows what he's doing, but I suspect he does it on purpose, and I want to cry with relief that he gets it.

"So, what are you guys doing this weekend?" Kenton asks, looking between the two of us.

I know what I want to do—I want to go back to bed and maybe have a good look at that piercing. I feel my cheeks heat up when I think about the way I felt when he was inside me, how alive my body felt when he made me orgasm with it, and how I really wanted another couple million of them.

"Baby, stop," Nico says, his mouth next to my ear, "I can tell exactly what you're thinking, and you're gonna make me be rude to my cousin, 'cause I'm about to pick your sexy little ass up, carry you to the bedroom, slam the door, and have my way with you again whether he can hear your screams or not."

I bend my head forward, blocking my face with my hair. My face feels like it's on fire. Apparently, I am now a super slut. "Sorry," I whisper.

"Don't be," he whispers back, his hand running along my thigh as he kisses my forehead. "I think we're just going to hang around here," Nico says, leaning his hip against the counter between my legs and picking up his coffee cup.

"You're not going home?

"Nah. Cash, Lilly, and the kids just got home from Alaska. Asher's praying over November's belly for a little boy, and Trevor is keeping Liz at home, waiting for her to go into labor."

"Jesus, you guys are like a baby-making factory," Kenton says, shaking his head.

"Nothing wrong with that," Nico mumbles, and I look at him and see that he is serious. His eyes meet mine and go soft before he leans in, kissing me once again.

"Shit, you too?" Kenton asks.

Nico nods before leaning back again.

"I knew, but I mean… I didn't know how serious you were."

"That serious, my man," he says, rubbing my thigh again.

I feel a nervous laugh climb up my throat; I cover my mouth, trying to hold it in, but I can't. Kenton looks at me and smiles, and Nico shakes his head.

"What's so funny?"

I shake my head before bursting out laughing. "Sorry." I laugh again and cover my face.

"You gonna let us in on the joke?" Nico asks, pulling my hands away from my face, smiling at me.

"Baby factory," I say, repeating Kenton's words, and I can't help but laugh again. I'm not even sure why I find it so funny.

"It's true, doll. My cousins are tryin' to take over the world with their offspring," Kenton says, smiling.

"Yeah? You wanna start your shit? How are things going with you and Autumn?" Nico asks.

Kenton's face changes completely. The smile he's wearing slides off his face, and he growls, "Don't start, Nico."

"What, you don't want me to tell you that you're a stupid fuck?"

"Fuck you," Kenton says, glaring at Nico.

"Nah, I'm good."

"You know, I came over here to get a break from that drama."

"You need to put an end to that drama, man, and just do what you both need."

"How can I when the damn woman won't listen to me?"

"Make her listen," Nico says, and Kenton glares, shaking his head. I feel sorry for him for some reason; he looks like he's really upset about whatever it is they're talking about. "Fix your shit."

"You think I haven't tried?" he asks softly, looking guilty.

"No, I don't think you have. I know you. I know that, when you want something, you make it happen. So you can sit there all day feeling sorry for yourself and talking bullshit, but I know if you wanted to, you would be at home with her right now instead of drinking my coffee and interrupting my day off with my woman."

"Hey." I hit him in chest.

"What? It's true." Nico shrugs like he wasn't just a giant jerk.

"It's not nice," I tell him.

"I don't need to be nice to anyone but you." His eyes meet mine and go soft, and I shake my head at his logic.

"I'm gonna head out," Kenton says, standing.

"You don't have to go," I tell him quickly, feeling guilty that he's leaving because I'm here.

"It's okay, doll. I got stuff to do anyways," Kenton says, taking one last drink from his coffee cup and putting it on the counter near the sink.

"Well, it was nice to meet you."

"You too." He smiles, making my heart do a little flutter.

Nico is hotter, but Kenton has his own brand of handsome with his shaggy dark hair, tan skin, blue eyes, and scruffy jaw—a look that says if you happened to get lost in the woods with him, he would be able to build you a house with his own hands then go out and find dinner with nothing but what he could find in the forest.

"I'm sure I'll see you around," he says, heading to the front door.

Nico follows him, talking softly. I don't know what he's saying, but Kenton shakes his head before giving a chin lift as Nico closes the door behind him.

"That wasn't very nice," I tell him as he walks back into the kitchen.

"I told you before—I don't need to be nice to anyone but you. Besides, he needs to get his shit straight."

"What stuff?" I ask curiously.

"Hold that thought, baby." He picks up his phone from the counter when it starts to ring. He looks at the screen and his eyebrows shoot together before he answers.

"Drake. What's up, man?" he asks, his hand rubbing absently along my thigh. "Like I told your dad, there isn't much you can do unless you can prove that shit." He shakes his head, looking off in the distance. "Don't do that crap; you will regret it, and it will give him the upper hand. Just do as I told you before. I got your back. Call if you need me," he says before hanging up.

"Is everything okay?" I ask, not liking the worried look on his face.

"Yeah. Don't worry about it." He pulls me forward on the counter until we're hip to hip. "You done eating? You want more coffee?"

"I'm done," I tell him as he pulls my legs around his hips and then my arms around his neck. "What are you doing?"

"We're going to shower."

"Oh," I breathe as he nips at my neck and walks us towards the bathroom.

"So, YOU'RE TELLING me you lost your virginity when you were twelve?" I ask in shock.

I look at Nico, who is sitting across from me on the bed, wearing nothing but a sheet. We had a shower, and then he brought me back to bed and did some crazy things to my body that had me screaming out his name before he was even inside me—once again, without a condom. When we were done and I reminded him we hadn't used one, he informed me that it was too late and there was nothing I could do about it. I'm not quite sure why it turns me on every time he says it, but it does.

Now, it's after ten at night. We're sitting in bed with a giant pepperoni pizza he ordered an hour ago for delivery between us. When it arrived, he quickly pulled on a pair of sweats, told me I better not get dressed, and left the room to answer the door, only to come back and get naked again.

"I lost my virginity at twelve. I had no clue what I was doing, but that was the first time I had sex," he says, taking a bite of pizza.

"That's crazy."

"I guess." He shrugs, taking a drink of beer.

"I always wanted to do it," I tell him, wiping my mouth. "I've just been too afraid."

"Thank God you hadn't done it before; I don't think I could've handled it if I wasn't your first. I don't even like thinking about anyone else looking, let alone someone touching what's mine."

"I don't know." I shrug this time. "I think it would be good to have experience. I have no idea what I'm doing."

I hear him growl, and my head flies up from where I was looking at the pizza.

"Don't even fucking say that shit," he says, his eyes going hard.

"What?"

"Anything you need to know, I'll teach you. You won't be having sex with anyone else. The only person you need to please is me, and I'm fucking thrilled with the way you take me," he says with a glare.

"I didn't say I was going to go out and start ho-ing around." I roll my eyes.

"You better not even think about what it would be like to be with someone else."

"I'm not." I frown, watching as he moves the pizza box from between us and sets it on the bedside table. "What are you doing?"

He pulls my paper plate from my hand, setting it on top of the pizza box. His hands go to my ankles, dragging me so I'm flat on the bed underneath him.

"What are you doing?" I repeat as his hands pull both of mine above my head.

"Going to make sure I'm the only one you think about," he says, rolling his hips into mine, making me gasp as his head bends forward, Then he takes one of my nipples into his mouth. I'm pretty sure every woman in the world would be thinking about him, and only him, if they knew him.

"Oh my God," I moan, shoving my head back into the pillow.

Suddenly, the doorbell starts going off. Daisy, who was asleep on one of the pillows, jumps up and runs into the living room barking.

"Fuck," Nico clips. "Do not fucking move." He kisses me once before jumping off the bed and leaving the room while pulling on a pair of sweats. After about five minutes, he comes back into the room with a scowl on his face.

"Who is it?" I ask, putting on one of his T-shirts and a pair of my cut-off sweats.

"Sven. I gotta go out of town for a couple days, babe. You gonna be good here?" he asks, and I can hear the concern in his voice. I know he hates leaving me alone. I hate when he leaves for any length of time, but I know he loves his job.

"Who's Sven?" I ask, cleaning up our mess on his nightstand.

"He's a friend of the family who recently moved out of town to Vegas. He needs me to fly back with him."

"Why?" I asked, confused.

"He opened a club and has been having some trouble."

"So what are you doing to help him?" I ask, getting nervous.

I watch him as he goes to the closet to pull out his black duffle bag. He shoves some clothes inside before walking over to the dresser and pulling out a black box, putting it in the bag too.

"Why do you need that?" I ask him as he pulls his gun out from the nightstand and checks the clip.

"You know I always have my gun."

He's right. I know he always carries his gun, but I don't like that he's going to Vegas and taking a gun with him when he just told me a friend of the family has been having problems at his club.

"I don't like this," I say, voicing my fear out loud.

"Baby, you know this is what I do," he says, coming to stand in front of me, his hands going under my jaw and tilting my head back. "I will be home before you know it, and we can get back to baby-making." He gives me a naughty grin before getting closer to me.

"You're crazy. Stop trying to distract me." I bat his hands away from my breasts, where his fingers started toying with my nipples through his shirt.

"I can't help it. I'm pissed I finally got you where I want you and now have to leave."

"You don't have to leave. You could stay home with me," I say, sliding my hands up his chest and watching as his eyes darken with my touch.

"Don't fuck around. You know I will have you bent over the side of the bed before you can say 'Nico,'" he growls, kissing me.

My clit pulses at his words. I want him to do that, and I really don't want him to leave.

"Yo! You ready or what?" is yelled from the living room, startling me and breaking the moment.

"Shut the fuck up and sit down!" Nico shouts back before placing his forehead against mine. "Be a good girl while I'm gone. Make sure to call me when you get home from work in the evenings, and don't forget to set the alarm when you're in the house."

"I know, I know." I roll my eyes. I get the same lecture every time he goes out of town.

"All right, baby. Come walk me out," he says, picking up his bag and the pizza box.

I follow him out of the room carrying the rest of the mess to throw away. When we reach the living room, the guy who must be Sven stands and runs a hand through his dark hair. He's pretty—like model-pretty—with dark hair, tan skin, brown eyes, and eyelashes any woman would be jealous of.

"Who do we have here?" he asks, his eyes doing a head-to-toe sweep, making me feel naked. I automatically grab the back of Nico's shirt for comfort.

"She's Sophie. She's mine and none of your damn business, so take your eyes off her," Nico growls, and the guy looks at him before smiling big and crossing his arms over his chest while rocking back onto the heels of his boots.

"Shit, you too, huh?" He shakes his head, laughing. I don't know what he's talking about, but he seems to think it's funny.

"Shut the fuck up and go sit down," Nico tells him again, shaking his own head.

I wonder if he talks to everyone like this. I have seen him talk to not only Kenton, but now Sven too.

"You're not very nice to your friends," I tell him when we reach the kitchen.

"What?" he asks, setting the pizza box on the counter before taking the garbage from my hand and putting it in the trash can.

"You're mean to your friends. You told Kenton he's stupid, and just now, you told that guy to shut up."

"Kenton needs a wake-up call, and Sven is the biggest player this side of the Mississippi and was looking at you. Again, as I told you before, I don't need to be nice to anyone but you."

"What about your family? Are you nice to them?"

"I love my family. I also love Kenton and Sven, but that doesn't mean I'm going to hold my tongue. If someone pisses me off, I let them know."

"Alrighty then," I mumble, not wanting to piss him off. It suddenly dawns on me I have pissed him off a few times already, and he had never said anything mean to me, so maybe I'm the exception to the rule. "What about your mom?"

"What about her?"

"Do you hold your tongue with her?"

"Hell yes! My mom is the one person on the planet I'm afraid of," he replies seriously.

"Really?" I ask, surprised.

"Really. She can put the fear of God in anyone."

"Wow." I bite the inside of my cheek, not very excited about meeting her.

"When I get back home, you will meet her," he says, setting his bag down before crowding me against the island, "and when you meet her, she will love you." His face goes soft.

"How do you know?" I look up into his eyes.

"It's hard not to love you." His soft words make my heart beat a little faster. His mouth touches mine in a soft kiss before he pulls his lips away, holding my face gently in his hands. "Now, be good while I'm gone." He smiles, kissing my forehead.

"Always," I tell him, getting up on my tiptoes to kiss him again. "But you be careful, and please don't do anything stupid."

"I'm always careful."

This time when he kisses me, it takes my breath away, and I have to unwind myself from him before he can pick his bag up. I follow him to the door, wanting so badly to tell him that I love him but not wanting to sound like I'm saying it because I'm afraid. He kisses me once more before he pulls the door closed behind him.

"I love you," I whisper, laying my forehead on the cool wood. I tried fighting what I'm feeling for him, and I tried to push him away even when I hurt myself in the process. He's right; I need to start living again. I don't want to push him away and one day have him finally give up on me. I know if I did, I would hate myself for the rest of my life.

Chapter 8

Nico

"SO, YOU REALLY done for, aren't you?" Sven asks as we make our way onto his private plane. Sven is from old money—his father's father's father found oil in Texas on their family's farm at the start of the oil rush. Since then, his family's role in the oil industry has only grown.

"We're not talking about Sophie"—I look over my shoulder—"ever."

"Jesus, it never takes you guys long to get pussy-whipped, does it?" He chuckles, sitting down across from me.

A stewardess in a small blue dress walks up the aisle towards us. Her eyes light up when she looks at me, and I shake my head. Chicks are all the fucking same. They all talk about how men only want one thing from them, but they are constantly throwing themselves at me, yet I never hit on them first. They want the bad-boy experience. Before Sophie, I would have been happy to take this chick into the bathroom to see what she could do with that mouth of hers—hell, I might have pulled out my cock and let her take me right here—but now, the thought of her anywhere near my junk has my shit shriveling up.

"Hello. Welcome aboard. Can I get you anything?"

"No, thanks," I tell her dismissively.

"Nothing to drink or eat?"

"No, thanks," I repeat.

"Are you sure you don't need anything?" she asks seductively leaning forward and giving me a shot of her breast.

My jaw clenches when I see the smile on Sven's face. I can't wait for him to find a woman. I hope when he finds someone that she puts him though hell.

"I don't need anything," I repeat, making each word clear.

"We're good, Stacy. Tell the pilot we're ready to go," Sven says, fixing his suit jacket.

She nods and walks to the front of the plane behind a small curtain.

"You're really gonna to pass up Stacy? She used to work for the circus," he says, and I shake my head, not even bothering to entertain him with that conversation.

"Tell me about what's going on with the club and why you need my help when you have bodyguards and people you pay to deal with this kind of shit," I say, leaning back in my seat.

"I don't trust anyone right now, especially those I have to pay. I don't know if someone's paying them more than I am," he answers, squeezing the bridge of his nose between his fingers.

"You've never trusted anyone," I remind him.

"You're right, but you forget I have a good reason. My mother—the one person my dad should have been able to trust—tried to kill him, and then she was going to do the same thing to me."

"Your mother was also crazy." I shake my head.

When we were young and Sven and his family moved into the area my parents still live in, his mom would make it her daily mission to come to the school and cause a scene. She was constantly accusing her husband and son of trying to kill her or being possessed by the devil; it was always some kind of drama. My father was repeatedly called to their home to settle some kind of domestic dispute. Then one night, Sven's mom went completely over the edge and stabbed Sven's dad six times in his sleep. He was half dead when Sven, who was ten at the time, heard what was happening, hid, and called 911. His dad was in the hospital for six months, and during that time, Sven lived with us. He became one of our brothers.

"You're right," he repeats, rubbing his forehead.

"Dude, what's really going on?" I ask, seeing the stress evident on his face.

"Someone's bringing drugs into my club. Not only are they dealing, but on seven different occasions, women have been roofied. I don't want or need that shit in my place of business. The guy I had asking questions ended up dead on my doorstep with a note telling me that they knew he was working for me." He looks out the window before his eyes come back to me. "Now you—no one knows you, and you sure as fuck look like you could hang with the guys who are dealing in the area. I need you to talk to them and find out who's behind this."

"I'm going to ignore the fact you just said I looked like a drug dealer." I narrow my eyes on him.

"Bro," he laughs, "you and I both know you look like you belong on the other side of the law." He shakes his head, looking me over. "That's why—I have to say—I was surprised to see your girlfriend. She couldn't be more opposite of you if she tried. Does she even have her ears pierced?" he questions with a smile.

"I'm not going to tell you again. You don't need to know anything about Sophie."

"You gonna marry her?"

"Yes," I state immediately.

"Jesus, you've known her for what—a day?"

"A few months, but I knew the moment I saw her," I tell him, watching his eyes widen.

"Why am I just learning about her then?"

"First, there is not one damn reason for you to know about her. Second, I know you bitches love to sit around and gossip like a bunch of women in a knitting club, but unlike you fuckers, my business is my business."

"Does Mom know her?" He smirks, and he knows she doesn't.

If my mom knew about Sophie, the phone chain would have been activated, and everyone and their mothers would know about her. That's why she will meet Sophie as soon as I get back into town; it would be fucked up to introduce Sophie to my mom after I've already married her and knocked her up.

"She'll be meeting her soon enough." I shrug.

"You are so fucked." He laughs, and I couldn't agree more.

Ma is going to be pissed that she is just finding out about her. I send Sophie a quick text telling her we're getting ready to take off in a few minutes and will call her when I land. She sends back a text telling me to be careful, with a small heart and some X's and O's.

I know she loves me; I have been waiting for her to figure it out. I have never been known for my patience, but with her, I want her to have time to accept things. Okay, that's a fucking lie; as soon as possible, I'm planting my kid in her whether she's ready or not. Shit, she could be pregnant now for all we know. I can see her behind my closed eyelids, holding our son or daughter and smiling down at them.

"What's that smile?" Sven asks.

I don't even open my eyes to reply. "Someday, dude, you'll understand," I tell him before zoning out and falling asleep.

"SO YOUR TELLING me that one of the biggest pimps in Vegas has been filtering drugs through my club…in hopes of recruiting new girls?" Sven asks, running his hands through his hair.

I have been in Vegas for over a week now. I didn't think it would take as long as it did to find out what was going on, but I hadn't realized how big this was. I thought for sure this was just some local drug dealer trying to sell his product in the perfect location.

"That's what I'm telling you. I also talked to local drug enforcement officers, and they said this has been happening all over Vegas."

"What do I do?"

"There is not really much you can do. There's no way to know who is bringing it in. Unless you hire some extra security and tighten that up, there isn't anything you can do at this point. People are always going to find a way to buy drugs, even if they do it outside the club. All I can tell you to do is keep an eye out and make sure the women who come into the club know what's going on."

"It's not like I can put up a poster saying 'You may be roofied. Drink at your own risk.'"

"That's not what I'm saying, fucker. You can have a guy you trust at the door giving wristbands letting people know not to leave their drinks unattended. Until the DEA has enough to build a case against the main guy behind this, there just isn't much you can do unless you want to close down your club."

"I'm not letting those fucks run me out of my own club," he growls.

"So, you know what you need to do," I tell him, sitting back in my chair.

"You sure you can't stay for a few more days?" he asks, sitting down behind his desk.

"Nah, man." I run a hand over my head and down my face, "Sophie has been on edge ever since someone tried to break into her house. She tries to hide it, but I know it bothers her."

"Why don't you just say you're pussy-whipped and want to go home to your girl?" he goads.

"When you find someone, you'll understand. Until then, fuck off."

"Why would I want to settle down when I have endless pussy at my disposal?" He shakes his head.

"You say that now."

"Just like you say you're ready to settle down with one woman for the rest of your life." He lifts an eyebrow.

"No, man. You think you will be happy banging some random chick every day for the rest of your life, but I can tell you now—eventually, that shit will get old. You'll start thinking about starting a family and having someone to go home to, someone who isn't after what you can do for them, but what they can do for you."

"You start working for Hallmark?" he asks with a smirk.

"Say what you want, man, but I know when I get home, Sophie will be waiting for me with open arms."

"When I get home, the hot blonde I met today will be waiting for me with open legs," he remarks.

"You're lying to yourself if you think that kind of life will satisfy you forever."

"Whatever, man," Sven grumbles, but I can see it in his eyes that he knows I'm right, even if he doesn't want to admit it to himself. "You know you're a brother to me. Thanks for coming out here on such short notice to help me out." He sighs, running a hand through his hair.

"I've always got your back," I tell him, meaning that shit. Sven is family, even if it isn't by blood.

"All right, before you start getting all sappy and shit, let me call and have the plane readied to take you home."

"That would be appreciated." I smile, ready to get home to my girl. After I make it onto the plane, I send a quick text to Sophie, letting her know I'll be home soon.

The cab pulls up in front of my house a little after seven that night. I start to make my way up the sidewalk when the front door is thrown open and Sophie—wearing a pair of sweats, a tank top, and her hair down, lying against the tops of her breast—runs to me at full speed. I drop my bag to the ground as she crashes into me so hard I'm forced to take a step back to catch her without toppling backwards. She wraps her arms around my neck and her legs around my waist. Her mouth crashes down on mine as one of my hands goes to her ass and the other to her hair so I can control the kiss. I pull her head to the side, opening my mouth under hers, her taste exploding in my mouth as soon as her tongue touches mine. Both of her hands move to hold on to my face as she kisses me back.

"I missed you," she breathes, pulling her mouth from mine to look down at me.

"Missed you too, baby," I tell her, pushing her hair out of her face. That's when I see the bags and dark circles under her eyes and know that she hasn't been sleeping. "Why didn't you tell me you haven't been sleeping?"

"I…I didn't want you to worry," she says, looking over my shoulder.

"Baby, even when I know you're okay, I worry about you." I pull her face back down for another kiss. When I pull my mouth from hers, I whisper against her lips, "You should have told me you needed me." I crouch down and pick up my bag.

"Let me down," she says, trying to unwrap her legs from around my waist.

"No," I growl as I squeeze her ass, pulling her tighter against me. "I'm not letting you down until I get you to bed, and then I'm going to fuck you so hard you won't have a choice but to fall asleep afterwards," I say. Her hips shift, rubbing against my erection. I can feel the heat coming off her pussy through my jeans and her sweats. "Are you wet for me?" I ask, dropping my bag just inside the front door. Daisy starts jumping around at our feet. I'll come back out and give her some attention, but only after I've gotten inside my girl and put her to sleep.

Sophie moans, her tongue licking up my neck to my ear before biting down. I stumble slightly before running us into the wall, holding her up with my hips.

"Fuck, baby," I groan, my hands ripping the front of her top down the middle, baring her tits to me. My head drops forward, pulling one nipple into my mouth while pulling and pinching the other between two fingers. I hear her head fall back against the wall with a soft thunk as her hips roll into me. "You wet now?" I ask, looking up at her.

She nods, and I shake my head.

"I don't think you're wet enough. I want you drenched when I eat you." I press into her harder; hearing her soft moan is music to my ears. "You want me to eat your pussy?" She shakes her head. "You don't?" I ask, surprised.

"No, I want you." She bites her bottom lip, shifting her hips against me.

"You're gonna get me, but I haven't had your taste on my tongue for a week. I need it, so you're gonna be a good girl and lay back and let me eat your hot little pussy until I'm full, and then I'll give you the dick," I promise.

She moans again as I pull her away from the wall, walking into my bedroom. Laying her on the bed, I look down at her for a second before pulling my shirt over my head and tossing it behind me, toeing off my boots and pulling off my jeans and boxers in record time. She watches my every move with her beautiful eyes clouding with lust, her lower lip caught between her teeth, and her thighs rubbing together.

Once naked, I go to the bed, and my hands go under her ass to pull her sweats off, along with her panties. Her eyes roam over me; I can feel them burning into my skin. I toss her clothes over my shoulder before my hands go to her thighs to spread them wide. My mouth lands right on her center, licking deep the first time. I missed her taste; I could never get enough of it.

I bury my face in her pussy, placing one hand on her stomach to hold her down when her hips try to buck me off. "Come in my mouth, baby. I want to taste it," I tell her before going back to licking and biting. I know she's on the edge by the way she's thrashing around on the bed.

I suck her clit into my mouth as I enter her with two fingers, scissoring them inside her. She comes on a scream, her taste flooding my mouth, her body convulsing around my fingers. I lay my forehead against her stomach, trying to calm down enough so that I won't hurt her when I take her. I feel her body stop shaking as her hand goes to my hair, running through it softly.

"Nico?"

"Just a second, baby." I take a breath; I can feel my cock throbbing. Having her taste in my mouth is not helping to calm me. It's been too long.

"Are you okay?" she asks softly.

My eyes meet hers, and I take another deep breath before moving up her body. Her legs open wider, making room for me. I run my hand up the smooth skin of her thigh as the other cups behind her neck to bring her closer.

"Fine, I just need to be inside you." My mouth opens over hers as I slide in deep. Her tight, warm heat has me pulling my mouth from hers to grit my teeth. "Fuck, your pussy is too fucking hot." I swivel my hips, keeping our bodies as close as possible. Her legs wrap around me, her hands going to my hair, holding me close.

"Nico," she whimpers, her legs pulling me closer.

"I'm here, baby." I hold her tighter, sinking into her, pulling out slightly, and sliding back in. I keep my strokes even, pressing into her fully and grinding my pelvis against her clit.

We're both breathing heavily, our breaths mixing between kisses. I can feel her heart beating rapidly against my chest. A thin sheen of sweat has started to slicken our skin. Her hands roam over me, her nails digging into my skin on each thrust. I can feel her getting closer as her hips tip, making me slide deeper. I know I'm close when I start to feel that deep tingle and my toes start to curl.

"I'm going to—"

"I know," I say, cutting her off, thrusting my tongue into her mouth as her pussy squeezes my cock. I bury myself balls-deep inside her, letting her orgasm pull me over with her. I hold her close as I roll, pulling her on top of me. "You okay?" I ask once my breathing returns to normal.

"Yeah," she whispers, cuddling closer. "I hated that you were gone, but hated it even more when you had to stay gone longer. I was really worried about you," she confesses softly. I can feel her tracing one of the tattoos along my ribs.

"I hated being away from you too. You know that, right?" I tip my head down to look at her.

"Yes." She nods, her eyes meeting mine, "I'm just glad you came home," she says, and my heart squeezes at the word home. She is my home now.

"I will always come home to you. I won't lie and tell you what I do isn't dangerous sometimes, but I'm always careful, and now, with you, I have a whole new reason to stay safe."

"Did you take care of whatever it was you were doing in Vegas?" she asks, and I feel my muscles tighten at her question; I'm not used to sharing things about my job with anyone but Kenton.

"I did as much as I could. Hopefully it won't take long for the police to get the situation figured out."

"What does that mean?" she asks, and I let out a long breath, wondering how much I should say. "You can tell me," she encourages.

"There are bad people in the world. You know that, Sophie. I just don't want you to know how bad some of them are, and I really don't want to talk to you about this right after I just got home and I'm still inside you in our bed. We should make a pact now to never talk about work stuff while we're in bed."

"Fine." She sighs before lifting her head and putting her chin on her hand. "You know how you want me to talk to you?"

"This is different. You and I both know it is." I run my fingers through her hair. "There are going to be times I can't or won't tell you about my job."

"Why?" she asks, shifting, making me groan and my dick jump.

"There are things I will always shield you from, and my work is one of them."

"Don't you think it's better for me to know?"

"No, I don't. If it's something you need to know, I will tell you. Otherwise, you're just going to have to trust me."

"Okay, but if something happens to you, I'm going to kick your ass."

I smile and flip her to her back, making her scream out in surprise. "How are you going to kick my ass when you can't even get out of this position?" I ask, bending down to pull one of her nipples into my mouth.

"I could if I wanted," she breathes, pulling my mouth closer to her breast.

"You think so?" I ask before moving to her other nipple.

"I know I could," she says, wrapping her legs around me; her hips rise up higher, causing me to sink deeper into her.

"Fuck," I groan, surprised to feel myself hardening inside her.

Her hands go under my arms, her fingers running along my back before hooking around my shoulders. She moans before licking up my neck, breathing into my ear. "Ready?" she says, biting down on my earlobe.

I'm so lost in her that I'm caught off guard when one of her legs unwinds itself from my waist and goes to the bed. Her arms shift, and then I'm suddenly on my back with her standing over me on the bed and looking down at me.

"Holy shit," I say in shock.

"Told you I could get out of it." She smiles down at me before sitting, straddling my hips.

"Where did you learn that?" I ask, running my hands up her thighs.

"Devon, Maggie's fiancé, is a cop and taught me some moves. He said it would help build my confidence back if I knew I could put someone on their back if they ever got me down."

"You're awesome, baby. I'm proud as fuck of you right now."

"Really?" She smiles.

"Really."

"Thanks," she says shyly.

"Come here, sweet Sophie."

I can see that she's tired. I pull her down to lie against my chest, running a hand over her hair and down her back. I hold her until I hear her breathing even out and know she's asleep. I roll her over and make sure she's covered before I leave the room.

Daisy's sitting outside the bedroom door when I open it. "Hey, girl." I scoop her up before going to the kitchen. "Things are going to change around here. First, I think you may be getting a friend to play with," I say, referring to another dog. "Then, we need to talk Sophie into moving in. Do you think you can help me with that?" I ask her. She doesn't care about anything except that I'm paying attention to her.

I walk over to the bag I dropped inside the door and pull out my phone. I slide my finger across the screen and make a call I've been avoiding since I met Sophie. I love my mom, but I also know her. If she knew about Sophie before, she would have been demanding I bring her around, and I couldn't do that. I needed to give Sophie time to get used to us being an us. Now, though? Now, I don't care. There will be no more of her not doing shit because she's afraid. I refuse to let her live the rest of her life like that.

"Hey, honey. Are you home?" my mom asks as soon as she picks up.

"Yeah. I got in a couple hours ago." I walk into the kitchen, setting Daisy down before washing my hands and going to the fridge to grab a bottle of water.

"How was your trip? Did you have fun?"

"It was work, Ma. I wasn't partying it up in Vegas," I tell her with a chuckle.

"Well, you were in Vegas. Why wouldn't you try to have some fun while you were there? You think I don't know what you do in your free time?" I can see her in my head rolling her eyes. "I know how you and your brothers act when you're single."

"Yeah, Ma, but I'm not single anymore," I declare, smiling.

"You guys are such man-whores. I swear—it's a wonder one of you didn't end up on that show 16 and Pregnant," she says, completely missing what I just said.

"Ma, stop talking for a second and listen to me," I say, waiting for her to stop rambling.

"I swear—Trojan owes me royalties for all the condoms I bought for you boys."

"Ma, listen." I shake my head.

"What?" she says, sounding annoyed.

"I found my girl, Ma."

"What do you mean 'found your girl'?"

"I mean I found the girl I'm going to marry."

"Is it April Fool's Day?" she asks jokingly, but I can hear shock and happiness in her voice.

"Nah. I wouldn't joke with you about something like this."

"When did you meet her? Who is she? When can I meet her?" she yells so loud I have to pull my phone from my ear.

"Her name is Sophie." I laugh. "I met her when I found her phone and retuned it to her. She is beautiful, smart, and so sweet, Ma—so sweet I don't even know how I got so lucky."

"You love her," she whispers in awe.

"More than love her." I can't even begin to explain the way I feel about Sophie, but I don't think it's normal love. It's something more. I love my family, and I love my life, but what I feel for the girl who's asleep in my bed right now goes beyond that.

"Oh, honey, I'm so happy for you," she says quietly, "but you should try to take it slow."

"Shit." I look down at the ground. "I've been seeing her for a while now, Ma."

"How long is a while?" she asks.

"A few months," I tell her softly.

"Why didn't you tell me?" I can hear the hurt in her voice. I knew this question was coming.

"She hasn't had the easiest life, Mom. I needed to give her time to trust me without overwhelming her with everyone."

"We wouldn't overwhelm her," she argues.

"Ma..." I say, the 'who are you trying to kid?' implied in my tone.

"Okay, okay," she concedes. "So when do I get to meet her?"

"Soon." I smile. "I'll call you tomorrow and we can set up a time for us to come for dinner."

"Okay, honey. I love you. And I'm so happy for you," she whispers.

"Love you too, Ma. Talk to you tomorrow."

"Bye, honey."

"Later." I hang up, setting my phone on the counter before looking at Daisy. "Let's go to bed, girl." I go back into the room and climb into bed with Sophie, who automatically curls into me. I hold her to me, kissing her hair before following her off to sleep.

Chapter 9

Sophie

"HI." I SMILE at David as he walks into the library. He's a pleasant-enough guy; he asked me out a couple of times, but I just couldn't go out with him. It's not that he isn't good-looking—he is—but he seems like he has to try too hard to be nice. It's odd.

"Hey, Sophie. How are you?" He leans on the counter in front of me.

"Good, and you?" I ask, typing in the call number for another book a teacher asked me to check out for their classroom.

"I'm good. I was wondering if you'd want to go out and get a bite to eat after work?"

"No, sorry. I can't." I don't even look up from what I'm doing when I respond.

"It must be hard for you moving to a new state all by yourself, living alone, and not having anyone around."

"Pardon?" I ask, finally looking up at him.

His eyes appear darker, and something about him just seems…off. A shiver slides down my spine, and I sit back in the chair. Something is telling me to get away from him.

"Oh shit, I'm sorry. You look scared." He laughs. "I didn't mean anything, Sophie. Just that, if you need me, I'm here for you."

"Thanks," I wheeze out, finding it hard to breathe.

"See you around," he says, smiling. He taps the top of the desk before leaving the library, and as soon as he's out of sight, I grab my keys and bag, turn out the library lights, and lock the door before rushing down the hall and out to my car.

My hands are shaking as I open my door, and once inside, I engage the locks. I start my car and lift my head when I feel eyes on me, my eyes landing on David's car a few spaces over. I can just barely make out David sitting in his car as he waves. I lift my hand quickly, put my car in drive, and speed out of the parking lot. By the time I reach Nico's, the strange encounter with David is just that—a strange encounter. David's always been nice. He knows I moved to Tennessee alone and was probably just worried about me being on my own all the time, and since he doesn't know about Nico, that would be understandable, I convince myself.

I turn the key in the door and open it to complete silence; this catches me off guard. Daisy always greets me when I get home. I walk into the kitchen to set my bag on the counter. I lift my foot behind me, ready to take off my shoes before searching for Daisy.

"Leave them on," is growled, and I look over my shoulder at Nico, who is shirtless, wearing a pair of jeans and nothing else. Seeing him makes me forget about everything. My heart kicks up when I see his face; his eyes are dark and hungry. "Been home all day, worked out three times, and still couldn't get the image of what you're wearing out of my head." He takes a step towards me.

I look down, confused. I wore a high-waisted pencil skirt with a white blouse, sheer stockings, and black suede stiletto pumps to work today. This is my normal attire when going out of the house to work. He has seen me in these kinds of outfits a million times.

"What?" I ask, my head tilting to the side, studying his expression.

His hands come up to pull the pins out of my hair, tossing them onto the island in the kitchen. Then they go to my top, unbuttoning it and pulling it to the side before undoing the front clasp on my bra, releasing it so my breasts are free. "You have this whole naughty-librarian thing going on." His hands lift my breasts as his head dips so he can lick each nipple before biting and sucking them, making me grab his hair. "Every time you leave the house in one of these getups, all I can think about is you on your knees in front of me, your skirt up around your waist while I watch you suck me off," he says as his hands begin to pull my skirt up my thighs and his teeth bite down on my earlobe.

"Oh," I breathe, feeling his fingers pull my panties to the side and then two fingers fill me.

"Look at how wet you are," he groans, pulling his two fingers up between us. He's not wrong; I can feel the wetness between my legs, and my clit is now throbbing. He puts his fingers in his mouth, his eyes on me the whole time. "So sweet." His hands go to my waist. Then I hear material tearing, and I realize that he is ripping off my panties. "I've had this fantasy since the first moment I met you. You were on your knees in front of me, your tits out," he says, rubbing his thumb over one nipple and then the other, "and your skirt up around your waist." He looks down, and I feel a hand on my bare ass. "The stockings... Those are a bonus," he growls, trailing his hand around before one finger slides over my clit. "Do you want to make my fantasy reality?"

I bite my lip, nodding my head. Without thinking, I sink to my knees in front of him. I look up, running my hands up his thighs before unbuttoning his jeans and pulling down his zipper. I hear a low rumble and my eyes lift to his, and then I watch as his nostrils flare. The second his jeans are unzipped, he springs free, bouncing against his stomach. Commando—so hot.

One of my hands goes to the back of his thigh, the other to the base of his cock, pulling it down towards me. Seeing his piercing makes my mouth water. Knowing the way it feels when he's inside me causes a whole new surge of wetness to spread between my thighs. I lick the head before closing my mouth over it. I can't get much of him into my mouth. He's too thick and long, so I use my hand, moving it along his shaft along with my mouth.

"Give me your eyes, Sophie."

I lift my eyes to his; watching his expression as I work him makes me want to please him that much more. I stroke him fast, and then his hands are in my hair at the sides of my head.

"This is better than any fantasy I've ever had," he groans, his head falling back and his hips pumping himself in and out of my mouth. "Shit, baby," he says, and before I know what's happening, he pulls out of my mouth, turns me around, and sinks into me from behind.

My hands go to the hardwood in front of me, my head bowing forward. Nico's hands go to my hips, lifting me higher, forcing himself deeper. He plows into me hard and fast. His hand slides around my waist, his fingers zeroing in on my clit. He circles it as his other hand goes to my breast, pinching my nipple. I cry out as I feel the first wave of my orgasm wash over me.

"Fuck," he groans, planting himself balls-deep and grinding his hips as he spills into me. "You okay?" he asks after catching his breath, sitting me up on my knees.

"I think so," I whimper as he pulls out of me.

His hands remove my shoes before wrapping an arm around my waist to help me up. "Shit, baby," he says, looking down.

I look at him then follow his eyes to my knees, which are red from the hardwood floors. "I'm okay." I smile, feeling my cheeks heat up. I'm still so dazed by that orgasm that I wouldn't notice any pain.

"Let's shower." He picks me up, carries me to the bathroom, and then helps me get undressed and into the shower before stripping his jeans off, following me in. "I have another fantasy," he whispers in my ear as his hands massage my breasts from behind.

"Oh yeah?" I ask, tilting my head to the side.

"Oh yeah," he says, nipping my neck before showing me a few other fantasies he's had. All of them are awesome, but my favorite has me with my thighs wrapped around his head.

"Tomorrow we're going to dinner at my parents so you can meet everyone."

I try to lift my head to look at him, but I'm just too exhausted. "Was this your plan? Wear me out so I don't argue?"

"No, but it sounds smart." I hear the smile in his voice and can't help but to smile back.

"I'm nervous about meeting them, but I also can't wait," I confess quietly.

"Really?" he asks, making me feel like a jerk.

I hate that he thinks I don't want to meet them. It's never been about not wanting to meet them. It's always been about being afraid of what would happen if I had a panic attack or something. I don't want them to think that their son should find someone else who's normal.

"Don't sound so surprised." I run my hand along his abs. "I want to see where you come from and meet the people who raised you. Plus, you've talked about your brothers and their families so much that I feel like I already know them."

"Thank you for doing this. I know it's not easy for you, but my family's cool. They're gonna love you."

"I hope so," I tell him, my eyes feeling heavy. I don't care who else loves me. I just want him to.

"Sleep, sweet Sophie," he whispers, his lips on my forehead.

"'Night," I mumble.

I feel his laughter against my cheek, making me smile before I drift off to sleep, completely forgetting to tell him about my strange reaction to David.

"YOU'RE HERE!" A woman yells, running outside and down the front steps to where I'm exiting Nico's car. I stumble back as she embraces me in a tight hug. "Welcome," she says breathlessly before her hands go to my face, her eyes soft as she looks at me.

"Hi." I can't help but smile as she pulls me back in for another hug. She doesn't seem so scary anymore. I almost laugh at my own fear.

"Hey," Nico says, walking towards us. The smile he's wearing is one I haven't seen before, but I have to say—it's probably one of my favorites.

"Hey, honey." She lets me go and walks to where he's standing, her hands going to his face this time. I hear her whisper something to him, but I can't make out what it is. His face goes soft, looking a lot like his mom as he nods before kissing her cheek. "So, I hope you two are hungry." She smiles, linking her arm with mine as we make our way into the house.

"Where's Dad?" Nico asks.

She turns to look over her shoulder to answer him. "He'll be here soon. He called to tell me he would be late," she says as we make our way inside.

The house is a beautiful two-story farmhouse. The outside is painted a pale yellow with white trim, and a large front porch sporting two rocking chairs completes the picture. As we walk inside, all I can think is how welcoming their home feels. The warm wood floors and country-style decor make me feel like I should be drinking a glass of lemonade while putting my feet up.

"I love your house," I tell Susan as we make our way into the kitchen.

"Thank you, honey. Nico's grandparents bought this house when they moved into the area. When they told James they were going to sell it, he bought the house from them."

"I would love to live in an area like this. The drive out here was beautiful. When I moved to Tennessee, I wanted to buy a house in the country on a couple acres, but I just couldn't afford it," I explain with a smile.

"I thought you liked living in a neighborhood close to the city?" Nico states as a question, wrapping his arms around my waist from behind.

"I don't mind it." I turn my head and look back at him. "But when I was little, I read all of the Little House on the Prairie books and dreamed of living in a house in the middle of nowhere with my husband and filling it up with tons of kids."

"We can definitely have tons of kids," he says, his eyes going dark.

He is on a baby-making mission. Since he got back from Vegas—unless I'm working—we've been in bed, and he's been doing everything in his power to put a baby in me. Not that I have been putting up much of a fight about it. After opening up to him about everything, I know that he is everything I want and need. I know that, deep down, even the night I ran away, I would have gone back to him; I wouldn't have been able to stay away.

"Nico, you wanna come help me out?" a guy yells into the house, my heart rate automatically kicking up.

We talked about this. This morning, he told me that everyone was meeting at his parents' for dinner. Like it told him last night, I am excited but still nervous. I know that I put this off for as long as I could. And honestly, it wasn't fair to Nico to keep pushing him away even if it was unintentional. When I told Maggie what was going on, I could hear her clapping and jumping up and down while we were on the phone. She loves that Nico is forcing me to step outside of my bubble. She is happy for me and excited to meet Nico.

"Yeah!" he yells back before kissing my neck and whispering into my ear, "You'll be okay. I'm here with you."

"Okay," I agree nervously. I just don't want to have some kind of breakdown in front of his family. Once, in Job Corps, I passed out when I was with a group of people at lunch. After that, I tried to just stick to myself.

"So, Nico said you work as a librarian?" Susan asks, smiling at me.

"Yes. Well, I do that part time. My real job is as a private insurance specialist." I watch as she goes to the stove and pulls out a giant ham, the kind you would have at Thanksgiving, with the pineapple and cherries on top of it.

"Wow, that sounds fun," she says sarcastically and giggles, making me laugh.

"Yeah, it's no fun, but it pays the bills." I shrug.

"That's always important."

"Well, really, the thing is—my shoe addiction isn't going to pay for itself," I say with a smile.

"You too, huh? I had to take a job working for my boys when their dad told me he wasn't going to give me any more money for shoes unless

I got rid of some first. I told him fine, I didn't need his money, and bribed my boys with cookies and started working for them. Needless to say, James had to build me a bigger closet." She laughs and shakes her head, and I burst out laughing too. I can't help it; she's so sweet and totally puts me at ease. "Can you help me out with the rolls and put them in the oven?" she asks.

"Sure," I say, going to the counter and putting a pan of Hawaiian rolls into the oven.

"Thanks, honey."

"You're welcome." I smile, feeling warm inside. I wonder if my mom would have been like her if she were alive. All of the memories of my mom are happy; she was always laughing and smiling.

"What's wrong?" Nico's arms wrap around me. I hug him back, breathing him in before bringing my hands to my face, wiping my eyes. "Talk to me," he says against my ear before kissing it.

"Nothing. Just thinking about my mom and wondering if she would be like yours," I tell him.

He tilts my head back with a finger under my chin. "You gonna be okay being here? If not, we can go," he says quietly, searching my face. Hearing him say that only makes me love him that much more. I know how much his family means to him. I know how much he wants me to get to know them, so his asking if I need to leave says more than words ever could.

"You love me," I whisper. It isn't a question; I know he does because I can see it in his eyes. I don't know how I missed it before.

"I do." He smiles, his mouth touching mine. "I love you, Sophie," he says softly for only me to hear.

"I love you too," I whisper, closing my eyes. I feel him smile against my lips before he kisses me again.

"Well, shit." He lifts his mouth from mine and I turn my head. "It is true. Fuck me—I thought Mom was kidding," a guy says, looking between Nico and me.

"Trevor, this is Sophie. Sophie, this is my brother, Trevor."

"Nice to meet you," I tell him, pressing closer to Nico.

Trevor is big, and we were in a kitchen, so I can't help but feel some fear as the thought of my attack in my childhood home's kitchen drifts into my mind. I try to fight it, remembering what my counselor said about not letting it control me, and I take a deep breath and put my hand out to Trevor, who immediately takes it. I scream when he suddenly pulls me to him, and it takes a second to realize that he's hugging me. My heart is pounding in my chest, but my breaths, which were coming in rough pants, slow, and I return his hug for a second before being pulled back by Nico's strong, tattooed arms.

"Aw, now you get it." Trevor smirks, shaking his head.

"I get it, and you got your own woman, so keep your hands off mine," Nico says, tucking me back under his arm.

Then a very pretty woman with long blond hair comes into the kitchen holding a little girl—well, trying to; it appears more like the girl is being detained, and the woman looks like if she moves wrong, her very pregnant stomach would explode.

"What did I tell you about picking her up, babe?" Trevor scolds her, taking the little girl from her and whispering something into her ear, making her laugh and yell out, "Daddy!"

"It was either pick her up or have your mom's house destroyed. She's just like you. She never wants to listen when I tell her no," she snaps at Trevor.

"You don't like telling me no," Trevor tells her with a smirk before gently pulling her forward by the back of the neck and kissing her. When his mouth leaves hers, she smiles then looks at Nico and me.

"Um," she mumbles, and I can't help but giggle. I totally get it; Nico has the same effect on me.

"Sophie, this is my wife, Liz, and my daughter, Hanna."

"Hi," I greet softly, lifting my hand in a small wave.

Nico pulls me fully against him until Hanna reaches out from Trevor's hold, latching on to Nico. I love seeing him with the little girl, who seems so fascinated by him.

"Oh my God, they were telling the truth," Liz says quietly.

My eyes go to hers, and she starts to laugh, making her whole belly bounce. I'm starting to wonder if she should even be out of bed with how large she is.

"Should you be doing that?" I ask her, watching her belly, afraid the baby is going to somehow become dislodged and come flying out.

"Do what? Laugh?" she asks, my eyes returning to hers as she smiles and shakes her head, laughing even harder. "I still have a ways to go, but this guy here is apparently going to be the biggest baby in the history of babies." She starts rubbing her belly, and I really want to rub it too to see what it feels like. "He's kicking. Do you wanna feel?" she asks, reading my face.

I take two small steps towards her, gently placing my hand on her belly. "Does it hurt?"

"No. It feels strange and uncomfortable, but never really painful, except childbirth. Now that is horrible, and anyone who says differently is a liar." She grabs my hand, pulling it around to her side and holding it there. That's when I feel a small kick, and then another, this one much harder.

"Wow," I breathe.

"Yeah. He's going to be a soccer player."

"He's going to be a football player," Trevor says, narrowing his eyes on his wife.

"Sure, honey." She smiles then rolls her eyes. "How long have you been seeing Nico?"

"Um…" Shit. What should I say? I look at Nico; he's so caught up trying to control the little girl in his arms and talking to Trevor that he's basically no help at all.

"You are seeing him, right? I mean, he's not just joking, is he?" she asks, confused.

"No, no, it's not a joke." I shake my head, my eyebrows coming together in concentration as I try to figure out what to say.

"Hey, I was just curious. You don't have to tell me anything," she says gently.

"I…I just feel bad. We've been seeing each other for a few months, but I just couldn't meet you guys yet. I was trying to work through some stuff first," I tell her quietly.

"I understand that. I had to work through some stuff for a while as well, so I know how you feel. Nico's a good guy though, so he'll help you."

"Yeah, he's kind of relentless," I reply, scrunching up my nose.

She smiles genuinely, transforming her whole face from pretty to stunning. "Well then I guess I should say welcome to the family." She shocks me, pulling me in for a hug.

"What?"

"Girl, now you're stuck. There's no way out of this. Even if you tried, he would hunt you down." She laughs.

"Yikes," I say with a fake grimace.

"Yep." She nods, and then I hear the front door bang open.

I jump and look at Nico. Then loud voices fill the front of the house.

"Ma?!" is bellowed. I look at Susan, who smiles and rolls her eyes.

"My oldest has no manners. Don't mind him," Susan says, walking around us and out of the kitchen.

"You called?" she asks with a laugh, and then there's a chorus of 'Grandma!' being yelled with happy squeals from what sounds like a troop of little girls.

"Come meet everyone," Nico says, walking me out into the living room with one hand against my lower back, the other full of a very excited little girl.

Once we make it around the corner, I stop dead in my tracks when I see two more beautiful men, a pretty red-haired woman, a beautiful woman with long brown hair, four little girls, and one little boy all gathering around Susan and yelling for her attention. The other two couples in the room are standing off to the side, watching and laughing while Susan's mauled by the group of kids.

"Uncle Nico!" a little girl wearing a tutu screams, running towards us at full speed. All the other kids in the room follow her lead and surround us.

"Who are you?"

I look down to see the only boy in the bunch looking up at me curiously. "Sophie. Who are you?"

"Jax," he says, tilting his head to the side and studying me. "I neber met you before."

"Nope, you haven't."

He looks at where Nico's hand is wrapped around my waist, and his little eyes narrow slightly. "You said girls are weird and that you didn't want one," Jax says, looking at Nico accusingly.

"I did, little dude, but that was before I met Sophie," Nico explains, and I want to laugh, but Jax looks very serious about this topic.

"But she's a girl," he argues, looking around at all the girls then back at Nico. "We already hab too many girls."

"He's right, you know. You are the one who's always said girls are gross," a guy in a baseball cap says, walking across the room and holding a woman's hand, both of them wearing wide smiles on their faces.

"Hi, Sophie, it's nice to meet you. This is my wife, Lilly. I'm Cash. This little guy here is Jax, and he is ours, along with Ashlyn," he says, pointing out one of the little girls.

"Nice to meet you too," I say as all the little girls it the room start running around us, yelling in their high-pitched singsong voices, "Uncle Nico's in love!" I can help but laugh.

"Welcome to the insanity," Lilly says, smiling, and that's when I recognize her from school.

"You used to work at the middle school, right?" Her hair is different, but I'm pretty sure it's her.

"That's why I recognize you!" She smiles excitedly. "Are you still working in the library?"

"Yes. I wondered what happened to you," I say quietly.

"It's a long story. One day when you have time, we'll meet for coffee so I can tell you all about it," she replies just as quietly.

I'm taken aback by her offer; even when she worked at the school, we never socialized. Well, I never socialize with anyone.

"I would like that," I say sincerely, liking the idea of having some friends here.

"It really is a small world." She shakes her head, looks at Cash, and smiles as he leans forward, kissing her forehead.

Then the other guy who arrived comes over, scooping up one little girl along the way. "Sophie, it's nice to finally meet you. I'm Asher, this is November, and those three girls are ours—July, June, and May," he says, pointing to each daughter as he says their name. If Nico hadn't prepared me for their names, I may have laughed, but thankfully, he warned me.

"Nice to meet you guys." I smile at both of them before taking a second to look around. Nico's whole family's beautiful...like, really beautiful.

"You okay, babe?" Nico whispers next to my ear, sending a small shiver down my spine. I nod and lean into him.

"All right, everyone. I need your help getting dinner on the table. Who wants to help Grandma?" Susan asks, and all the kids start yelling about who gets to help set the table, who gets to butter the rolls, and all sorts of other tasks they clearly do often.

"We call it controlled chaos," November says, watching as all the kids follow after Susan.

"I just call it insanity," Trevor says, walking into the living room with Liz, who he helps sit down before putting her feet up on a pillow.

"Honey, I told you I'm fine," she grumbles, but seeing the size of her ankles has me wincing and thankful she's off her feet.

"Well, be fine sitting your pretty little ass in here with your feet up," he replies, kissing her hard before going back into the kitchen.

"He's so bossy," Liz says, but I can tell she really doesn't mind that he's bossy with her.

"So, you sure you're ready to be a part of this craziness?" Asher asks me, wrapping an arm around November's waist.

I look at Trevor, who comes in to give Liz a glass of water, and then Cash, who is whispering something into Lilly's ear making her smile. I glance at November, who is looking at Asher like he holds the secrets of the universe, and as I feel Nico's hand on my side, his fingers running along the skin between my shirt and jeans, in his touch alone, I feel love.

"It may take some getting used to, but yes, I'm ready," I tell Asher, and Nico's fingers give me a squeeze.

"I'm still trying to get used to it, but as long as you have a backbone and don't let these guys boss you around too much, you'll be fine," November says, smiling.

"Hey, I don't boss you around," Asher says, glaring at November.

"I know you don't." She pats his chest then rolls her eyes, making me giggle.

"Dad's home," Nico says as we hear a loud diesel engine pulling up outside, and before I have a second to gather my thoughts, "Grandpa's here!" is yelled and a swarm of children run into the living room then out the front door.

My heart swells as we walk out onto the front porch. There's obviously a rule in place and the kids must do this often, because they all stay on the porch until the truck is shut off. The second the engine dies, the kids all run full speed down the steps. An older man—who is still very handsome and looks a lot like his sons—hops out of the truck. Then chaos ensues, and the kids are on him, jumping up and down, and all of them talking to him a million miles a minute at the same time. He takes his time, greeting each one, picking one up, and giving them a second of his time before kissing them on their head and putting them down until every single one of them has had their turn.

I fall in love with Nico's family right then and there—his mom, brothers, sisters-in-law, and now his dad—and I can tell without a doubt that they all genuinely love each other. They are the definition of family and exactly what I never knew I wanted for myself.

After all the kids have their time with their grandfather, he makes his way up the porch steps with a wide smile on his face holding Jax.

"So I hear Nico's in love. That right?" he asks, looking at Nico and then at me.

I bite my lip to keep from smiling at Jax, who looks utterly annoyed with his uncle. "Um…" I don't know how to respond.

"He is, Grandpa. He was wookin' at her all funny and everything," Jax says, crossing his arms over his chest with a huff.

"Well then, I'm James, but you can call me Dad. Welcome to the family." I'm about to put out my hand and introduce myself, but I'm suddenly pulled into a bear hug that forces Jax between us.

"I'm Sophie," I tell him, hugging him back.

"Nice to meet you, Sophie," he says, pulling away to set down a wiggling Jax.

"You too." I smile up at him, seeing that his eyes look exactly like Nico's.

"All right, you guys. Come inside. Dinner's ready," Susan says as she comes outside, wiping her hands on a dishcloth.

James pulls her to him with an arm around her waist and kisses her once before patting her butt and sending her inside in front of him. Now I know where the Mayson boys get it from, I think, looking up at Nico with a smile as we follow his parents into the house.

"So how's work been, son?" James asks Nico.

We're all sitting around the table and eating, and the conversation has mostly been about my history. I've tried to steer things away from what happened after my mom died and before I went to Job Corps. I feel a little like I'm lying, but there are some things I just can't bring myself to talk about. I look at Nico curiously when he avoids the question his dad just asked him and completely changes the subject.

"How do you guys feel about the fact that Cash and Lilly ran off and got hitched?" he asks with a smirk, and everyone at the table stops looking at him and turns to stare between Cash and Lilly. I look at Nico funny, knowing he's avoiding talking about his job. I'm happy to know I'm not the only one he keeps his work-life separated from, but I really hope he talks to someone about it. I can't imagine doing what he does and not having someone to vent to.

The rest of dinner is spent talking about Cash and Lilly, their time in Alaska, and their quickie Vegas ceremony. I also spend most of dinner with different kids in my lap, each asking me questions of their own. First, it is July asking me about my nail color and if she could borrow my polish. The next is June, who has a hundred questions about me and Nico, and then May wants to know why she's never met me before and asks me every question under the sun, from my favorite food to if I had any pets. By the time Hanna comes to sit on my lap, I am thankful for the little girl because she only wants to talk about books. Ashlyn is the last to sit with me. I tell her all about Daisy, who she has only met a couple of times but has fallen in love with her. Jax is quiet during most of dinner. He sits on the other side of Nico, who I guess from their talks is his idol—well, until I came along. Apparently Nico broke his trust when he got a girlfriend.

After we've finished our dinner and each had a piece of homemade lemon meringue pie, it is almost nine and time for us to go home.

"Are you sure you can't hab a sleepober wif me?" May asks, bending her little head backwards so she can look up at my face.

"I'm sorry, honey, but your uncle Nico would be sad if I didn't have a sleepover with him," I tell her. Leaning forward, I can't help but kiss her head. "I promise you we will have a pajama party soon though. We can watch movies, paint our nails, and do all kinds of fun things."

"Mommy! I get to have a sleepober wif Aunt Sophie!" May yells, jumping down off my lap, and then all the kids run into the dining room and swarm me, asking if they can have a sleepover too.

"Yes, you can all come and have a sleepover." I laugh as they all run off to their parents, yelling about a sleepover at 'Uncle Nico and Aunt Sophie's house.'

"When you have this sleepover, I'm gonna make sure I gotta work," Nico says, making me narrow my eyes.

"No, I figure this will be good practice for you, Mr. I-wanna-get-you-knocked-up."

"Touché." He smiles, kissing my nose. He wraps his arms around my waist, and I lean into him. "You ready to go home?"

"Yeah, if you are," I tell him before getting up on my tiptoes to kiss him. Today has been awesome. I now know that I have nothing to worry about. His family is sweet. I'm happy to know them and glad Nico has them at his back, and I can't wait to spend time with them again soon. "I love your family," I tell him as I kiss the underside of his jaw.

"They love you too baby."

"I love you," I tell him with a smile.

He leans forward and kisses my forehead before leaning back his eyes meeting mine. "Love you too, sweet Sophie." I smile and shake my head. "All right. Let's get out of here. I need to be inside you," Nico says, making me tingle.

I nod and make quick work of saying goodbye to everyone, including all the kids, who make me promise again that we will have a sleepover soon.

"WHAT DO YOU mean Jax and Ashlyn are missing?" I ask, watching as Nico pulls on a pair of jeans and boots, and I immediately hop out of bed and start to get dressed.

Not long after I met everyone, Lilly was arrested, and Nico worked hard to get her released. This morning, he found evidence proving that Lilly had been wrongfully accused. I hate that they are being forced to deal with more drama, and I feel nauseated just thinking about something happening to the kids.

"Cash couldn't say much, just that he and Lilly had been home with her parents and the kids. Lilly noticed that the kids were quiet and went out to check on them. He said they've searched everywhere and still came up with nothing."

"Okay, so we can help them look," I tell him, pulling on a hoodie along with my Chucks.

"Sorry, baby. No way."

"No way, what?" My eyebrows draw together.

"You're not going with. I won't be able to focus if you're there."

"I wanna help," I tell him firmly. There is no way I'm going to be sitting here worried out of my mind while he is searching for the kids.

"No. No way." He shakes his head.

"I wasn't asking you for permission." My hands go to my hips.

"I don't have time to argue with you, Sophie," he growls, pulling a shirt on.

"Then don't argue." I leave the room and head to the kitchen to grab my bag.

"You're not fucking coming!" he yells behind me. Once he comes into the kitchen, he grabs his keys and heads for the front door. I quietly follow behind him, thinking maybe he won't even notice I'm there. "Baby, serious as fuck, I don't have time for this shit right now. Please put my mind at ease. Stay here and wait for me," he says, turning around, his hands going to my face. I can see in his eyes that he is stressed, and I don't want to add to it. As much as I want to go with him to help look for the kids, I know I can't add to his worry.

"Okay," I agree reluctantly.

"That's my girl." His mouth drops to mine, and before I can kiss him back, he's opening the door.

"Call me the minute you find them!" I yell as he's getting in his car. He gives me a chin lift, so I figure that's basically an affirmative.

I don't know how long I pace back and forth between the living room and the kitchen, but it must be a couple of hours. I give in and call Lilly, who's a wreck and can't even get a word out without breaking down into tears. I can't imagine what she's going through, but I tell her that, if she needs anything at all, I'm here.

After I get off the phone with her and another hour passes, the phone rings and I jump to answer it, thinking it's Nico with good news. I'm disappointed when it's November and Liz calling to see if I've heard anything. They both know as much as I do, which is nothing at all. Halfway into our conversation, November gets a call from Susan, who says they found Jax and are on their way to get Ashlyn. She doesn't have a lot of information, but I feel better knowing that they are on the right track. I want to help, and I hate that I'm stuck at home and can't do anything. By the time Nico calls to tell me they have Ashlyn and that Cash is heading to the hospital with both of the kids in an ambulance, I'm a mess.

"Should I meet you there?" I ask, holding my breath.

"No, baby. I'm just going to take care of a couple more things and then I'll be home. We can go and see the kids tomorrow, but right now, I think Cash and Lilly just want to be alone with the kids," he says quietly.

I want to cry; I feel horrible not being there with him. "Are you sure? I can meet you at your parents'. That way, if they need us, we're close."

"Baby, I swear if I thought for one second that would be best, I would have you come here, but as of right now, everyone's going home. Asher wants to go sit with his girls, Trevor told me he needs to be with his, and I want you at home."

"Okay," I whisper, hearing the stress in his voice.

"Be home soon," he says, hanging up.

I sit there for a few minutes, going over everything that happened to Lilly—and now the kids—and also what November told me about her story and what Liz explained about hers while we were on the phone. I look at the picture of Nico and me on the screen of my phone and swear to myself right then that I will do everything in my power to be worthy of Nico. It's not that I don't still have fears, but knowing how life can change so drastically in the blink of an eye makes me want to live my life completely. I'm in love with an amazing man who looks at me like I'm his reason for breathing when, in reality, he's mine. I want to be the strong person he sees me as. He deserves that and more.

"HE'S SO CUTE," I tell Nico, looking from Trevor and Liz's new son to his smiling eyes.

"He is, babe," he agrees, his face soft as he looks at his nephew.

"Here. You hold him." I hand Cobi over to Nico, helping to situate him in his arms before smiling up at him.

His eyes drop to my mouth before he leans forward to kiss my forehead. I feel warmth flow through me. I love Nico's family. That's why, when Trevor called to say that Liz had gone into labor, I freaked out and ran around the house in a hurry, wanting to get to the hospital as soon as possible.

By the time we arrived, Liz was already seven centimeters. Two hours after we got there, a smiling Trevor came out to tell us that baby Cobi had arrived and he was nine pounds and six ounces. When he made this announcement, my first thought was, Oh my God, I can't wait to see him! Then my mind wandered to the bag of flour I had to carry around in junior high during sex education that weighed ten pounds. And then I thought about something that size coming out of my vagina and wanted to stop having sex altogether. The idea of that coming out of something so small made me feel uneasy.

The second I had Cobi cuddled to me, all thoughts of teeny, tiny vaginas and giant babies left my head, and I knew that, no matter what, when you'd hold your child, whatever you went through would be completely worth it.

Chapter 10
Nico

"YOU SURE YOU don't want me to go with you?" I look at the GPS, seeing that I should be in the Nashville area in about two hours.

"I'm sure. I just need to get some clothes and check the mail. I won't even be there for more than thirty minutes."

"Just wait for me and I'll go with you," I try again.

"You and I both know that, when you get home, you're not going to want to leave the bed, let alone the house."

"Shit," I groan, getting hard just thinking about being inside her. "You say it like it's a bad thing."

"It's not a bad thing. That's why I want to go to my house. I don't want to leave the house either once you get home," she says shyly.

"Be naked in bed," I demand.

"What?"

"You heard me. I want you naked, spread eagle on the bed so when I get there, I can get my taste before fucking you."

"Nico," she breathes, but I can hear the hunger in her voice.

I've been out of town for three days. The whole time I was gone, all I could think about was the news we found out right before I left. Sophie had woken up sick a couple of days in a row. I had my suspicions, but there was no way to know for sure without her taking a test. On the third day, I said fuck it, got up, and went to the pharmacy near the house. I knew she was afraid to take the test after the last few times she had taken one and they'd come back negative.

I sat there with her in the bathroom, refusing to leave even when she peed on the thing. I knew in my gut that this was it; just like I knew she was my forever, I knew our child was growing inside of her. Those three minutes were the longest of my life. All I could think was, How the fuck can a piece of plastic that probably costs one cent to make in China hold such an important message? When the screen flashed and the word 'pregnant' appeared on the screen, I looked at Sophie, who was staring at the screen in complete shock. The only thought in my head then was how much I fucking loved her.

"Holy shit," she whispered, her eyes meeting mine. I could see tears beginning to form. "We're going to have a baby."

"We are," I confirmed as I pulled her against me, burying my face in her neck. "I love you, baby. Thank you for giving us this," I whispered against her skin.

"We're having a baby," she repeated, this time sobbing into my chest.

I pulled her face away so I could look at her. "You okay?"

"I'm scared, but so happy," she cried and smiled at the same time.

"Me too, baby. But I know everything's going to be perfect." She nodded, and then she smiled a smile that lit her whole face—a smile that, even thinking about it now, makes me feel like king of the fucking world.

Knowing that Sophie is pregnant—fuck me, if that shit doesn't make fucking her even hotter. I can't keep my hands off her. I love knowing that my kid is growing inside her. After that shit with Cash's ex and the kids going missing, I spent all my free time trying to get Sophie pregnant. Not that I hadn't been on a mission before that, but knowing how short life is only made it that much more important. Next on the list is giving her my last name. Yes, I'm doing shit ass-backwards, but I don't give a fuck.

"Babe, seriously—when I get home, you better be in bed, butt na-ked, and ready for my mouth," I tell her, coming out of my daydream.

"You can't talk to me like that and expect me to get anything done," she cries, making me smile.

"You better hurry. You have a little less than two hours to get your shit done before I'm home and you're mine. Besides, what do you even have at your old place that you could possibly need? The last time I walked into our bedroom, all your shoes, clothes, and other shit were spread from one side to the other."

"I'm not that bad," she says low, probably looking around the bedroom at the disaster she has turned our room into. "I have to get my suitcase and the stuff for Maggie's wedding."

"You need to just put that house on the market and stop saying the market's shit. Who cares if you take a loss? You know I got you."

"You can't tell me to take a loss on my house," she huffs.

"We're not talking about this right now." Every time we discuss her house situation, she gets upset. "Just get you're shit and then be naked when I get to the house."

"Maybe," she says, but I can hear the smile in her voice and can't help but smile too.

"Don't fuck with me, Sophie," I growl before gentling my voice. "How's my baby doing?"

"Good. Making me tired, but good." She sighs.

"I'll have a talk with him when I get home."

"It could be a girl." She laughs. I swore up and down to her that it is going to be a boy, but something keeps telling me it's going to be a girl.

"It's not." I smile.

"Love you," she says quietly, making my heart squeeze like it always does when she says those words to me.

"You too, babe. See you soon," I tell her, hanging up.

I'm about twenty minutes outside of Nashville when my phone rings. At first, I think about not answering it, knowing that I will be home soon, but I know that, if my friend Leo—a cop in Nashville—is calling, he probably has a job for me or needs my help with something. I reluctantly answer on the third ring.

"Yo, Leo. What's up?"

"Mayson, I need you to meet me at your girlfriend's house."

"What are you talking about?" I ask, dread creeping up my spine.

"Look, I wanted to give you a heads-up. I don't want you to get here and flip your shit. Therefore, I'm telling you now so you have time to calm down."

"What the fuck is going on?" My adrenalin surges; he's fucked if he thinks I can calm down before I get there when he starts a conversation out like that.

"I called Kenton. He's on his way. Someone got into her house when she was inside."

"Tell me she's okay."

"She's fine. Has a couple scratches, a bump on her head, and she's pretty shaken up, but she's all right, man."

Fuck, my heart is beating out of my chest. I press down on the accelerator, needing to get to my girl. "Put her on the phone," I bark.

"Give me a second. She's in the ambulance," he says, and my fucking fingers feel like they're going to make dents in the steering wheel.

"Why the fuck is she in the ambulance? You said she's okay."

"It's a precaution. You know that shit."

"Man, she's fucking pregnant," I bellow into the phone. I do not care about anything except her and finding out she's all right.

"Fuck me," he growls. I can hear the wind moving down the line, indicating that he's running. "Sophie, Nico's on the phone," I hear him say, and then the line is quiet for a second.

"Hey." Her sweet voice is like a balm to my rage.

"I'm almost there, baby."

"Okay," she says quietly, and I want to fucking scream because I can hear the fear in her voice. She's been so good—no freak-outs, no worries. She's settled in and started coming around…and now this.

"Talk to me, baby," I say soothingly.

"About what?"

"Are you okay? Are you hurt?"

"I…I'm okay." I can feel her anxiety through the phone. My foot eases off the gas as I exit off the highway.

"How's my son?" I ask, hoping to get her to relax a little.

"It could be a girl," she tells me quietly before taking a deep breath. "I think she's okay. I...I didn't hit my stomach or anything."

"It's a boy, babe. I keep telling you this," I prod.

"You don't know that," she replies, sounding annoyed, making me smile slightly as I turn onto her street.

I park on the curb, seeing not only an ambulance, but three squad cars. The minute I shut off the car, I hop out and jog to the ambulance. Leo's standing in front of the open doors of the ambulance with his arms crossed over his chest and his feet planted apart. I can't see her until I'm right on them. The minute my eyes lock on her, my slightly calmed rage erupts once again.

There's a scratch down the side of her face and a dark mark under her jaw that looks like a bruise, and the top she has on is ripped at the neck. I take a second to get myself under control before she sees me. I don't need her feeding off the anger I'm feeling. The second her head turns and our eyes lock, tears fill hers to the brim. Fuck, I hate seeing tears in her eyes, and knowing that she's scared isn't helping settle my rage any. I hop in the back with her, getting down on my knees in front of her. The EMT starts to say something, but I give him a don't-fuck-with-me glare and he backs off.

"Hey." I hold her face between my hands. She's so fragile, so fucking breakable, and the most important thing in my life. If something happened to her, I don't know what I would do.

"You're here." She presses her face deeper into my hand.

"Told you I was close."

"Sir, I'm gonna need you to wait outside," a different EMT says, hopping into the back with us.

"And I'm gonna need you to cut me some fucking slack. My woman was attacked, and I need to see for myself that she's okay. As soon as I'm done, I will let you do your job, but don't fuck with me right now," I growl.

"Give him a minute, man," I hear Leo say from outside.

The EMT looks at me and nods before jumping out. My eyes go

back to Sophie's; I study the marks on her, swearing that whoever did this to her won't be able to walk again after I find them.

"You sure you're okay? No cramping or anything, right?"

"No, nothing like that. My head just hurts." Her hand goes to the back of her head, and mine follows her movement. The second I touch the bump on the back of her head, she flinches, and I let off a string of expletives. "You know you can't cuss like that when the baby gets here, right? The last thing we need is for his first word to be fuck," she says softly.

"You finally admitting it's a boy?"

"No." She rolls her eyes then winces. I lay my forehead against her stomach, just taking a second before asking her more questions. "Are you okay?"

"No... Fuck no," I choke out.

"I'm okay." She runs her fingers over my hair, down the back of my neck. I can't believe she's trying to comfort me right now.

I finally build up the courage to ask. "What happened, baby?" I hear her take a deep breath, and I lift my head to look at her.

"I was getting all my stuff together for the wedding when I heard someone in the living room. At first, I thought it was you getting home early and you stopped by to help me. I called out your name and you didn't reply, and then I thought maybe you were trying to scare me. It took a second to realize you would never do that to me." She shook her head. "I started heading for my phone when a person wearing a ski mask and all black clothes came and stood in my bedroom doorway. As soon as I saw them, I started screaming and put the bed between us. I looked for a weapon, but there was nothing near me. I was so scared." I can hear the fear in her voice again, and I run my hands up and down her arms, trying to calm her. "The guy grabbed me and started dragging me out of the room. I wiggled out of his hold and got in a good kick to his crotch. I was almost to the front door when he grabbed for me again; that's when I got this scratch," she says, pointing at her face. "He got ahold of the neck of my shirt and it ripped, which made me fall backwards and hit my head on the coffee table. Then someone started pounding on the front door and he took off."

"Jesus, baby." I pull her closer, needing to know she's safe, "I'm sorry I wasn't here."

"It's not your fault."

"I should have made you wait for me," I insist.

"Please stop," she says quietly, her arms squeezing a little tighter.

"I'm gonna let the EMT finish checking you out. I'll be right outside talking to Leo." She nods, and I put a finger under her chin, lifting her face up so I can look in her eyes. "You're safe. I love you."

"I know." She rests her head against my shoulder, and my hand goes to her stomach, where my child's growing.

"All right, baby. I'll be right back." I kiss her forehead then her lips. I give the EMT a chin lift, letting him know he can get back to checking her over as I hop out the back of the ambulance. "Talk to me," I say to Leo, handing him his phone back. He starts to take a step away from the ambulance, but I shake my head no. I need to have an eye on Sophie.

"All right, man. I heard what she told you."

"Yeah?" I prompt.

"The neighbor who pounded on the door told us they were walking their dog when they heard her scream. At first, they were just going to ignore it, not wanting to get involved in a domestic dispute. When they heard the second scream though, they decided to act."

Fuck me. I know many times people ignore a scream or yell thinking it's nothing or not wanting to get involved. Who knows what would have happened to Sophie if someone hadn't knocked on her door and scared the person away? I shake my head, not allowing myself to think like that. I look into the back of the ambulance at Sophie, who's talking with the EMT. She's a little roughed up but safe, and that is all that matters.

"The neighbor said he banged on the door before trying the handle, which he was surprised when it opened. He found Sophie in the living room. She was out of it but talking. He said he helped her to the couch then called the cops." He shakes his head, running his fingers through his blond hair. "When we got on the scene, she asked us to call you first. I thought she was a client or something, so I had one of the guys call Kenton. That's when I found out she's yours." I watch as he looks in on Sophie, his eyes going soft. "How did you find this chick?" he asks quietly.

I know we don't look like we match—she's the soft to my hard, the light to my dark, the blatant innocence to my roughness—but I couldn't give a fuck if people look at us and wonder why we're together. I don't like the softness in his eyes when he looks at her. Leo is a good ol' boy. He grew up on his family's farm, comes from old money, played high school and college football, and could have gone pro if he wanted to, but he always dreamed of being a cop. He's about six foot two and two hundred and eighty pounds of pure muscle. He's the kind of guy a sweet girl like Sophie could take home to her parents, or vice versa. Too bad for him she's mine and will be until God sees fit to take her from Earth.

"Do I seriously need to tell you not to check out my girl right now?" I glare at him.

"Sorry. It's not that. She's just so not your type."

"Really?" I raise a brow at him, ready to put my fist in his face. "I'm pretty sure my kid growing inside of her tells you just how much of my type she is," I say through my teeth. "Besides, you have your own woman," I tell him, missing the way his jaw ticked.

"Leo, shut the fuck up. Don't dig yourself any deeper. My cousin's a little sensitive where Sophie is concerned," Kenton says, walking up on our conversation. "You good man?" I lift my chin before looking in on Sophie again. "What do we know?" Kenton asks, looking at Leo.

I half-listen as he retells what happened and what Sophie told me. "How'd they get into the house?" I ask, focusing back on the conversation.

"There was no forced entry, so at this time, we're unsure. Sophie said she locked the door when she entered her residence, but she never checked the back door to make sure it was secure as well."

"Did anyone see anything or anyone?" Kenton asks.

"No one saw anything. The person who stopped the assault when he entered the residence didn't see anyone but Sophie," Leo says.

"So basically, we got nothing?"

"Afraid so. Unless you have someone you suspect, then we got nothing to go on," Leo says.

I'm frustrated as fuck. This is not what we need right now. "Jesus, this is so fucked," I growl. "This isn't the first time someone has tried to break into her house, so this isn't some random act," I tell Leo.

"Yeah, I saw the previous report. She got any enemies?" Leo asks.

"No. No one."

"Maybe an ex?"

"No, man. Nothing. There is no one in her past. She hasn't even been in Tennessee long."

"You sure she doesn't have an ex? That's normally the first person we suspect."

"No one," I repeat, starting to see red. This isn't the first time I've thought about this shit, but no one stuck out to me. The only person who kept popping into my head was Sophie's dad. "I need to make a call," I say, looking between Kenton and Leo.

"Sure, man," Kenton, says.

"Keep an eye on Sophie for me."

He lifts his chin as I make my way to the side of the ambulance. I pull out my phone, find the number, and hit dial.

"Yello," Justin answers, and I shake my head; this kid is a fucking mess.

"Justin."

"You got me, daddio. Congrats on that, by the way," he says cheerfully.

"Jesus, you guys really do love to fucking gossip."

"We're friends. Friends share happy news."

"Can you stop yappin' like a forty-year-old housewife for a second?" I run a hand over my head, my eyes dropping to my boots.

"What's up, man? Talk to me."

"Someone broke into Sophie's old place while she was inside. I need you to do a background on her dad. I want everything."

"Shit, man. Is she okay?"

"Yeah, she's fine. A little shook up, has a scratch and a couple bumps, but for the most part, she's okay."

"Jesus, dude. Give me the name you want me to run," he says seriously, a tone I rarely hear out of him.

"His name is William Grates, and his last known place of residence was Seattle, Washington. He's Sophie's dad, so maybe you can trace him that way."

"I got this. I'll call you later with what I find out. Just go be with your girl."

"Thanks, man."

"Later," he says, hanging up.

I walk back to where Kenton and Leo are still talking and look inside the ambulance. When Sophie's eyes meet mine, she gives me a small smile before turning back to talk to the EMT. Something about that smile lets me know that everything will be okay. I look back at Kenton and he nods. My cousin is crazy as fuck, and as long as he's in my corner, I know Sophie will be safe.

"GET BACK HERE." I pull Sophie back under me after she tries to roll away. "Where are you going?" I kiss the skin of her neck. My hand runs along her thigh, up under my shirt she has on, along the smooth skin of her stomach, and then up to cup her breast.

When we got home last night, I helped her shower—even though she insisted she was fine—and carried her to bed so I could hold her close. I haven't let her out of my grip since.

"Oh," she breaths, and I watch as her head tilts back, giving me better access to her neck.

"Sensitive?" I question, running my thumb across her nipple. Last night, she said that her nipples were extra sensitive when I was washing her in the shower. She nods as I tilt her face towards mine so I can take her mouth in a deep kiss. "What about this one? Sensitive?" I ask, traveling my hand to her other breast, tugging on that nipple.

"Yesss…" she hisses out, pressing herself deeper into my hand. Her hand closest to me travels down my abs and grips my erection, pumping once before her thumb slides over my piercing at the tip. My hips automatically shift, wanting closer to her.

"What about this? Is it sensitive?" I ask, running a finger over her folds before dipping in and then circling a finger outside her entrance.

"Oh, please," she cries, making me smile. Her head turns, her eyes open, and they lock on mine as her fingers dig into my bicep.

"How did I get so fucking lucky?" I lean forward, kissing her mouth before kissing her chin, each nipple, and below her belly button, where I kiss my child.

I look up at her, pulling one of her legs over my shoulder before licking her in one long stroke. She's gotten sweeter since becoming pregnant. Her taste hits my mouth and I can't hold back; I take her aggressively, burying my face in her pussy until I can hear her screaming my name.

Chapter 11

"BUT WHERE ARE you going? Where in Seattle? Have you ever even been here before?" Sophie asks in rapid-fire succession.

We got to Washington yesterday for her best friend's wedding. I hate fucking lying to her, but there is no way I'm telling her that I'm going to meet her dad. She doesn't even know he's in prison, and the last thing I want right now is her worrying.

"Baby"—I finish tying my boot and grab her hand before sitting back so I can pull her onto my lap—"I go to cities I know nothing about at least once a month. Don't worry about me. I won't be gone long." I run a hand down her back, the other lying over her stomach.

Her eyes go to her lap before meeting mine again. "I hate being away from you."

"You're safe here," I tell her. Since the attack, she hasn't left my side. I hate having her away from me, but because we're so far away from Tennessee, I know I can relax a little.

"It's not me I'm worried about."

"I'm always safe. Besides, I'm not working. I just need to go out and pick something up."

"What could you need to pick up in Seattle?" she asks, obviously frustrated.

"If I told you, it wouldn't be a surprise. Now go back to sleep. You need your rest."

"I'm not tired," she huffs.

"I can see the bags under your eyes, Sophie. I know you're tired." I run my fingers under her jaw. Yesterday was a long day of traveling, and I pray we won't have to do it again while she's pregnant.

"Sheesh, you're a charmer." She shakes her head.

"You know you're beautiful. Now stop being difficult and lay down. I'll be gone three hours tops."

"Okay, but you owe me cake—chocolate cake. Wait, no, chocolate cheesecake. No—just chocolate cake." She bites her lip, and I burst out laughing, pulling her closer to me.

"How 'bout I get you both? That way you don't have to choose."

"I'm going to be as big as a house by the time this is over." She sighs.

"You will always be beautiful," I assure her.

"Even if I weigh four hundred pounds?"

"Hell yeah," I smirk. "Big girls are hot."

"What?" she asks, searching my face.

"I don't discriminate, babe."

"You don't?" she asks, her eyes narrowing.

This is one thing about Sophie being pregnant—she is moody as fuck. One minute, she's happy-go-lucky, and the next, you would swear she's possessed by the devil.

"I didn't before you. Women of all shapes and sizes are beautiful."

"I get that." She nods, looking off in the distance before her eyes come back to me. "I totally feel that way about guys. You know, skinny, muscular, jock, nerd—they all have something I find attractive," she says, and I growl deep in my throat. I do not ever want her to check men out...ever.

"You better not be checking dudes out," I tell her, watching her try to hide her smile. "You fucking with me?"

"No. Why would I do that?" she asks innocently, batting her lashes.

"Just for that, when I get back and I'm inside you with you begging me to let you come, it's not gonna happen." I watch her breath pause before speeding up. "I should tie you up and torture you." Her thighs tighten together and she squirms on my lap, rubbing against my dick, which is ready to go. "Seems like you like that idea," I whisper against her neck before biting down on her earlobe. I slide my hand from her stomach to her thigh. "When I get back here, this is mine." I run my finger up the center of the panties before pulling her in for a kiss. I end it quickly, knowing how fast things can get out of hand with her. "Be back soon." I kiss her once more before picking her up off my lap and heading out the door.

"Be careful."

"Always, baby," I tell her, shutting the door behind me.

When I finally get to the prison and make it past security, I know I'm going to be late making it back to Sophie. Not only do I have this stop, but I have to pick up her ring from Tiffany's. Maggie and Devon want me to ask her when they are there to see it. It's fucked up, but the only time I can do it is at their wedding. They're leaving town in the morning to head out for their honeymoon.

I walk down a long hallway with phone booths and Plexiglas lining one side. "Wait here," a guard says before going to stand near the door. I take a seat, watching as a man wearing an orange jumpsuit enters. He's short with a stocky build, dark, greying hair that's tied back into a ponytail, and a face that is weathered and aged. If not for eyes perfectly matching Sophie's, I would have no idea that he's her father. His eyes meet mine through the glass, and I can see the confusion on his face; I know he has no clue who I am or why I'm here. He sits down across from me and nods to the phone, lifting the one on his side to his ear as I do the same.

"I don't know you," are the first words out of his mouth.

"No, you don't."

"Why are you here?" he asks, his eyes looking me over.

"You and I have someone in common."

"Since I've been here for the last almost eight years and you look like you're young enough to be my son, I doubt that," he says and starts to pull the phone from his ear.

"Sophie," I say, and his face pales, his eyes go wide, and his grip on the phone tightens so much that his hand and knuckles turn white.

"What did you just say?"

"Sophie," I repeat and watch as he leans back in his chair, his hand going to his mouth, covering it.

"How do you know Sophie?" he asks as his hand moves from his mouth to run over his head.

"She's going to be my wife," I tell him bluntly.

His eyes look me over again before narrowing slightly. "Not my daughter." I'm slightly taken aback by the adamancy in his voice. "She's a sweet girl."

"She is," I agree. "So tell me why the fuck you didn't protect her?" Even though this isn't my reason for being here, knowing the shit she went through after losing her mother, I had to ask him.

"I...I was lost." He takes a breath.

"You were lost?" I repeat, wondering what the fuck that even means.

"After her mother died, I was lost. I tried to be a good dad, but I couldn't even look at my own daughter without hating her."

"What?" I growl.

"She looked just like her mom. I know it was fucked up, but I hated looking at her and seeing my wife. Do you know how fucked up it is to look at your only child and wish they would have died with their mother just so you wouldn't have to see the disappointment in her eyes when she looks at you?"

"You're one stupid motherfucker." I shake my head in disgust, wishing the glass weren't separating us.

"You think I don't know that? You think I don't regret the way I treated her?"

"I don't think you do. You left her to the wolves."

"I was fucked in the head after losing my wife," he says, shaking his head.

"I get that, man. I really fucking get that. I honestly don't know what would happen if I lost Sophie, and I pray to God I'll never have to know what that feels like, but if she left me with our child, I would always make sure my kid was safe. No way would I fuck my kid's life up just to make mine easier to deal with."

"I fucked up!" he shouts this time, making the guard take a step towards us.

"You did, but what I want to know is—are you still fucking up?"

"What do you mean?"

"You said earlier you wished Sophie had died. Do you still feel that way?"

"Do you know why I'm in this fucked-up place?"

I do know. I know he's in here for murder. "I do," I reply, looking him dead in the eyes.

"Do you know who I killed?"

"No." When Justin told me where Sophie's dad was and why he was there, I didn't ask any more questions.

"I killed the guy who touched her. It was two days after she left. I had been sober for two whole days, looked around, and realized what I was doing to myself and what I let happen to my daughter. I tracked the guy down that hurt her and killed him. I'm in here for the next fifteen years. I do not regret for one second taking that fucker's life. I know I should have prevented it from happening in the first place, but I didn't, so I made it to where it would never happen again."

"Holy shit." I sit back in the chair, my body sagging.

"I know I fucked up with her, but I never wanted her to be afraid again," he says softly.

I shake my head, still in shock from what he just said. "Someone has tried to hurt her twice since she moved to Tennessee."

"That's where she went?"

"What do you mean?"

"I had someone keeping an eye out for her, and then one day she was just gone."

"Yeah. She's in Tennessee with me."

"How long have you been in the picture?" He cocks his head to the side.

"A while."

"How is she?" he asks, closing his eyes, but not before I catch the look of pain in them.

"Good, but I really need to know who's after her. Do you know of anyone here from her past who would be messing with her?"

"The only threat she had is dead." I nod. "What's your name?" he asks.

I debate for a second if I should tell him, but seeing him in here behind bars and knowing the reason he is here, I quickly make up my mind.

"Nico Mayson."

"And you're with my daughter?"

"Yes."

"Is she happy?" he asks quietly, hopefully.

"Very," I tell him.

His eyes search my face. "Take care of her," he chokes out before hanging up the phone and standing. He leaves me sitting there in shock.

I still know nothing about who's after Sophie, but I do know that her dad loves her, and now I have to figure out if I should tell Sophie about him.

"Fuck," I grumble out before hanging up the phone and getting the fuck out of there.

Sophie

"GIRL, YOU KNOW I don't do the whole 'white meat' thing, but that man of yours is seriously fine. I mean F-I-N-E," Maggie says, throwing herself down on the bed next to me.

"I know." I smile.

"I've never seen you this happy."

"I've never been this happy before. He makes everything okay. With him, I feel safe, like I can explore or just be me and know he will watch over me."

"Yeah, I saw that. He's kinda scary," Maggie says quietly.

"He told me he doesn't have to be nice to anyone but me," I tell her, watching her eyes widen.

"Wow." Her head turns towards me, her lips parting slightly.

"You know, when I first met you, I wondered how the hell this little ol' white girl was gonna make it in the world if she couldn't even be around a group of people without freaking out. Then you surprised me by never giving up. Yes, you did freak the hell out every time, but you never quit trying. You're one of the strongest people I know, Sophie. So yes, that man will probably kill anyone who ever tries to harm you, but your strength is internal," she says, and I start to cry immediately.

"Don't mind me. This baby has me all messed up," I say before thinking. No one knows I'm pregnant. Well, no one except Kenton, Nico's friend Leo, the EMTs, and a whole bunch of cops. Okay...so a lot of people know I'm pregnant.

"Did you just say what I think you said?" I squeeze my eyes closed and shake my head. "You did! You just said, and I quote, 'Don't mind me. This baby has me all messed up.'"

"Um..."

"Holy mother of God! Sophie Jean Grates, you're pregnant!" Maggie yells as she climbs up to stand on the bed. "You're pregnant and you weren't going to tell me?" She starts to jump up and down, and just like that, my stomach flips, I stand up and run to the bathroom, and proceed to get rid of my breakfast and lunch. "Oh shit, I'm so sorry! I didn't even think."

I feel a cool, wet washcloth run across my forehead. "It's fine. Just the whole jumping-on-the-bed thing was a little much," I say, flushing the toilet before taking the washcloth out of her hand and bringing it to my mouth.

"Why the hell were you jumping on the bed?" I hear growled.

Maggie and I look at each other in shock before turning our heads to the open bathroom door.

"Seriously, babe. You have a hard-enough time keeping food down as it is, so tell me why the hell you would feel the need to jump on the bed," Nico demands, walking into the bathroom.

He is so hot that I have to look at Maggie and see if it's just me who is affected by him. Nope. The look on her face says that he does it for all women. Today, he has on jeans, boots, and a black Henley with the neck unbuttoned, showing off his tattoos. The area between my legs starts to tingle just from looking at him. I watch as he gets out my toothbrush before putting some toothpaste on it and setting it on the side of the sink. Then he walks over to where I'm still sitting on the floor, picks me up, and places my butt on the bathroom counter.

"You said you were only going to be gone a couple hours," I complain right away. He has been gone for the last six hours. I try to avoid pouting out my bottom lip like a two-year-old who's not getting her way.

"I know. I got held up. Now open," he instructs, and I do before I realize what he's doing.

"I can brush my own teeth," I grumble, pulling the brush from his hand to clean my own teeth, and shake my head at him.

"No more jumping on the bed, okay?" he prompts. He looks really worried, and I don't think it's from seeing me sick.

"Are you okay?" I ask, searching his face.

"I hate seeing you sick."

"She wasn't jumping." Maggie laughs, looking between us. "I... Well, she slipped up about the baby, and I was excited, so I started jumping on the bed."

I watch as Nico's eyes start to narrow, and I pull his face towards me. "Maggie is my friend. I don't care what you say about not having to be nice to your friends, but you treat mine like you treat me. Got it?" I say, waving my toothbrush around, foam flying everywhere.

"I don't like you getting sick."

"Well, then you shouldn't have gotten me pregnant."

"I like you pregnant." His eyes go soft before he runs his hand along my stomach like he often does. I smile then realize I probably look like an idiot with my mouth full of foam and a big cheesy smile on my face.

"You guys kinda make me want to vomit," Maggie says, making me laugh.

I LOOK ACROSS the room at Nico, who has his head tilted towards Devon. They're both standing next to the bar wearing suits, and each has a glass of what looks like scotch in their hands. Whatever they're talking about looks really serious.

"What's that about?" Maggie asks, coming to stand next to me.

"No clue." I shrug, not taking my eyes off the guys.

"Well, Nico has Devon's seal of approval."

"Really?" I ask, finally looking at Maggie, who looks beautiful in her wedding dress. The creamy color against her dark skin is stunning.

I look back at the guys, thinking how much the two men are alike. Devon is one of the hardest people to get along with. His childhood made him into an adult who doesn't easily trust, yet he always sees the glass as half full. He is also very protective of those he cares about; he is a lot like Nico in that aspect. He is one of the first people who made me feel safe. I knew when we were in Job Corps together that Devon would hurt anyone who even thought about messing with Maggie or me.

"Really. I guess they have a mutual friend, and Devon said he heard about Nico Mayson a long time ago."

"Seriously?" I whisper, this time in shock. Tennessee and Seattle are really far apart. Knowing that someone in Seattle heard about Nico makes me a lot more curious about his job.

"Yep. Seems your man has made a name for himself."

"I knew he was good, but wow," I breathe, my heart filling with pride.

I look over at Nico and Devon again, seeing that they both have their heads turned towards Maggie and me. Nico's eyes travel from my head to my toes, and I can see the hunger in his eyes. I have the urge to pull him into the bathroom.

"So how does it feel to be married?" I ask, turning back to Maggie.

"No different, I guess." She shrugs her bare shoulder. "You know, we've been living together so long we may as well have been husband and wife already. This is just a piece of paper that says we're married."

"I can't wait to have that piece of paper," I mumble under my breath.

Yes, I'm living with Nico, and yes, I'm pregnant with his child, but I want his last name. I want his ring on my finger, and I want mine on his. I really wanted it after the one night I was looking at all his tattoos and he told me why he didn't have one on his left ring finger when he has them on all the others.

"When we get married, I'm gonna tattoo your name there," he said, and I felt my heartbeat double-time at his words. I want my name on him. I love that idea, but I want him to wear a wedding band as well.

"Do you know the history of the wedding ring?" I asked him, tracing the empty space between his knuckles.

"No. Tell me."

"In ancient times, the circle was the symbol of eternity, no beginning or end. The hole in the center of the ring also had significance. It wasn't just considered a space, but rather a door leading to things and events for the couple. When an Egyptian man gave his woman a ring, it signified his never-ending love. Later, when the tradition was adopted by the Romans, the ring symbolized ownership. They also believed the ring should be worn on the left ring finger because they thought there was a vein in that finger, referred to as the 'Vena Amoris,' or the 'Vein of Love,' that was said to be directly connected to the heart."

"How do you know that?" he whispered.

My eyes met his, which were warm and soft. "I read it somewhere." I shrugged like it wasn't a big deal. I had been fascinated by that little piece of gold on my mom's finger since I was a little girl.

"Now tell me the truth about how you knew that," he said, running his hand over my hair.

I sighed, loving and hating how he could read me so easily. "When I was little, I used to play with my mom's wedding band on her finger. I remember always being curious about what it meant. I knew it meant forever. I just wanted to know why. So one day, my mom took me to the library, and we found this old book about the history of the wedding band. The first ones were made out of grass then later out of ivory or wood, depending on your wealth. But no matter what they were made from, the meaning was always the same."

"Jesus," he growled, flipping me onto my back, and before I had a second to think about what was going on, he was inside me.

"Sophie? Sophie?"

"Wh…what?" I ask, snapping out of the memory.

"Wow, that man must have it going on if you can stand in a room full of people and still be with him somewhere else."

"It wasn't that." I blush, lowering my eyes.

"Uh-hummm. Whatever you say, girl, but I know that look anywhere. Hell, I plan on wearing that look later tonight."

"What are you to talkin' about?" Devon asks, walking up and putting his arm around Maggie's waist as Nico does the same around mine.

"Girl talk, and you know we can't tell you."

"You and Sophie's girl talks always mean trouble," Devon says with a smirk. "Man, you gotta watch out for these two. They've always been nothing but trouble."

"That's a lie." I laugh. "You were always trying to get us in trouble."

"I'm a cop. I take offense to that."

"Whatever." I roll my eyes and shake my head.

Devon was always trying to talk us into doing things we weren't supposed to. Job Corps was very strict; we weren't allowed to leave the grounds unless you had earned it. We had a curfew and other rules as well, and he was always breaking them and dragging us along with him.

"Sophie loved the drama." Maggie smiles.

"Anyways, are you excited to go to the Bahamas?" I ask, changing the subject.

"Yes! Two weeks of beautiful beaches and sun. I love Seattle, but I hate that it rains all the time. It will be nice to get out of town," Maggie says, leaning deeper into Devon's side, smiling up at him. It used to make me jealous watching them, but now I have that kind of love for myself.

"That's one thing I don't miss. I love Tennessee," I tell them, feeling Nico's fingers flex on my hip.

"We'll come visit after you have the baby," Maggie states, and Devon looks at me, his eyes getting big. Crap.

"You pregnant, Sophie?"

"Yes," I say quietly.

"How did this happen?"

"Well, you see, when a man and—" I start flippantly.

"Cut the crap. You gonna marry our girl?" Devon asks, glaring at Nico. Nico—being Nico—glares back at him, putting his arm around my shoulders.

"You really want to ask about that at your wedding?" Nico asks.

"Hell yes. Everyone in this room loves Sophie, and no one here will be happy to know she's pregnant with no ring on her finger."

"That so?" Nico asks, looking around at the people in the room, who have all started to watch us.

I can feel my cheeks heating up. I know Devon thinks of me as family, but this is crazy.

"Devon, please sto—" I start, but suddenly Nico gets down on one knee in front of me. "What are you doing?" I whisper, watching as he pulls a small, turquoise box from inside his suit jacket.

"I knew from the moment I saw you that I would do everything within in my power to make myself worthy of you. I was going through life one day at a time, and then you came along and gave me a reason to plan for tomorrow. Every second, every minute, and every day, I will prove to be a better man, a man worthy of you, a man who will love you the same way you love me—for who I am, not what others see me as. I promise to love and protect you until my last breath, Sophie Jean Grates. Will you marry me, baby?" he asks, pulling a diamond solitaire ring from the hinged case in his hand, dropping the box on the floor, and pulling my hand towards him.

Before I can even think or he can get the ring on my finger, I tackle him. "Yes." I push him backwards, climbing on top of him and kissing him all over his face. "Yes," I repeat, holding his face between my hands and looking into his eyes. "I love you, Nico Mayson."

"I love you too, baby." He slides his hands through my hair, pulling my face down to his. Loud applause fills the room, and I feel myself turning red as he kisses me again, only to pull away and whisper against my lips, "Let's get off the floor, crazy girl."

I nod and climb off of him, fixing my dress. As soon as were both up, he slides the ring on my finger, pulling it to his mouth and kissing it then kissing me.

"I love you, girl," Maggie says, pulling me into a tight hug.

"I love you too. I can't believe he asked me in front of everyone," I say, still in shock.

"We knew yesterday," she tells me then moves to Nico before I can ask her what she meant.

Devon holds his arms open to me; I automatically go to him, wrapping my arms around his waist.

"You did good," he whispers before kissing the top of my head. I nod, feeling tears filling my eyes. "I know you understand what you got in our girl, man; just take care of her," Devon says over the top of my head before turning me around and handing me off to Nico.

"You happy, baby?" Nico asks, bending down to kiss my forehead.

"Yes," I tell him, tilting my head back to get a kiss.

When his mouth leaves mine, I hold my hand up to his chest, looking at my ring. This is what my mom had with my dad; even if she only had it for a short time, I know this is what she felt.

"I love this dress," Nico says from behind me later that night as his fingers run across my bare shoulders, making me shiver, "but I really love what's under this dress." He kisses my neck.

I feel his fingers on my zipper as he begins to pull it down. My breathing picks up as my dress starts to fall from around me. His hands go to the back clasps of my bra and it falls to the floor.

"Put your hands around my neck," he says against my neck as my hands go over my head and behind his neck. His hands run over my hips and up my stomach before cupping my breasts in his big hands. "I want to try something with you. Will you let me?" I nod. There is nothing I wouldn't try with him. "Tell me."

"Yes!" I cry out as he tugs on both of my nipples at the same time. Since becoming pregnant, my breasts have become extra sensitive, and I swear they are directly connected to my clit now.

"Lie on the bed on your back and close your eyes."

I step out of his embrace and walk to the bed, where I climb on, wearing nothing but a pair of pale-yellow lacy boy shorts that match my bra and dress perfectly. I lie on my back, feeling the wetness between my legs with every movement. I get comfortable and close my eyes, but I can't help but to peek at what he's doing—not that I can see anything. His back is to me, and his shirt is now off.

"Close your eyes. You peek again and I won't do what I've got planned."

I slam my eyes closed and feel my pulse start to race in excitement. I hear some clinking, the shuffle of feet on the carpet, and then the bed depresses next to me.

"Tell me you want this." I nod, clenching my fists. "I need you to say the words out loud, Sophie," he says, running a finger from the bottom of my foot to my inner thigh.

"I want this," I tell him.

"Good. Lift your hands over your head."

I take a second but do as he says, and then I feel something smooth wrap around my right wrist then my left. They're drawn together and lifted higher, and I automatically tug my hands and feel that they're tied to the headboard.

"Oh shit," I moan. I know he's joked about this, but I never thought it would really happen.

"Relax." I feel his fingers run from where my arms are joined, down one, and then along my side and under each breast. "I have imagined this over and over again."

I feel the bed depress. Then his hands travel from my ankles, spreading my legs wider as they travel up my knees, pulling my legs apart. His body comes over mine, his tongue licks over one nipple then the other, and then his hand at my side leaves and I hear clinking again.

Suddenly, the cold feel of an ice cube is circled around my right nipple then the left, causing my nipples to become even harder. I grit my teeth then cry out as the ice cube travels down my stomach, around my belly button, and then over the lace that is covering me.

"I need to cool you down, baby. You're really hot down here," he says, but then the ice is gone and I hear some kind of metal-on-metal sound.

I scream when my nipple is pinched, and not by fingers, causing my eyes to fly open as I look down.

"Eyes closed," he growls, making me wetter.

I close my eyes and squeak when he treats my other nipple to the same treatment as the first. The image in my head is strangely beautiful. He's attached small, golden clamps to my nipples. I can feel the pressure, but it's odd, because at the same time, I can feel the connection from the clamp to my clit like a live wire.

"Perfect." This time, his mouth comes down on mine, his teeth biting my lip, drawing my tongue out to play with his. His mouth travels down under my chin, between my breasts, and around my belly, and then I feel him sit away from me as his hands slide under my ass, pulling my panties down then off. His hands come under me again, lifting my ass of the bed.

"Now you can open your eyes." I do immediately; our eyes lock and his tongue licks right up my center. "Did you know you're so fucking sweet that I could eat you for hours? I love how wet you are for me." He sucks my clit into my mouth, my back bows, and the clamps on my nipples shift, making me cry out. I tug my hands against their bindings, trying to get them free, but it's no use. I'm completely at his mercy.

"I'm going to come," I pant, feeling the pull and knowing I'm getting ready to crash over the edge. His mouth leaves me, his fingers running over me in soothing strokes, making me jolt and cry out. "I was so close," I tell him, lifting my hips.

"I got you," he breathes against my pussy before licking me again. His fingers slide inside, and I cry out again as he flicks over my clit with his tongue. I'm close again, so I squeeze my eyes closed and lift higher, only to have him pull away again.

"Oh my God, I'm going to kill you!" I shout. His chuckle has me trying to kick him.

His hands grab my ankles then thighs, holding tight before his mouth is on me again. This time, his fingers fill me, his mouth covers me, his tongue thrashes before pulling my clit into his mouth, my head presses deeper into the bed, and I scream as I come harder and longer than I ever have. I feel like I'm floating on a cloud before I slowly come back to my body. The feeling is so overwhelming that I feel tears spring to my eyes.

He pulls the tie at my wrist, flips me over onto my stomach, lifts my hips, and slides into me, slowly filling me inch by inch; I can feel his piercing dragging inside me, hitting all the right spots. The nipple clamps attached to my nipples pull them down, and the feeling of them dragging against the sheets causes me to moan. I arch my back, lifting my ass higher wanting it deeper.

"Shit, baby," Nico groans from behind me, the noises he's making spurring me on. His hands go under my arms, lifting me up and impaling me on him. Then one arm goes around my chest and the other hand slides down to my clit. With each thrust, my breasts bounce, causing a jolt of electricity to shoot from my nipples to my clit. "I need you to come, Sophie. Come with me."

Nico shouts his release, pulling off the clamps one at a time then slapping my clit. The shock sends me over the edge and lights flash behind my closed eyelids. I can feel Nico deep inside me, his come filling me. We're both breathing heavily as he leans us forward, falling into the bed with him behind me, wrapping himself around me.

"That was wow," I say once I can talk.

"Yes, it was wow." His lips travel up my neck to my ear. "So when are we getting married?" he asks, pulling my hand up.

I look over my shoulder and see that his eyes are on the ring on my hand. "Whenever you want."

"Do you want a big wedding?" he asks, looking at my hand then me.

"Honestly, I'm okay with just getting the license then doing dinner or something." I don't want a big thing; I don't really have anyone I would invite besides Maggie and Devon.

"I don't care either. I just need you. The rest doesn't even matter."

"Then we agree?" I ask.

"I do want it done before the baby gets here."

"It's not a chore." I roll my eyes.

"Baby." He chuckles, kissing my shoulder again. This time, I bite my lip. My hormones are turning me into a crazy woman.

"Okay. Before the baby gets here," I agree before turning around to face him. "I'm so sleepy."

"Let me get you cleaned up so you can sleep."

I watch as he walks into the bathroom of the hotel room. I hear the water running, and then he comes back to me and gently cleans between my legs before tossing the washcloth towards the bathroom. I lean over and turn off the lamp as he gets into bed, pulling me into him and the blanket over us.

"I love you," I whisper, cuddling deeper into his side.

"You too, baby. Sweet dreams." He kisses my forehead, and before I can reply, I'm asleep.

I UNLOCK THE front door and run to the phone, trying to reach it before the answering machine picks up. "Hello?" I breathe when I finally get it to my ear. Tossing my bag on the counter, I unhook the rest of the shopping bags from my arms.

"This is a collect call from Seattle Correctional Facility from inmate"—the automated voice clicks off and a man's voice comes on the line—"William Grates." Then it's back to the automated voice. "Do you accept this call?"

I stand there, frozen. I can still remember the sound of his voice after all these years. It's like nothing has changed.

"This is a collect call from…" the automated voice repeats itself.

It takes me a second to realize what the voice said—Seattle Correctional Facility. My dad is in prison. I quickly slam the phone down into its cradle and take a few deep breaths. I can't talk to my dad now; there's just no way. Why the hell is he calling me, anyways? Better yet—how the hell did he get this number? The phone starts ringing again and I have the urge to run away and hide.

"Babe, you gonna get that?" Nico asks, walking into the living room. Not having noticed that he's home, I jump and my hand goes to my chest, trying to calm my pounding heart. "Babe, answer the phone," he says this time, walking towards me.

"It's no one, just a telemarketer." I lift the receiver then hang it back up.

"Who was it, Sophie?" His eyes narrow as he starts prowling towards me.

"It's no one. I already told you it's just a telemarketer." I walk into the kitchen to put away the groceries, praying the phone doesn't ring again.

"I can tell by the look on your face that it was someone."

"Drop it. It was no one," I grumble, going about putting the groceries away.

Just then, the phone starts ringing again. I try to beat him to it, but with his size and height, there's no way to get the phone out of his hand.

"Hello," he answers, holding me tight against his side with one arm under my breasts. "What the fuck?" he growls, throwing the phone across the room, shattering it against the wall. "Fuck me," he says, pulling me around in front of him. His hands hold my face.

"I don't know how he found me," I tell him, closing my eyes. I have never seen him this mad.

"I know."

"We can change the number," I tell him, laying my head against his chest.

"No, baby. I mean I know how he got this number." He picks me up, carrying me into the bedroom and crawling into the bed with me in his arms.

"What's going on?" I ask, reading his face.

"Your dad's in prison."

"I know. I heard the recording when he called."

"That's not how I know." He runs his fingers through the hair at the side of my head. "When you were attacked again, I had him looked into and found out he's in prison. I needed to see if he knew anything about what happened to you, so while we were in Seattle, I went and saw him." He pauses, looking down at me, studying my face. "While I was there, your dad asked for my name. He knew that I lived in Tennessee. It wouldn't take him much to figure out how to find me and, in turn, find you."

"You think my dad had something to do with me getting attacked?" I ask, skipping over everything else he just said.

"I wasn't sure, but now, no." He shakes his head.

"Why's he in there?" I ask even though I don't know how I feel. Part of me cares, but then the other part—the part that was abandoned by him—doesn't care at all.

He lets out a long breath then pulls me up his body so I'm lying on top of him before he rocks my world—and not in the good way. "Your dad's in prison for murder," he says, and my stomach rolls, making me hold my breath, praying for the nausea to pass. I can't imagine my dad killing anyone. Even when he was at his worse, he was never violent.

"I feel sick."

His hand goes to my back, rubbing it in soothing strokes. "I gotta tell you the rest, but I need you to know it has nothing to do with you," he warns.

"Okay," I say, bracing myself.

"Your dad killed the man who attacked you."

"What?" I scream, trying to jump out of the bed.

"Baby, calm down. This is why I didn't want to tell you," he growls, holding my wriggling body, which is trapped to his by his muscular, tattooed arms.

"You can't tell me to calm down! How can I calm down? My dad is a murder! He killed someone because of me! How is this not my fault?"

"Your dad made his own choices. This does not reflect on you."

"I'm gonna be sick," I tell him, and this time, he must know that I really am going to be sick because he releases me immediately so I can run to the bathroom. I lean over the toilet, gagging.

I can't believe this. My dad is a murder.

"Take some deep breaths for me," he says, laying a cool washcloth against the back of my neck.

I sit back on my calves and take a few deep breaths before he picks me up off the floor, carrying me back to the bed, tucking me in front of him.

"Okay. I think you can tell me the rest now," I tell him, wanting to get this over with.

"After I saw your dad, I did some research about what happened. I knew you would feel guilty about this, and I didn't want that for you." His arms wrap around me tighter, making me feel safe. "When you left, your dad sobered up. He finally realized what he did—or I guess, didn't do. The court documents say your dad started asking around about the guy who attacked you and found out you weren't his first victim."

"Oh my god." I close my eyes. I never even thought that what happened to me could have happened to someone else.

"He molested a girlfriend of his young daughter and then raped another woman."

"No." I shook my head not wanting to believe how really horrible that guy was.

"I'm sorry, baby." He kisses my forehead, pulling me closer to him. "Your father went to his house to confront him about what he had done. He said the guy attacked him first, but your dad had no wounds or anything that proved his claim. Your dad killed him." He pushes the hair away from my face, his lips going to my forehead again. "I know you feel differently than I do. I'll be happy if our child has your kind of compassion, but I'm glad he's dead. He deserved what he got. Actually, he deserved a lot worse for the things he did."

I'm glad he's dead too. I'm glad he isn't alive to hurt anyone else. I still feel guilty though. I don't even realize I'm crying until I feel Nico wiping the tears off my cheeks.

"Please don't cry, baby," he says quietly, running his hands over my head.

"Why's my dad calling?" I wonder out loud.

"I don't know, but I'll find out before he calls again." He rolls me to my back, his body leaning over me. "You know I love you, and there is nothing on this earth I wouldn't do for you. I would kill for you, walk through fire for you, and fight your demons if that's what you needed from me." He wipes my cheeks again before kissing me softly. "This is something I'm going to need you to fight through with me though. I know it'll be hard for you, but I think it may help heal some of what he broke in you if you talk to him."

"I don't know if I can. Why is he doing this now when before he couldn't care less?"

"He had someone checking on you while you were in Seattle."

"What?" I breathe. I look into his eyes, and he nods then shakes his head.

"He told me he had someone checking in on you, making sure you were okay, but then one day, you were just gone and he didn't know what happened to you."

"Okay... I don't know how I feel about that."

"I think he was doing it so he had peace of mind. When I met your dad and he talked about what happened to you, I could see how guilty he feels. He feels responsible for what happened to you, but he also feels guilty for your mother's death."

"He told you that?" I look at him, wide-eyed.

"He didn't have to. That's why I think it would be good if you talked to him."

"Can I send a letter or something first? I don't know if I'm ready to talk to him on the phone yet."

"You can do it however you need to," he says, kissing my forehead before pulling me into his chest. I'm not sure I'm ready to face my past, but I know that, as long as I have this man with me, I will be okay. I also know that, deep down, he is right; I need to face my past so I can move on to a future with Nico.

Chapter 12

Nico

LOOK OUT the window of the nursery and rub my hands over my face. For the first time since I started doing what I do, I feel out of control. I got in early from a job today and went to meet Sophie for lunch. When I got out of my car to head into the building, I noticed a paper under her wiper blade. At first, I didn't think much about it. I wasn't even going to look at it until something in my gut told me to turn around and grab it. As soon as I opened the letter, my stomach dropped.

After you have his baby, you're mine. I haven't forgotten about you.

The words were typed out on simple white copy paper. They were enough to send me into a rage and bring me to my knees all at once. I have no idea who had attacked her. I don't know how safe she is working at the school anymore. She already had to have someone stay with her when I was out of town for work. She hates feeling like she needs to be on guard. I have no idea what to do. I don't want her any more stressed out than she already is. Dealing with the situation with her dad already has her up late at night worrying. I don't want that for her, and I don't want that for my child. The fact she is now showing in her pregnancy is starting to freak me out. Not the showing part, but the part where she is very obviously carrying my child, there is someone after her, and they have been around her to know that she is pregnant.

"What are you doing in here?"

I turn to look at her as she enters the room we chose for the nursery. She's so fucking beautiful that I have to ask myself, Why me? How did I get so lucky? Today, she has on a high-waisted skirt that ends right under her tits, and the fit of the skirt shows off her very rounded stomach and ends right above her knees. At only three and a half months, you would think she is farther along than she is with how large she is already. We still don't know what we're having. People have already been making bets, so we've decided to keep it a surprise for D-day, as Asher always calls delivery day.

"Baby, you know you're not supposed to be wearing those shoes." I shake my head as I watch her heels move across the carpet.

"These are not even that high," she defends, doing a one-leg lift to show off one of the shoes. They are tall. They bring her forehead up to my mouth. When she's barefooted, it reaches my chest. These are all lace with a long, wide heel. "Besides, I think this is the last day of heels for me until the baby gets here anyways." She pouts then places one hand on my chest, lifting her foot behind her to slip off her shoe before doing the same with the other, causing her to shrink in height.

"What's wrong?" I rub her belly, loving the look of pregnancy on her. The first day I came in and saw her naked with the small bump that had formed overnight, I freaked, realizing that it's real. She really has my baby inside her.

"My feet are swelling today." She wraps her arms around my waist before laying her head on my chest.

"No more heels. They're not safe." This isn't the first time we've had this conversation. Talking to Sophie is like talking to a wall—I tell her one thing and she agrees then does whatever the hell she wants.

"I've been wearing heels forever. I'm probably safer in heels than sneakers." She laughs, hugging me.

I hold her a little tighter, putting my lips to the top of her head. Our problems are a lot bigger than her wearing heels though. I hate not knowing who I'm after. With my job, there is always a suspect. I always know exactly who I'm looking for and what they are capable of. This situation is out of my hands, and that scares the shit out of me.

"We gotta talk, Sophie."

"You're using my name, so that tells me it's something I won't want to talk about." She sighs.

"Sorry, baby, but we gotta." I lead her out of the nursery and into the kitchen, where I carefully put her up on the counter. "You hungry?"

"No, and you're the one who wanted to talk, so why are you avoiding it now?" She watches me as I go to the freezer, pulling out a pizza before turning on the oven.

"I found a note on your car today when I came to meet you for lunch." I go about taking the pizza out of the box before putting it on a pan.

"What kind of note?"

"Fuck." I run my hand over my head. "I don't want to tell you about this. If there was a way to keep this from you while keeping you safe, I would."

"You're scaring me," she states, looking at my fist clenching and unclenching at my side.

"I don't want you to be scared. That's the last thing I want, but I would rather you be afraid and cautious than you not know what's going on, not pay attention to your surroundings, and then have something happen to you because you didn't know you were in danger."

"Tell me," she prompts.

I walk back to her, fitting myself between her legs. I pull the copied note out of my back pocket to show her. I handed the original off to Kenton to take to Leo. I also checked with the school to see if they had any cameras on the premises, but they didn't have any. I still have no leads. The note has no prints besides mine from grabbing it from the windshield. I watch as Sophie reads the words and her face goes pale, and I see the worry etched in her eyes when they meet mine again.

"Who's doing this?" she asks, one hand covering her stomach, the other covering her mouth as tears begin to fill her eyes.

"I don't know. I've asked myself that same question a million times and keep coming up with nothing."

"I don't know anyone here. I've always kept to myself," she sobs, making me feel helpless.

"We'll figure it out, baby. I just don't know about you working at the school anymore. I don't think it's safe." I hold her until her tears start to die down.

"I feel like I'm letting whoever's doing this win by quitting, but I know I can't work there and feel safe. I hope this ends soon. I don't want to have the baby and be looking over my shoulder every time I leave the house."

I wipe her face, kissing each of her eyelids before taking the note from her and putting it back in my pocket. "I hate this for you, but things are going to have to change until I find out who it is."

"I'll do whatever you need me to do," she says, and in those few words, I know how much faith she has in me. Her faith alone makes me want to fight that much harder to end this.

"From now on, when I'm out of town, you're gonna stay with Mom and Dad, and tomorrow, we're going to get you a gun and I'm gonna teach you how to shoot." I put my mouth to her forehead, kissing her before looking into her eyes again.

"Do you really think it's necessary?"

"Absolutely. I need to know you can take care of yourself. Your self-defense moves aren't going to be as helpful when you've got a belly to contend with."

"Do you really think I need to stay at your parents'?"

"Yes. The person has proven that he knows where you lived and now where you work. Who knows if he's figured out that you now live here?"

"I hate this, but okay," she agrees reluctantly.

I hate that she is being forced to change her life while whoever is doing this is out there living normally and probably getting off on her being afraid. But I'm stuck. I cant risk something happing to her.

I kiss her forehead again then try to make her forget about everything by turning off the oven and carrying her upstairs, where I make love to her until we both fall asleep.

"AIM TO KILL, baby," I tell Sophie as I wrap my arms around her and help her line up the shot. "I want you to take a deep breath, and when you let it out, I want you to squeeze the trigger, not pull it."

"Got it," she says shakily.

I listen as she takes a deep breath, letting it out slowly. Her hand steadies, and she lets off three rounds, one after another, all hitting near the center of the target. Her aim is nearly perfect for someone who has never even held a gun until today. I hit the button, bringing the target closer so she can she what she did.

"You're a natural," I tell her with pride etching my voice.

"Really?" she asks, setting the gun down before turning to me.

"Really. Look at what you did. All three of your rounds are near center of the bull's-eye."

"This is kinda fun." She laughs, and suddenly her eyes go wide and she grabs my hand, pulling it to her stomach.

"What?" I ask in a panic, and then I feel the slight movement under my palm. I immediately fall to my knees in front of her, both hands holding her stomach. "Holy shit," I choke out, looking up into Sophie's beautiful, glowing face then back down to where my tattooed hands are in stark contrast to her white maternity dress.

"I know," she whispers, dragging my hands around her stomach so I can feel the baby moving. "The shooting must've woken her up."

I nod then shake my head. I never thought this would be something I would experience. I look up at her again, seeing her beaming down at me. Her hair is braided back away from her makeup-free face, but little pieces have come loose and are flying around her in the wind.

"Can I shoot again?" she asks, making me laugh.

"I was having a moment...and you want to shoot?"

"Well, it was fun."

I shake my head and kiss her belly once before standing. "All right. This time, I want you to aim at the head."

"I can do that," she says with confidence, giving me an instant hard-on.

She refused to get a gun at first…until she saw a white Ruger LCP .380 with pink flowers all over it. I almost refused to let her get it—no gun should have flowers on it—but I figured that, if she was carrying it and it could kill someone if she was in danger, I didn't care what it looked like.

I press the button on the machine, sending the target back out. I put my arms around her again, this time resting on her belly. With every shot, she makes the baby move inside her, making her laugh and miss the target the first three times. I reload her gun, giving her advice on how to focus before sending a new target out with instructions that I want two in the head and three in the heart. This time, she focuses and hits her target with ease.

"You're a pro."

"Really?"

"Really, baby." I kiss her temple. Knowing that she can shoot has some of my stress easing.

"Maybe when the baby gets here, I can work for you."

"That's never gonna happen." I have a friend who works with his woman, but I can't imagine having Sophie with me on a job. I wouldn't be able to focus.

"I could be your backup."

"Not happening," I state.

"Aww, come on. You said I was a great shot. I could dress like a ninja. I would be like your secret weapon. People would be like, 'Oh, we got Nico,' and then I would show up and take them out," she says, doing a strange-looking karate chop.

"As entertaining as that would be, it's still not happening."

"Fine. I guess I'll give up my dream." She sighs, making me laugh.

I take her hand and make our way out to my car. After I get her in the passenger's seat, I jog around and hop behind the wheel.

"How you feeling?" I drive out of the parking lot before taking her hand in mine and pulling it to my mouth.

"Okay. Just tired."

"I want you to ask the doctor if he has any suggestions for that."

"Sleep." She laughs.

"Very funny, smartass, I'm serious though."

"I know you are." I hear the humor in her voice, and it makes me smile.

"It's the doctor's job to answer questions," I remind her.

"Yes, but when you call him at midnight to ask him if it's normal for me to have heartburn, I think that may be overkill."

"He told me to call if I had any questions. Besides, you ate a whole container of Tums in one night"—I look over at her—"like they were candy."

"Don't remind me. That was not one of my crowning moments." She laughs. Then her voice goes quiet. "I can't believe you won't be here for my appointment."

"Sorry, babe." I hear the regret in my own voice. I hate not being able to go with her, but after this job, I'll be taking some time off until the baby gets here.

In reality, the more I think about leaving Sophie and the baby after he or she gets here, the more I start hating my job. Leo told me the other day that they have a couple of spots opening up in his department. He could get me in if I wanted. My first thought was no, but then he explained that their captain lets them do their own thing as long as they're closing cases. Knowing that, if I took the job, I would no longer be going out of town and leaving her alone made me think harder about it. I want and need that. I hate the idea of her being home alone with a new baby. Yes, my family will be around, but it's not the same. I never want to miss out on important occasions with my family.

"Mom's gonna go with you so you won't be alone."

"I know, but it's not the same," she says, repeating my thought. It's crazy to think how much my life has changed since I first laid eyes on her.

"I know it's not."

We drive the rest of the way home in silence. When we reach the house, I pull into the garage and help Sophie out of the car before heading to the mailbox.

"Nico," Deb calls from two houses away, where she's outside watering her lawn.

I lift my chin then shake my head at her. I don't know how her husband puts up with her shit, but he's a better man than I am. If I ever found out that Sophie was outside watering the lawn and wearing practically nothing, I would go postal.

"Hi, Deb," Sophie calls, waving at Deb, who gives a small wave back. She presses her tits into my arm before sticking her hand in my back pocket, leaning deeper into me.

I bite my cheek to keep from smiling. It's cute that she's protective, but she never has anything to worry about.

"Did we get anything good?" she asks innocently, looking at the stack of letters in my hand.

I shuffle through the mail then stop when I come across the letter Sophie has been waiting for. In a way, I'm glad she's here as I'm checking the mail. If I were on my own, I don't know if I would have given her the letter. Yes, I want her to work through her past, but it's engrained in me to protect her from anything that might potentially cause her pain.

"He wrote back," she whispers, looking from the letter to my eyes.

I put all the mail in one hand before cupping her cheek with the other. "You don't have to read it right now. You never have to read it if you don't want to."

"I want to." She swallows, leaning her head deeper into my hand. "You're right. I need to see what he has to say so I can put it all behind me. I don't want this hanging over my head anymore, and I don't want to worry about it when the baby gets here."

"So we read it then burn it, making it history."

She nods, not saying anything.

Running my thumb over her jaw, I lean in and kiss her once before tucking her under my arm to lead her inside. Once I get Sophie situated out on the back patio with a glass of tea, I go get a lighter and my metal trash can from the garage and take them out with me. I hand her the letter before pulling her onto my lap. Her hands start to shake as she rips the envelope open, and I watch as she pulls the letter out, unfolding it.

Dear Sophie,

I don't even know where to start. I got the letter from Nico after I tried to phone you. I understand why you didn't want to talk to me, but I wish I could hear your voice. Maybe one day, we can talk and I can hear for myself that you are well and happy. I know from your boyfriend that you have become successful and are leading a life that would make your mother proud. She was always proud of you. You were the most important thing in her life, and I know her death was hard on you. I wish I could explain to you the reasons I did what I did, but there is no excuse that will justify my actions and the way I neglected you when you needed me. Your mom would hate me if she knew what happened after her death. I regret few things in my life, but my treatment of you is something I will regret until the day I die. I'm sorry.

I know it would be nearly impossible for you to forgive me, but if you could find it in yourself to offer me a few words every now and then, I would enjoy that. Your boyfriend is very different from anyone I thought you would end up with, but he seems to love you and to be very protective, and even though it's not my right as your father, I couldn't ask for more. Your mother would have been thrilled that you found someone who obviously loves you so deeply. I love you, Sophie. I know I didn't show it when I should have, but there isn't a day that goes by that I don't think about you and the woman you have become. I wish I could have been a better father to you. I just didn't know how to do that after your mom died. I'm so sorry.

I hope this letter finds you happy.

Love,
Dad

I pull a sobbing Sophie into my chest, rocking her back and forth like a child, trying to offer her some comfort. After reading that letter, I hope she will be able to find some closure.

"I got you, babe," I shush her, rubbing her back.

When the sobs racking her body start to die down, I pull her face out of my chest, taking a second to look at her. Even with her face splotchy with tears, she's beautiful.

"I know that was difficult, but how are you feeling?"

"Torn," she says quietly, grabbing my wrist. "I feel like I want to talk to him. He's the only connection I have to my mom. I feel sad that it took him so long to realize what he had, and the other part of me hates him for not being there for me when I needed him. That's the part I don't like. I don't want to hate him. My mom loved him. They were so in love that, even as young as I was, I could see their love was the kind that would never die. When I was young, my dad would come home from work and walk into the house, and the first thing he would do was go to my mom and kiss her, even if I was waiting by the door for him. Then he would come and pick me up." I don't tell her that that's fucked up. Our kids will be just as important as her. "When my mom died, I felt like my connection with him died too." Yep, totally fucked up. "I think I need time to think about this."

"You have all the time you need."

"Thank you for being here with me." She does a face-plant back into my chest, making me smile.

"Nowhere else I would want to be."

"Do you remember when I told you I used to want a tattoo?" she asks quietly.

"Yes." I run my hand down her back, holding her tighter against me.

"My dad had my mom's name tattooed along his ribs. I wanted that, only with my husband's name, but then I lost my mom. And not long after that, I lost my dad, and I stopped believing love could last. Now I know it can. After I have this baby, I want a tattoo like that of your name along my ribs. I belong to you—will always belong to you. You brought me back to life." She lifts her head to look at me. Her finger runs along my jaw then up to trace my bottom lip.

I can't talk with the emotions choking me, so I pull her in for a deep kiss, gently pressing one hand to her stomach. After I find my voice again, I tell her, "If you want that, baby, I'll take you."

"Thank you," she whispers

"There is nothing in this world I wouldn't do for you, sweet Sophie." I pull her closer to me and smile into her hair, thinking about my name being tattooed onto her perfect skin.

"YOU SURE HE'S here?" I ask Kenton, looking at the run-down house across the street from us.

"Yeah. When Ian called, he told me that Justin found a hit on his credit card. The stupid fuck ordered shit from Amazon and had it deliver here."

"How the fuck did he run drugs without being caught for so long?" I shake my head. I swear I don't know how most criminals are able to get away with the shit they do. Half of them are dumb as fuck.

"I don't think he was the one in charge," Kenton says, shaking his head.

"So what do the cops say about him?"

"They think his partners are turning on him. They want to offer him a deal, but they haven't been able to track him. You know they always have too much red tape when it comes to this shit. Their hands are tied, so they want us convince him that he needs to come in."

"So what's the plan?" I look across the street again, seeing that the only light on is the one in the basement.

"We go in and do just that—use the power of persuasion to convince him to do the right thing."

"And if he doesn't agree?" I ask with a smile, knowing what the answer will be.

"By the time we leave him, he will be running to the cops."

"Sounds good." I nod. What I do isn't always smiled upon, but knowing that one more fucked-up criminal will be off the streets before my child comes into this world makes me feel that much better about doing what I have to do. "Lets roll."

I open the door to my car, getting out at the same time Kenton does. We don't even bother with the front door. We walk around the side of the house, checking windows until one opens. Kenton goes in first and I follow behind him when he gives me the signal that it's clear. After that, we search the house, making sure that no one else is inside. By the time we make it to the basement Meyer Bulger is in the middle of getting a blowjob. The chick that was sucking him off runs out of the room screaming when she sees me. I let her go, knowing that she was paid for her time and is not likely to get involved.

"Meyer," Kenton says, sitting down casually across from the guy.

"What are you doing here?" he finally asks, his eyes are glossed over from the cocaine he was shoving up his nose.

"We came to have a chat," I tell him, setting my gun down on the table in front of me. His eyes go wide and his hand moves to the left. "Try it and I will put a bullet in you."

His eyes search my face, and I know that he can tell that I'm not fucking around. His hand that had been reaching for his piece moves back to his lap.

"What do you want?" he asks, looking between Kenton and me.

"You," Kenton says with a shrug.

"What the fuck does that mean?"

"You know what it means, Meyer." I shake my head.

"I'm not a snitch."

"Then you're dead," I tell him, starting to stand.

"No, you don't understand."

"I do understand." I look him over. "I can see it now. You probably started using your own product when no one was watching. Eventually your addiction caught up with you and you couldn't get enough. When that happened, you started fucking up, and the people at the top of the food chain didn't like that much. Now they want you dead. So tell me. What's it going to be?"

"You know if I talk to the cops I'm signing my death warrant."

"You have a better chance of surviving if you work with the cops," Kenton tells him.

"Fuck." He shakes his head, his eyes falling to his lap, and just like that, I know we won.

I look at Kenton and smile, ready to get the fuck home to my girl.

"MA, WE'RE NOT moving," I state firmly then watch Sophie's bottom lip wobble. Fuck, I hate when she cries, and she cries about everything lately. "Baby, please don't cry." I pull her into my side, kissing her head.

"I always wanted to live in the country, and the money from selling my house can buy it. Please just look at it before you say no," she says, looking up at me with tears filling her eyes.

"You're not buying our house." I look at the ceiling, praying for patience. "Ma, do you see the trouble you're causing?" I narrow my eyes on my mom. "I leave my girl with you for three days, and this is what you do?"

"Your mom's not causing trouble." Sophie sighs, looking at my mom then me.

I see something pass between them. "What?" I look at my mom and then back to her.

"I have something to tell you," Sophie says, biting her bottom lip while avoiding eye contact.

"What?" I repeat.

"I think you should sit," she says, wringing her hands together.

"I don't need to sit. Is it about the baby?" I ask, feeling sick all of a sudden.

"I really think you should sit, honey," my mom says quietly, causing me to panic.

"Tell me," I growl.

"We're having twins," Sophie blurts then covers her mouth, looking at my mom with wide eyes.

I stare at her blankly for a minute. I don't make her repeat herself; I heard her loud and clear. "I need to sit," I mumble, walking over to the couch where I plop, putting my head between my knees. "How did this happen?" I wonder out loud. Hearing my mom laugh, I lift my head to glare at her.

"I'll be in the kitchen," Mom sings, walking off.

"Are you okay?" Sophie asks, coming to sit next to me and running her hand down my back.

I sit back, pulling her into my lap to run my hand over her stomach. I can't believe this; it's like hitting the kid lotto.

"You're okay with this, right?" she asks, and I realize I haven't spoken to her; I've just been staring at her stomach, running my hands over her large bump.

"Shocked as hell." I shake my head in disbelief. "We're having twins." I smile then feel it fall from my face. "They're both okay, right?"

"The doctor said they're perfect."

"Why are we just finding this out?" I rub her stomach again, amazed that two babies are growing in there. I can't imagine how large her stomach will be when it comes time for her to give birth. She's so tiny, and her stomach is already large at just four months along.

"The doctor wasn't sure why the other baby didn't show before now, but he was suspicious when I told him we could feel him or her moving already, so he did an ultrasound to see what was going on. That's when we saw that there were two of them, and he assured me that everything's fine," she explains with a beautiful smile that lights up her whole face.

"Do you really want to move?" I pull her head down to lay against my chest. I love the townhouse, but I can't see us raising our kids there. The neighborhood is mainly single people and couples with no children.

"I know you love your place, but I want my kids to grow up close to family. Well, your family, anyways," she says softly.

"They're your family now too, and my place is always your place."

"I know."

I can hear the smile and tears in her voice, so I pull her face away so I can look at her. "All right, baby. We're gonna have to move anyways. One baby would be okay in our place now, but two would be pushing it."

"Really?" she asks happily.

"Anything for you, sweet Sophie," I tell her, watching in fascination as she laughs and cries all at the same time.

Chapter 13

Sophie

"I CAN'T BELIEVE how much has changed. I mean, you got married, you are not only pregnant but you're having twins, and now you're moving into a new house," Maggie says, coming to sit down next to me on the couch. "I should have guessed that you're having twins though. You're really frickin' huge," she says, rubbing my large belly.

I know she doesn't mean it in a bad way, but her words hit me wrong and I start to cry. My boobs are giant, my belly is so big that I can't even see my feet, and my legs are swollen and probably hairy.

"Why are you crying?" she asks, looking at me like I'm crazy. I probably am crazy.

"I'm a big, fat, hairy beast," I tell her on a sob.

"Oh God, you're so dramatic." She laughs, making me cry harder.

"Why's my wife crying, Maggie?" Nico growls, walking into the house, Devon following close behind him, carrying a box.

We're in the process of moving from the townhouse to our new country home. The process took longer than we'd planned. The house was a short sale. The bank took two months to get back to us that they had accepted our offer.

I wipe my face, trying to get rid of the tears; I don't want Nico to see me cry. He's so amazing and supportive while I'm horrible with my constant complaining and crying. I start crying harder as I think about what a bad wife I am.

"Geez, girl. You need to calm down. We can shave your legs if it's bothering you that much." Maggie rolls her eyes, handing me another tissue. I blow my nose then look up when I see a shadow fall over me.

"You know I hate to see you cry," Nico says softly, putting one hand on the armrest of the couch and the other on my neck. "If Maggie's the reason you're crying I'm gonna make Maggie leave," he says, making my eyes narrow.

"If you try to make my friend leave, I'll leave with her."

I watch as one side of his mouth quirks up before he replies, "You can't. You have two of my kids growing inside you. So basically, your body is half mine until you're no longer pregnant. Not only that, you have my last name, meaning I own you." He smirks.

"Holy shit," I hear Maggie say from beside me. She doesn't sound pissed, which is surprising.

"I can't believe you just said that to me," I tell him, ignoring Maggie.

"Believe it."

"I really cannot believe you just said that," I hiss, glaring at him.

"Would rather have you mad than crying," he says before leaning forward, kissing me until I can't breathe, and then standing and leaving the house.

"I'm not sure what just happened, but that was hot. So hot that I want to drag Devon into your spare bedroom," Maggie says, and I look over to see her leaning back, fanning herself.

"He just did that so I would stop crying," I tell her in shock.

"He did," she agrees, smiling.

"He's crazy." I grin back at her.

"Crazy hot." Maggie giggles, and I look at her in shock; I have never in my life heard her do that.

"Did you just giggle?" I ask.

"Absolutely not." Her eyes get big. "Holy shit, I fucking giggled. What the hell is wrong with me?"

"I don't know, but you should get that checked out," I tell her with a straight face.

"Your man turned me into a giggling school girl." She sighs, laying her head back against the couch, a large smile on her face.

I smile and then look around our new home. The house is a newer two-story brick home with a location perfect for being close to family. Our new living room is much larger than the townhouse's, with dark bamboo floors, tall vaulted ceilings, and large windows that look out to the forest behind the house. The kitchen is also large and has all new appliances, with a large island that can seat five barstools. Next to the kitchen is a small dining room that was built into a rounded section of the house that is surrounded by floor-to-ceiling bay windows.

I love this house. I love that the backyard is huge and already has a play set for kids. I love that all the bedrooms are on the second floor so we won't have to be separated from the babies when they get here. What I really love is that Nico loves it as much as I do. I know he loved his townhouse and his neighbors, but when he walked into our new house for the first time with me, I could see it on his face that he loved it. Or maybe he just loved the fact that he'd have a three-car garage and two of his brothers as our neighbors.

"Aunt Sophie!" I hear yelled in time to see July running into the living room, carrying a very annoyed Daisy in her arms.

"Hey, honey." I sit forward on the couch as she runs to me.

"Uncle Nico said you're getting another puppy."

"He did, did he?" I look over at Maggie, who shrugs her shoulders.

Nico hasn't said anything to me about getting another dog, but with him, I never know what's going to happen. He never even told me he wasn't going to be working for Kenton anymore or that he was taking a job with the MNPD working with Leo until he had to be gone for a week to do some training and testing. When I first found out, I was upset; I didn't want him to change jobs because of me. Then he sat me down and explained that, with the babies coming, he didn't think he would be able to handle being away all the time, and taking the job with Leo meant he would have more stability. I told him that was good, but if he didn't like it, he should go back to working for Kenton.

"Yes, but Daisy's still my favorite," July says, and I laugh as she pulls a wiggling Daisy up to her face to talk to her. "You will always be my favorite. You're so cute and small and fluffy," she tells the Pomeranian before bringing her down to her chest for a hug. Poor Daisy looks like her eyes are going to pop out of her head, making me wince.

"Honey, why don't you let Daisy down for a bit and go wash your hands? Maybe we can make some sandwiches for everyone."

"Uncle Nico ordered pizza," she says, holding Daisy tighter against her, making her squirm.

"Daisy may need to pee."

I guess those are the magic words, because she immediately puts the dog down. I watch as Daisy jumps off the couch, quickly running away, probably trying to find somewhere to hide.

"I don't want her to pee on me. May peed on me one time when I was holding her, and that was gross."

"That is gross." I laugh at the squeamish look on her cute little face.

"Now that you live here, can we have more sleepovers?" she asks, looking around.

"We can." I don't tell her that it won't be for, like, ten years. She doesn't need to know that. I'm still trying to recover from the last sleepover we had.

"Good! The last one was so much fun!"

I smile and shake my head. Having six kids over for a sleepover was insane, and not something I want to repeat anytime soon. The first couple of hours were fine, but then it came time for bed and none of them wanted to sleep, except Jax, who was hanging with his uncle most of the time. Then there was a lot of crying. We had to take all of the kids home at around two in the morning, so it really wasn't a sleepover; it was more like an extended visit. I love them all, but I won't be doing that again for a long time.

"Uncle Nico," July says as soon as she sees him walking into the room carrying a box, "Aunt Sophie said we can have a sleepover."

"Did she?" he asks, smiling at her. I bite back my smile when his eyes come to me and narrow slightly.

"She did."

"After the babies are born, we will talk about it," he tells her, carrying the box somewhere into the house and getting out of Dodge.

"Where are your sisters, honey?" I ask her before trying to stand.

"Outside with the other kids."

"All right. You go get them and bring them in here. When all of you wash your hands, we can get you guys some juice for when the pizza gets here," I tell July, and she runs off. "I'm gonna go check on Nico," I say, looking at Maggie, who is lying on the couch with her eyes closed.

"Sure, whatever. Leave me to my dirty fantasies about your husband."

"Whatever you say." I laugh, leaving the room. When I get to the office, Nico's there with his back to me, putting something up on one of the shelves built into the walls.

"We are not having a sleepover," he says without even turning around.

"I agree—no sleepovers." I walk behind him, wrapping my arms around his waist, laying my head against his back.

"I set up the bed in our room. Why don't you go lay down for a while?"

"I'm not tired."

I look over his shoulder to see what he's putting on the shelf and see the picture of us on our wedding day. We're both in profile. I'm in my dress, standing in front of him in his suit. My head's bending forward, my forehead pressed to his chest, his lips on the back of my head. Both of us have our hands on my belly. Every time I look at that picture, all I remember is how loved I felt right then. We had just walked down the aisle after saying our 'I do's.' Through the whole ceremony, the babies had been going crazy, so I'd stopped Nico at the end of the aisle and pulled his hands forward, splaying them on my belly. He had said something sweet, making me lean into him, and I could feel his mouth on the back of my head where he kissed me.

With the way the picture was taken, you can't really make out our features, but out of all of our wedding pictures, it's my favorite. I never would have thought I'd want a big wedding, but the minute I saw my wedding dress through the shop's window, I knew I needed to have one so I could wear that dress; it would have been a sin to waste it on a courthouse wedding. The dress was white—so white that, if you looked at it in the sun, you might go blind. The top had slim sleeves that hung off my shoulders, and the waist was taken in with a simple white ribbon tied under my breasts, showing off my baby bump. It was perfect.

After I found that dress, everything else fell into place. All the Mayson women were more than happy to help plan everything. We decided to have the wedding in November and Asher's backyard. The boys built a bridge over the pool with a perfectly placed altar in the middle, and the colors were pale yellow and cream. Nothing was like anything we'd planned all those months before while we'd lain in bed. We had over a hundred guests, most of them I didn't know, but all of those people there to see Nico and me get married, and that made it that much more perfect. We had a huge three-course dinner and a six-tier cake for dessert. That night, I learned that my new husband loved to dance. Every chance he got, he dragged me out onto the dance floor to hold me close through every slow song.

"Baby, you really need to rest. It's not good for you to be on your feet for so long," Nico says, bringing me back to the present.

"I've been resting all day," I tell him as he turns around to face me.

"You're so damn stubborn." He shakes his head but looks at me lovingly.

"You're not?" I smile, looking up into his eyes. "July said you ordered pizza?"

"I did. Devon went to pick it up." His hands hold my face and he kisses me.

"I'm starving," I say against his lips.

"You should have eaten earlier," he scolds, running his fingers through my hair.

"I did, but I want to eat again. I always want to eat," I tell him. He knows this because he does at least one late-night grocery run every week.

"My boys are going to be strong."

"I'm not even going to argue with you. As you know, they could be girls. Two girls," I taunt him.

"You're only allowed to give me one girl."

"Really? You're going to allow me to give you one girl?"

"Yep. Just one," he says, smiling.

"All right, but don't come crying to me if these are both girls," I say with a smirk and rub my belly.

"If you're all healthy at the end of the day, I don't really care what they are," he confesses softly.

"Good answer." I go up on my tiptoes while pulling his mouth down for a kiss.

"Ewww! Gross," I hear from behind me. I turn my head to see Jax looking at us. "Pizza's here," he says before running off. I giggle, turning back to face Nico.

"He can't wait until Cobi gets big. He hates being the only boy old enough to voice his opinion on how gross girls are," Nico says.

"I can't wait to remind him about how gross girls are in about fifteen years."

"You and me both. Now, do I need to give you something to help you sleep?"

"What do you have in mind?" I question innocently, getting as close as my belly will allow.

"When is everyone leaving?" he growls, nipping my neck.

"I don't know. How much longer until we're all moved?" I tilt my head while grabbing a handful of his hair.

"We have one more load." He licks up my neck, kissing below my ear. "I need everyone gone so I can be inside you."

It still surprises me that he wants me as much as he does, even with how pregnant I am. He never makes me feel like I'm unattractive; if anything, I feel like he wants me even more.

"I need you," I moan, shoving my face into his chest, my hands fisting his shirt.

His hands go to mine, pulling them away before leaving me standing there, watching as he walks to the door. Then he shuts and locks it before coming back to me and helping me up on the desk. When he's done with me, I'm starving and ready for a nap.

"ARE YOU SURE this is a good idea?" I look at the giant dog Nico just brought home.

Daisy's excited about him, and he seems like he's tolerating Daisy, but I'm not so sure. He's huge; his head comes up to my waist when he's on all fours. I have never been afraid of dogs, but he puts some fear in me.

"Danes are good dogs. They're loyal and very smart," he says from where he sits on the couch.

"Where did you even get him from?" I back up when the dog starts to come towards me.

"Baby, do you honestly think I would ever bring a dog into our home if I didn't know for certain you and our babies would be safe with him around?" Nico asks, watching me and the dog closely.

"It's not that I don't trust you… It's just… He's so big that my head can fit in his mouth. Daisy can fit in his mouth! I love Daisy. I don't want to look for her one day then a couple hours later have him go outside to do his business and his business is a ball of fur that was once my Daisy."

He laughs, and the dog takes another step towards me, forcing me to take another step back. "Baby, he isn't going to eat Daisy. He doesn't even notice her."

"You say that now, but what happens when we're not home and they're alone together?" I ask, watching as Daisy runs in and out from between the big dog's legs then jumps up and down, trying to get him to play with her. "Okay, so maybe they'll be okay, but I just don't know."

"Come here, Sophie." Nico holds out his hand in my direction. I scoot around the dog before taking his hand so he can pull me onto his lap.

"I think I'm getting too big to sit on your lap," I tell him.

"Never." He kisses the side of my head. "Now come here, Goose."

"Goose?" I repeat quietly, watching the dog come towards us. "What kind of name is Goose?"

"Goose is his name because he's as white as a goose."

He is white—pure white, with one black ear, a pink nose, and blue eyes. Nico holds my hand out for him to smell. I have been around Asher and November's Beast a few times. He's a nice dog, great with all the kids, and very protective. He's just so big. I always try to avoid him.

"Relax, babe. He's a good dog."

I un-ball my fist, cautiously holding my hand out to him. His cold, wet nose touches my palm, and then his tongue runs over my skin. Daisy jumps on the couch so she can get closer to Goose, and once she's in front of him, she starts licking his face and barking, trying jump on him. He pushes her out of the way with his head, forcing her to the side so he can lay his head on my lap. His nose goes to my stomach, and I wonder if he smells the babies. Daisy's still going crazy trying to get his attention, but he just ignores her, pressing himself even closer to me so I'll pet him.

"The best part is he's already house broken, and he's full grown."

"Where did he come from?" I ask, starting to relax and enjoy the comforting feeling of his big, warm head against me.

"A friend of mine who's in the military is getting ready to go overseas and can't take him with him."

"So we're going to have to give him back in a couple years?" I wonder out loud, not liking the idea of getting attached to him and then having him taken away in a few years when his owner comes back.

"No, babe. He's ours permanently," Nico assures me.

I laugh as he rubs his big head against my stomach, wanting me to pay attention to him. "Okay, so he's kinda cute," I finally agree.

"He's well trained. That's what's important."

"You're not still worried, are you?" I ask. Since moving, I never even think about what happened at my old house.

"I will be worried until we find out who the person behind what happened to you is."

"Nothing has happened in forever. Maybe what happened before was a complete coincidence." I shrug my shoulders, the movement making Goose look up at me with big puppy-dog eyes.

"Maybe, maybe not, I'm not willing to take that chance."

"So I guess we just got a new dog." I sigh, finally placing my hands on each side of the giant head nuzzling my belly and stroking his short but surprisingly soft fur.

"Glad you're seeing things my way." He smirks.

"I love when you ask me how I feel about something, knowing you're just going to do whatever you want anyways." I scratch behind Goose's ears and giggle when one of his back legs starts to shake.

"When it comes to your safety, I will do what's necessary." He kisses the side of my neck, and Daisy decides to jump up on the back of the couch, where she can prop her front paws on Nico's shoulder and lick both of our faces.

My hormones take over for a moment and my heart swells. "Two fur-babies before our two real babies get here. It's gonna be a full house."

I SIT DOWN in the glider that was just delivered for the babies' room and tap my pen on the paper in my lap. I need to reply to my dad's letter. I've been putting it off for a long time, trying to figure out what I want to say, what I really want our relationship to be like, or if I even want a relationship with him at all. The closer my due date gets, the more I think about my babies having their grandfather—not just Nico's dad, but my dad as well—at least in some capacity. I know it's what my mother would have wanted. I look down at the paper again, wondering how to even start the letter off. Do I write Dear Dad, or do I write his name? Why does this have to be so difficult?

"Whatcha doing in here?" I look up when I hear Nico's voice.

"Sorry?" I ask him, lost in the way he looks. His torso is covered in sweat, his tattoos even more pronounced from the sun shining into the room, his body looking bigger than it used to for some reason.

"What are you doing, baby?" he repeats.

"Trying to write my dad," I mumble out, my eyes locked on the V of his hips. "Did you have a good workout?" I look up when I hear him laugh. "What's funny?"

"Baby, the look on your face makes me think you didn't get enough this morning."

"Sorry." I smile. I'm not really sorry; my hormones are insane. I want him all the time, but the part that sucks is that we are forced to only use a couple of different positions with how large I have gotten.

"Don't be sorry. Come shower with me." He bends over me, his body caging me in with an arm on each side of the chair.

"I really need to write him. I keep putting it off."

"You can write when you're ready."

"I have been ready. I just don't know what to say. I don't even know how to address the letter. I mean, do I say, 'Dear Dad,' or something else?" I sigh, leaning my head back against the chair.

"What do you feel like addressing him as?"

"Dad… I don't know." I close my eyes and then open them when his lips touch my forehead. "He's my dad, even if he didn't act like one, but after everything that's happened…I just don't know."

"You address him and talk to him about anything," he says softly, his words spoken against my skin. "He'll be happy to hear from you, no matter what you say." He kisses my forehead again and then my lips before running a finger down my cheek and leaving the room.

I watch the spot he just left for a long moment before putting my pen to the paper for the hundredth time.

Dear Dad,

How are you? This is awkward, and I don't really know what to say, but as Nico told me once, awkward is okay as long as you don't feel uncomfortable. I don't feel uncomfortable. I feel like this is some-thing I have needed to do for a long time. I have thought about your letter a lot since I read it. I have been trying to understand where you were coming from and what you must have been going through after Mom passed away. Now that I have Nico, I can't imagine him being taken away from me without warning. I pray I never have to go through something like that.

I wish I could say I forgive you for everything, and hopefully, with time, I'll find a way to do that. I want you to know your grandkids. Nico and I are expecting twins. We don't know the sexes yet because we want to be surprised when they get here. Everyone has been making bets since we found out we were pregnant. I think they are both girls, but Nico swears they are boys, but I can tell he really wants at least one girl. I know he is going to be a great dad. His family is amazing. His parents are very supportive and loving, and they have accepted me as I am. He has three brothers, and each of them is married and has kids of their own. I hope you don't think I'm saying these things to upset you. That's not what this is. Honest-ly, before Nico, I had Maggie, Devon, and a few other friends, but now my life is full and I'm happy.

Nico also just bought us a beautiful home in the country—a house Mom would have loved. I sometimes sit out on the front porch at sunset and read. I hope when the babies get here I can sit outside and read to them like Mom used to read to me. I wish I had some of the photos of us so I could show them my side of the family when they get older.

Well, I don't know how to end this letter, but I hope you are okay and that when you read this, it brings you some kind of happi-ness.

XOXO,
Sophie Mayson

I set the letter down on my lap and close my eyes. When they open, I look around the nursery at the light-grey walls Nico and his brothers painted last week. Then I look at the mural of a white tree with silver leaves his mom just painted. My gaze drifts over the two cribs that were added to the room two days ago, with a changing table between them. The room is beautiful and will be perfect for either sex once the babies get here. The room represents so much—not only the start of our family, but also Nico's family, the love they have for each other, and what it means to have a real family. I smile and stand up, going in search of my husband and praying that I find him before he gets dressed.

Chapter 14

Nico

"CAP' WANTS YOU to start," Leo says, and I sigh into the phone and look out from the patio into the backyard, where Goose and Daisy are playing. Well, Daisy is playing; Goose is just walking around while Daisy jumps in and out between his feet.

"I can't, man. I hate leaving Sophie right now. She just reached the eighth-month mark, and the doctor said she could go into labor any time. Her doctor's appointments have moved to every week. They're concerned because she's already begun to dilate."

"We could really use you right now."

"I told you before—Sophie's my priority," I remind him. When this whole thing started, I told everyone that I'm not going to start working until after the babies are born and I know Sophie will be okay on her own with them.

"I know. I just thought you would relax some after you moved," he confesses.

"I can't relax. I still have no clue who was after her or if they still are. Now, with her due date getting closer, I've gotten even more nervous. I swear I feel like I'm constantly on edge. I know something's going to happen. I just don't know when or how to prepare for it."

"Has anything happened?"

"No, nothing." I rub my hand over my face.

"You're probably just nervous about becoming a dad. When Jenna had Lynn, I was a nervous wreck."

I'm not nervous about becoming a dad; that's the one thing I never really worry about. I know that, with Sophie as my kids' mother, the rest will fall into place. Plus, I have a shitload experience with kids now. I'm not nervous about having my own; I'm ready for that, even knowing how much work it will be.

"How are Jenna and Lynn?" I forgot all about his fiancée and daughter because he never talks about them.

"Jenna is a bitch and Lynn is beautiful."

"What? I thought you guys were getting married."

"Yeah, I thought we were getting married too until I found out she was sleeping with her high school sweetheart behind my back," he growls into the phone.

"Shut the fuck up. She did that?" I knew Jenna had a tendency to act like my old neighbor Deb, but I never imagined her cheating.

"She did. And had been doing it for about six months when I found out."

"Why didn't you ever say anything?"

"You mean why didn't I tell everyone my ex-fiancée was having an affair when she was supposed to be at work? I felt like an idiot, and when I caught on to what was happening, she blamed me and my job, saying I wasn't around when she needed me."

"Shit. I'm sorry," I tell him, rubbing the back of my neck.

"I'm not. I'm glad I found that shit out before I gave her my last name."

"True, man. How are things with Lynn? She's what, three now?"

"Perfect. If it wasn't for her, I would be pissed I wasted so much time on her mother. That's why I'm tellin' you Sophie's safe. You're just nervous about having not only one, but two kids."

"It's not that, man. You're a cop. You know that feeling you get in your gut when something is off. That's what I feel. It's not nerves." I shake my head.

"You want me to do anything?"

"I don't think there is anything anyone can do right now. That's the fucked-up part. I have done all I can to make sure she is safe and that, even if I'm not around, she will be okay."

"Well, you know if you need me I'm here."

"Thanks. As soon as I know when I can start, I'll let you know."

"Looking forward to it. Everyone's excited to have Nico Mayson on board. Cap' wanted me to see about Kenton joining the team too, but I told him that shit was not gonna happen." He chuckles.

"Yeah, not happening, especially not right now."

"Why? What's going on right now?"

"Nothing. Kenton just doesn't like red tape."

"Your cousin's crazy."

He's not wrong; Kenton does his own thing and doesn't like anyone telling him when or how it should be done.

"All right, man. We'll talk soon."

"Yeah, man. Talk to you soon." I hang up, watching Daisy and Goose for a few more minutes before heading inside to check on Sophie. I still have that feeling in my gut, and I have no idea what I'm going to do to get rid of it, but I want it gone before my kids are born.

"GOOSE, WHAT THE fuck?" I yell, chasing him up the stairs to where Sophie is supposed to be taking a nap. The moment I get to the second floor and look down the hall towards our bedroom, I see the giant dog scraping the door, trying to get inside. "What the hell?"

I run to the door, swinging it open. Sophie's on the floor, her body wrapped around her belly. Her face is red and sweaty, and tears are running down her face onto the hardwood floors.

"Baby." I get down on my knees in front of her, running a hand over her head.

"Something's wrong!" she cries out, wrapping herself tighter around her belly.

"Are you having contractions?"

"Yes, but I think there's something wrong," she cries harder, her body trembling. My first instinct is to pick her up and get her to the car, but something is off, and I don't want to make this worse for her.

"I don't think I should move you," I tell her, grabbing the phone off the nightstand and dialing 911.

Once the dispatcher answers, I tell her what's going on. She tells me that I need to check Sophie over, so I lift the bottom of her nightgown up to her waist before helping her onto her back and pulling off her panties. I spread her legs and don't see the babies, so I take that as a good sign. I tell the woman on the phone that there is no blood or anything else I can see just as I hear sirens outside.

"Oh God!" Sophie screams, shoving her face into my lap, and then, without warning, I feel her teeth sink into the skin of my thigh. I grit my teeth, running a hand down her hair. Whatever pain I'm feeling right now is nothing compared to what she's feeling.

"I gotta get the door, babe," I tell her becoming more concerned.

Her face has paled, her breathing is more shallow, and her skin is now cool and damp. She doesn't say anything, but she whimpers when I stand to leave.

"I'll be right back. Goose, come." I point to the floor where Sophie is. He whines, laying his head on top of her arms still wrapped around her waist.

I run down the stairs and throw the door open, not even bothering to make sure they're following before I run back up the stairs. "My wife is eight months pregnant and was laying down for a nap. I found her on the floor of our room, and she said she's having contractions, but something's wrong."

"We'll take care of her," one of the EMTs says.

As soon as we enter the master bedroom, Goose stands up in front of Sophie and growls. I knew he was a good dog before that, but guarding my girl just earned him free rein—especially since he's the reason I knew something was wrong to begin with.

"Goose." I point to the floor next to the bed, and he immediately goes there to stand guard. The EMTs hurry over to Sophie. I kneel above her head, putting my lips on her forehead, telling her softly that everything will be okay.

"We need to get her to the hospital," one of them barks at his coworker.

Everything is such a blur around me that I don't even have time to think before they're carrying her downstairs on a gurney. I see my dad's cruiser pull up as I'm climbing into the back of the ambulance. He nods, letting me know that he will follow as the doors close behind me.

"What's going on?" I ask when there is a lull in activity.

The one carefully placing an IV in Sophie's arm looks at me, his face telling me more than I want to know right now. "We're not sure, but we think one of the babies' cords is tangled, and she's going to have to have an emergency C-section as soon as we get to the hospital."

I look down at Sophie. She's the most important person in my life. I can't imagine something happening to her, and that thought alone scares me more than anything else. I nod at the EMT and hold her hand a little tighter, my other hand going to her belly and rubbing it once before closing my eyes. As soon as we arrive at the hospital and get her out of the ambulance, they run us down the hall towards an operating room that I hear a nurse say is already prepped and waiting.

"I'm here, baby. Everything's going to be okay," I tell her, seeing her nod as tears begin to form in her eyes.

"It's going to be okay," I repeat as the bottom of the gurney she's on slams through the door ahead of us.

"Sir, I'm sorry, but you're not allowed past this point," a small woman wearing scrubs says, wrapping her hand around my arm.

"That's my wife and kids," I growl.

"I understand, sir. I'm sorry, but until I get the okay from the doctor, you're not allowed," she says calmly.

"Go get the fucking okay from him then. My wife is in there alone. I promised her—" I hear the break in my voice and try to swallow it down. Sophie's back there by herself and scared, and there is nothing I can do for her.

"As soon as they get her prepped for surgery, I will talk to the doctor. For now, why don't you come with me and get changed. That way, you're ready if you're allowed to be with her." I immediately follow the nurse into another room, where she hands me a stack of clothes. "Just put these on and I'll be back in a few minutes," she says quietly.

I jerk up my chin and start pulling on the baggie scrubs over my clothes and then slip the shoe covers over my boots before taking a seat. I don't know how long I'm in that room alone, but I know I pray more in that time than I have in my whole life.

"Sir, you can come with me." I look up to see the nurse standing in the doorway. I get to my feet and follow her out of the room, down a well-lit corridor. "Now, when we get in there, you need to stay near her head unless instructed differently."

I nod and follow her the rest of the way in silence. Once we reach the end of the hall, she grabs my arm and leads me into the room. Everyone is moving around quickly while people yell back and forth to each other around her. When my eyes land on Sophie, my stomach drops. She's lying on her back, her head the only thing I can see. Her hair is covered, and they are getting ready to put an oxygen mask over her face. I pull my arm free from the nurse and go to her.

"Hey, baby." I bend down, breathing her in.

"You're here," she croaks out.

"Nowhere else I would want to be."

"All right, Mr. and Mrs. Mayson. Are you guys ready to have some babies?"

I look across the blanket at the doctor, whose cheerfulness relieves a little bit of the claustrophobic tension that's been building inside me since I heard Goose barking.

"You ready, baby?" I run a finger down her cheek. She nods and closes her eyes. "We're ready when you are," I tell the doctor.

"Then let's get started," he says before disappearing behind the curtain.

The nurse comes back over, bringing a rolling chair for me to sit on. I thank her and put my face near Sophie's.

"All right, you're gonna feel some pressure, Sophie," I hear the doctor say above the beeping of the monitors.

"You okay, baby?"

"Yeah." She nods, squeezing her eyes closed.

"There we are! We've got baby number one," the doctor says happily.

I want to stand and look over the curtain when a loud cry fills the room, but instead, I sit there, not breathing, holding Sophie's hand.

"Okay, Mom and Dad, baby number one is a girl." I smile down into Sophie's face, quickly drying the tears starting to fall from her eyes.

"Just a quick hi so I can get her cleaned up," the nurse says, bringing our daughter over to us.

"She's perfect," I whisper to Sophie, looking at our little girl, seeing her cute little face and headful of dark hair.

"Let's go get you cleaned up," the nurse coos before taking her away.

"You're doing great, baby." I smile down at Sophie, so fucking proud of her.

"Okay, Mom and Dad, we've got baby number two, and she is a pretty girl as well! I'll let you see her after I have her checked over," the doctor says.

"Two girls." I laugh, looking down at Sophie, who looks worried. "You did great, baby."

"Rr-ee."

"What?" I ask before pulling the mask away from her face so I can hear what she's saying.

"I'm worried."

"Everything's okay, baby. You and the girls are okay." I kiss her before putting her mask back in place and smoothing her hair away from her face.

"Two girls... Can you believe that?" I ask her, shaking my head. I certainly can't.

I smile when I see a small one forming on Sophie's face, and I'm so happy to see that smile again. At that moment, a second cry fills the room, forcing me to let out a long breath. All three of my girls are alive and healthy; nothing would ever matter as much as that.

"See, baby? They're already showing off. Listen to those lungs."

"Okay, girl number one is four pounds and seven ounces and seventeen inches long. Girl number two is four pounds and three ounces and sixteen inches long," one of the nurses yells from across the room.

"They're so small," I whisper and watch across the room as a nurse puts one of the babies in an incubator.

"Why are they putting her in that?" I ask, my heart starting to pound.

"Her O2 level's a little low, but that machine will help bring it up."

"Are they both okay?"

"Twin number one is doing great, and twin number two needs oxygen but looks great otherwise," the doctor says, calming me.

"Baby"—I look down at Sophie—"we really need to give them names. I think they may get upset with us if we refer to them as twin numbers one and two for the rest of their lives," I tell her, trying to change the look of worry I see in her eyes.

I move the mask away from her face again, and she answers, "Willow and Harmony."

"Those are perfect." I kiss her forehead.

"Are you mad you didn't get a boy?" she asks with genuine concern.

"How could I be mad when I have two beautiful girls?"

"I can't wait to hold them," she says softly.

"Me either."

I LOOK DOWN at my daughter, Harmony, who's been sleeping quietly in my arms for the last hour. Her sister, Willow, is still in ICU being monitored. They said that it's just a precaution; they were worried about her oxygen levels. I'm willing to do whatever is necessary for her to get healthy so I can take all my girls home. Sophie is still out of it from the drugs they gave her for the C-section. She's been asleep since they brought her into this room.

I look over at Sophie and can't believe that it was just a few hours ago I was worried out of my mind, not knowing if she or the babies were going to be okay. After Sophie was brought into the room, I went out and saw my family to let them all know that she and the babies were doing great and I would call them the next day when they could come by for a visit. They were all worried, and as much as I wanted them to meet my girls, I didn't want anyone near them yet.

"How is she?" I look up from Harmony's sleeping face to her mom's beautiful eyes.

"Perfect."

"And Willow?" Her voice cracks, and I hate that she's upset.

"She's fine, baby. The doctor said she should be in here with us by tomorrow morning. They just want to monitor her for now."

"Can I hold her?"

"Of course you can. Let me lay her down so I can help you." I carry Harmony over to her bed before going to Sophie to help her sit up, adjusting the bed and pillows around her. Once she's comfortable, I bring her Harmony and watch as tears fill her eyes.

"She is perfect." Her eyes meet mine, and this time, they're smiling.

"She is, and so is her sister."

"I can't wait to have both of them with us," she whispers.

"Soon, baby."

"I can't believe how much I love them already." She traces a line down the center of the baby's tiny nose. I nod; I can't talk with the tears clogging my throat.

We stay close the rest of the night, and the next morning, when they bring Willow in, I lose it completely. Seeing my wife holding each of my girls to her breast while they feed is a moment I will never forget. I can't believe how perfect my family is. My girls are both gorgeous. Harmony has dark-brown hair like her mother, and Willow's hair is dark blond like mine. We won't know what color their eyes are for a while, but I pray they're brown with golden flecks like Sophie's.

"I want you to sleep for a while, baby. I'm gonna have a nurse help me take the girls out to meet everyone while you rest."

"They can come in here," she says quietly, looking down at the girls, who are both sleeping.

"No way, baby-mama. You need your rest, and I know if we stay in here, you won't sleep."

"I don't want to miss anything," she complains with a pout.

I smile then bend forward, kissing her. "I won't let you miss anything. They'll probably sleep the whole time anyways."

"Okay, but if they smile or do anything cute, you need to take a picture."

"Promise." I press the call button for the nurse so she can help me take the girls to see my family.

I carry Harmony while the nurse carries Willow into the waiting room. Everyone is excited to see both of our girls, but with the babies being so small and Sophie being out of my sight, I want to get them back to the room as fast as possible. I don't know how I'm going to stand going back to work. I don't even like to think about not seeing them for any length of time.

"Where's your wife?" the nurse asks when we walk into the room.

I look at the bed expecting to see Sophie there, and it takes a second to realize that she's not in bed. The blankets are half on the floor, and the bed they brought in for the girls is pushed to the side. My heart starts slamming into my ribcage when I see that the bathroom door is open, letting me know that Sophie isn't in there either. I walk to the bed, pressing the call button before pulling out my cell phone and calling Kenton.

"We're just getting in my car. You need me to bring you something?" he asks as soon as he picks up.

"Sophie's not in the room. I need you back in here. Now," I tell him, trying to stay calm. Something isn't right.

"What do you mean she's not in the room?"

"Exactly what I just said. Get back in here now." I hang up.

"Did you need something?" a second nurse wearing bright pink scrubs asks, stepping into the room.

"Do you know where my wife is?" I ask, not wanting to hear the word 'no' come out of her mouth.

"She's not here?" she asks, looking at the nurse holding Willow then around the room before walking into the bathroom and turning on the light.

"Get security for me," I growl impatiently.

"Yes, of course," she mumbles, looking worried. She leaves the room, and I look down at Harmony then over at Willow.

"Anything?" Kenton asks, coming into the room.

"I'm waiting for security to get here before I go look for her myself. Do me a favor and take Willow." I motion for him to take my daughter from the nurse, and he does immediately. "Go check and see what's going on with security," I tell the nurse, and she nods, leaving the room quickly.

"We'll find her," Kenton says with conviction, looking down at Willow.

"I know." There isn't any other option.

I know that, wherever Sophie is, she's scared, and it's fucking with my head. I've made sure since we got together that she always felt safe. Knowing that she just had emergency surgery to have our daughters and is still recovering is only making my anxiety heighten.

It takes about five minutes for security to show up, and once there, they tell me that the nurse explained what's going on. They've put the hospital on lockdown and are searching for Sophie.

I take a second to call my mom to let her know that I need her here and to bring Dad. As soon as they arrive, I give her Harmony and Willow and a strict instruction to not leave the room for any reason. I leave her and Dad in the room, along with a guard at the door, and follow the head of security down the hall to the security office. Once there, we go into a small room holding the CCTVs. An older gentleman with short white hair is sitting in front of the screens, playing back a video from the camera in front of the room Sophie was in.

"You find anything yet, Charlie?"

"Not yet. Still looking," the guy mumbles.

I watch the screen as well, trying to catch a glimpse of anything out of the ordinary. Five minutes into the video, I'm ready to start breaking shit. I need to be out looking, but I know this is the first step in the process. I watch the video of me leaving the room with the nurse and heading to the waiting area, taking my girls to meet our family. About two minutes after we leave the room, a guy wearing a long doctor's coat and pushing a wheelchair enters Sophie's room. He's facing away from the camera, so I can't see what he looks like, but I feel bile in the back of my throat as I watch him enter the room. I don't know what happens when he is in there alone with her, but I do know I will find and kill him. About four minutes after he enters her room, I watch as he leaves, pushing a passed-out Sophie in the wheelchair, and I finally see who the fuck it is.

Rage fills me when I see that the man pushing the chair is the same man who's had a hard-on for Sophie since she started working at the school. David goes out of camera-view before reappearing in the next shot. He pushes Sophie casually down three halls before wheeling her out of the front door of the hospital. My body is literally shaking with adrenalin. I cannot imagine what he wants with her or how he even found out she was here.

"I know who that is. I'm gonna call Justin and tell him what I know about this guy to see if he can lead us to where he lives or where he might have her."

"Who is it?" Kenton asks.

"He worked with her."

"Why would he take her?"

"He wants her. He's had a thing for her since she started working at the school," I growl.

"Call Justin," Kenton says as I pull my phone out of my pocket, putting it to my ear.

"Hidee-ho, Ranger Joe," Justin answers in his usual chipper voice.

"Cut the shit," I snap, running a hand through my hair. "I need everything you can get on a guy named David who works at the same school Sophie did."

"You got a last name?" Justin asks, his voice now all business. I guess he must hear the seriousness in my tone.

"I think it's Rasmussen, but I'm not sure," I mumble, hating that I didn't dig into the fucker when I should have.

"Give me five and I'll call you back with everything I find."

"Thanks," I say, hanging up. "Justin's on it. He said five, so let's be ready to roll when he gets back to me." Kenton nods, and we head outside just as the cops start to show up. "Look, I'm gonna call Leo and fill him in on what's going on. I don't what the local PD in on this right now."

"Agreed. Too much red tape," Kenton mumbles, typing something into his cell.

I dial Leo's number once I reach to the truck, and he answers on the second ring.

"Nico?" He sounds tired.

"Yeah, man. Look, I don't have a lot of time because I've got a call coming in, but I'm going to need backup from your boys."

"What's going on?" I can tell my words have woken him up and piqued his interest.

"Sophie went missing from the hospital"—I pull my phone away from my ear, looking at the time—"twenty minutes ago. I got footage of the guy that took her. I need you to be ready to roll when I text you the info my man sends me."

"Shit," he growls, and I can tell he's up and moving. "Hit me back when you got something. Do you know who we're looking for?"

"Yeah, man. A guy Sophie worked with at the school. His name is David, and I think his last name is Rasmussen. He must have been watching her for a while."

"Fuck. All right. I'll get the guys rounded up. As soon as you know where you want us, text me."

"Thanks." I hang up with him just as Justin calls.

"Go," I say, opening the door to my car.

"His address is 382 Donner Street in Springhill. It says he has another house over on Commerce in the same area. His background is pulling up all kinds of fucked-up shit, man. He was married twice, and both times, his wives went missing. The first one was when he was nineteen and his wife was eighteen, and they had dated throughout high school. The second wife was when he was twenty-eight and she was twenty-three. She went missing a year after they got married. He was suspect number one in each case, but the police couldn't find any evidence."

"Jesus."

"That's not all," he says, and my gut goes fucking tight. I can't imagine anything worse than what he just told me.

"What?"

"Seems he moves around a lot."

"And?" I prompt.

"Each place he has lived, there have been women who come up missing, and not long after they go missing does he move from the area."

"Fuck," I roar. That sick fuck has my woman. She's still recovering from the C-section she just had, and he fucking has her when she's in no state to fight back.

"Go get her, man," Justin, says before hanging up.

I look at Kenton, giving him a silent signal to get into the car.

"Talk to me," he says as soon as I hit the gas.

I don't know what to say; I don't want to say out loud the fucked-up shit I just heard.

"We're going to get her back," he says, filling the silence. I pray he's right; I can't imagine having a life where there's no Sophie in it.

"The guy who took her has a history of women disappearing," I choke out, feeling bile crawl up the back of my throat.

"Fuck," Kenton clips.

"I need you to call Leo and have him go to the second address Justin gave me. Tell him about his history and let him know I want that fucker dead."

"If he doesn't get taken out by one of us tonight, the second he's in jail, he's dead," Kenton mutters.

I know he has that kind of power, has people everywhere who owe him. I want that. Either way, the motherfucker's gonna die for even looking at Sophie.

I STOOP, MAKING my way in front of one window then another until I'm at the back of the house. I can hear arguing from inside, and I signal for Kenton to follow. I take three steps, my back hitting the wall near the back door before I turn the handle. It clicks open, and I lift my Glock, pressing the door open with it. I search both ways while stepping into the kitchen. I hear Kenton behind me as we scope out the first two rooms we come to.

"It's all clear down here," he whispers.

I nod then point up the stairs. We make our way to the top, and there are two doors; one has a light penetrating from the bottom of it. I gesture to it with a tilt of my gun, and Kenton signals over his shoulder to the door behind him. He cautiously opens it to find it empty, and then I lean forward, trying to hear anything from inside the lit room. I hear two male voices and a whimper.

I have been moving on autopilot since she was taken, just doing what was necessary to get her home. I know the minute I open the door that I'm going to kill whoever is in that room with her.

Kenton nods to the room he just checked, motioning with his left hand to show me that he's about to set off a distraction. It takes two seconds for the flash bang to go off. The door to the room I'm covering flies open, and one guy comes out. I shoot him in the head without a second thought. The second guy we heard inside points a gun at Sophie.

"Drop the fucking gun," I tell him, my gun aimed at his head, ready for the smallest opening.

"You killed my brother," he says, looking down at the man at my feet.

I hear Sophie whimper and look at her for the first time. Her eyes are full of tears, she has a gag in her mouth, her face is pale, and she is tied to a chair. All I can think about is getting her out of here to somewhere safe.

"I should fucking kill her. You killed my brother!" he yells, and I watch his finger tighten on the trigger.

"Drop the fucking gun, David," Kenton says this time from behind me.

"Fuck you! I'm not David. I'm Dustin." He looks at Sophie. "I fucking told him you weren't worth it. You didn't even know, did you? He's my twin. We like to pretend to be the same person. It's a fun game, and no one ever figured it out until it was too late."

"Eyes on me, fucker," I growl, his eyes coming back to me. "You're dead. There is nothing you could say or do to get out of this."

"It wasn't supposed to be like this. This is all your fault." He points the gun at me. "You and your brother Cash's fault. I thought I had chance at something real with Lilly, and then he came along and took her from me—just like you took Sophie from David."

"Fuck me," I breathe.

"You're crazy," Kenton says calmly.

Before I have a chance to blink, there's a loud explosion in the hall, and Dustin moves his gun towards us. I take my opening and shoot once, hitting him between the eyes. Blood goes everywhere, including on Sophie, who starts to scream against the gag in her mouth.

I go to her side, carefully pulling the gag out before untying her hands and feet, wrapping her in my arms. She starts sobbing, her fingers digging into me, her face going into my neck. I pull her away, wanting to check her over.

"I got you, baby. You're safe," I tell her, cupping her face. I check her over and see nothing until I reach her stomach, where the nightgown she has on is covered in blood across her lower abdomen. If those fucks weren't dead, I would kill them all over again. "I'm gonna get you to the hospital, baby." I put my arm under her knees and pick her up.

"Leo's here," Kenton says, coming back into the room. Two seconds later, Leo and two other men I met recently walk in behind him.

"Ambulance is en route," Leo says, looking at Sophie, who is clinging to me.

"We'll get this cleaned up. Take care of her," Kenton says.

I nod, carrying Sophie out of the house and down the stairs, and as soon as I reach the front door, the ambulance pulls up.

"I got you, baby," I tell her, not sure if I'm reminding her or myself at this point.

"Our girls?" she asks against the skin of my neck.

"They're at the hospital with Ma and Dad." I kiss her temple. The ambulance door opens and I don't even stop; I just carry her right inside, laying her down on the gurney. "She just had a C-section. I think her stitches are torn," I tell the EMT, watching as they start to pull up her nightgown. "You wanna shut the fucking door and get a blanket to cover her first?"

"I'm okay," Sophie says, palming my cheek.

I look down at her and shake my head. "You're not okay."

"I am. You found me." Tears start to fall from her eyes again.

"I will always find you," I tell her, kissing her forehead.

The door to the ambulance closes, and a blanket is laid over Sophie's lap. I sit back and watch as they lift her nightgown, showing her waist and the incision from the C-section. The wound is open, and I can tell she's in pain. I grit my teeth, not wanting to flip out and make this harder for her.

The guys clean up her wound as best as they can, and as soon as we reach the hospital, she is rushed back into surgery while I'm forced to wait for her outside. I call my dad and mom to make sure they're okay with the girls up in the nursery of the hospital. Ma tells me that they are fine and that Kenton called as soon as we were in the ambulance to let them know that we were on our way back to the hospital.

I feel like crying in relief that the situation is finally over, but at the same time, I know going through something like this is going to fuck with Sophie's head when she just started getting over what had happened to her when she was younger. Hell, I don't know how I'm going to deal with it. I hate that I wasn't able to protect her when she needed me. I vow right now that nothing else will ever touch her again. I don't care how small or big—she will never be worried or scared as long as I walk this earth.

Chapter 15
Sophie

"NICO, WHY IS your mom calling to tell me you're not letting anyone see the girls?" I ask, walking into the nursery where Nico is sitting, holding Willow.

"The girls are too small to have everyone over right now," he grumbles then smiles over at Harmony, who is now awake and cooing at her daddy through the slats of the crib.

"Honey, they're old enough to have people over to visit." I roll my eyes.

"They're too small. Look, she fits in one hand," he says, proving his point by putting Willow in one of his hands.

"Your hands are freakishly large," I argue.

"You like my freaky hands." He smirks before looking down at Willow as he tells her, "Your momma is a dirty girl." He laughs when she smiles at him.

"Nico, don't tell our daughters that," I growl. "This is getting ridiculous." He is so overprotective of the girls and me. I'm lucky if I'm able to go to the bathroom alone.

"Baby, I'm not ready."

"They're family." I run my hand down the back of his hair, trying to get him to relax.

"They've seen them," he grumbles sullenly, making me smile.

"Call your family and tell them to come for dinner."

"My mom talks too much." He looks up at me with puppy-dog eyes, making it hard to fight to do the right thing.

"Your mom wants to get to know her granddaughters. There is

nothing wrong with that," I tell him, walking over to pick up Harmony, who sees me and begins to fuss.

"I hate when they come over. They are all like, 'Oh, just let me hold her for a couple of minutes,' and then they don't give them back when I tell them to," he complains, looking completely serious.

I shake my head. I want to laugh at how ridiculous he's being about this, but I can't. He loves his girls; he's hands-on with everything. I don't ever need to ask for help. He's always there the second one of the girls starts to fuss.

"Honey, you need to get over what happened. You can't lock us away forever," I tell him quietly. I hate that what happened to me is so hard on him. I haven't even had one nightmare about it. He has woken up twice drenched in sweat. The minute he knows where he is and I'm there, he's on me. I know it's his way of reassuring himself that I'm okay, but I hate that he still thinks about it when I never really do.

"I can't get over it." He shakes his head. "I will never get over thinking you were lost to me and our girls."

"I wasn't, so please try for me and the girls to be reasonable about this."

"I want you guys to myself. I only trust us with my most prized possessions."

"As much as I love you for that, I know that, even if we were in a room full of the most dangerous criminals in the world, you could and would protect us. But, honey, the people who want to come over are not criminals. They're your family. They love you, the girls, and me. They would never hurt us, and even if they tried, you wouldn't let them."

"Fine. Dinner. The minute dinner's over, I want them gone."

I avoid rolling my eyes in front of him and sit down in the rocker next to him, pulling my tank top down and freeing my breast for Harmony.

"Four days," he says under his breath, making me smile.

I can't wait until we can have sex again either. The next four days can't come fast enough.

Nico

"MA, I DON'T care," I tell my mom, who has been hogging Willow and Harmony since she walked into the house.

"Nico, go away. I'm their grandmother. I want to spend time with them." She blows me off then smiles down at my girls, who are lying on the floor smiling up at their grandma.

I shake my head and look at the clock on the wall, counting down until everyone is out of my house. It's not that I don't love my family or want them around; I just want my own little family to myself. I hate sharing them with everyone.

"Son, come outside," my dad says.

I look at him, then down at my girls, then back through the house to the kitchen where Sophie's sitting, talking to November, Liz, and Lilly. I nod, looking back at my dad before following him outside.

"What's up?" I ask, standing near the door so I can look inside through the glass window at the girls and Sophie.

"Relax, man," Trevor says, handing me a beer. I don't even know how to relax anymore. My body is wired lately.

"This is an intervention," Asher says before taking a drink of his beer.

"Yeah, bro. You need to fucking chill," Cash says, and I wonder how the hell he could seem so calm when the same sick fucks who took my wife had wanted his.

"You guys don't have a clue," I tell them.

"I understand what you're going through. The thing is, this is not healthy. You need to go back to work soon. You need to understand that the girls and Sophie will be okay at home without you."

I know they're right, but a permanent, cold dread settled inside me once Sophie was taken. Knowing now what the men who had taken her wanted to do to her and that I would have been left with two baby girls to take care of—looking at my girls every day and knowing I had failed them—I never want to feel that kind of fear ever again.

"We'll all stop by and check on them while you're at work so you can have some peace of mind," Trevor offers.

"I don't know." I rub the back of my neck.

I have enough money to live comfortably for at least a couple of years, but I know Sophie's ready to kick my ass if I don't back off a little. It's unbelievable to me how she acts like nothing happened, like she has no fears, while I spend every day worrying from the time I wake up until I go to sleep.

"We're all worried. You need to talk to someone about what's going on," my dad says.

I look at my brothers and dad, seeing concern etched in their faces. I know Sophie's worried, and now, seeing that everyone feels the same way, I know I need to get help.

"Okay. I'll talk to someone," I agree, taking a swig of my beer.

"Thank God," Trevor groans and sits down, "I thought I may need to beat the shit out of you to get you to listen."

"When was the last time you were able to take me?"

"I could take you," he says, puffing out his chest.

"I'm gonna let your mouth slide this time, but only because I don't want to embarrass you in front of Liz. I doubt she would want to sleep with you anymore if you cried like you did the last time I kicked your ass." I smirk.

"Fuck you! You kicked me in the nuts. That shit doesn't count."

"Whatever," I mutter, fighting back laughter.

"This is what I missed," Cash says, sitting down.

I take a seat as well, and when I look inside the house through the glass doors, Sophie's eyes meet mine. She gives me a smile I haven't seen in weeks. That's the moment I realize how worried she is about me. I take a breath and mouth the words, "I love you," before going back to talking to my brothers.

"Why do act like nothing happened?" I ask Sophie, who is sprawled out on top of me later that night.

"What do you mean?"

"You act like nothing happened, while I relive that shit over and over again."

"I know you'll protect me. I think about it sometimes, but really, I think about the girls and you and how lucky I am to be with my family. I know I could've died that night. I know what David wanted to do to me," she whispers, clinging to me. "He told me about the other women he and his brother hurt. His brother, Dustin, told me what they had planned to do to Lilly, but when she got fired from the school because of Cash's ex, it threw a wrench in their plan. I was afraid, but I knew you would find me, and I guess I deal with it because I know what I could have missed out on," she says, cuddling closer.

"Shit," I whisper, finally getting it. I don't know how I missed it before. I'm doing to her what she did to herself for years. I hate that I'm trying to shove her back in her bubble when she has a million reasons to be out enjoying life.

"Yep," she whispers back. "Now I just need you to start living life with me again."

"I love you, sweet Sophie."

"Love you too," she mumbles, and I kiss her head.

I think about my girls and my need to protect them and their mother, and then I think about being their father and what that means. I can't be the reason they're never able to experience life to the fullest. I would hate myself if my own fears stunt their growth or turn them into fearful adults.

What I didn't know was that, when my girls became teens, I would wish I had made them fearful of everyone, especially the male population.

Epilogue

"T HEY'RE GROUNDED UNTIL they're forty," I tell Sophie as I watch both my girl across the football field. "Why did you encourage them to be cheerleaders?" I grumble as I watch one of the football players come off the field, giving Harmony a smile. "Yo! Hands off!" I stand and shout when another player picks up Willow and swings her around in a circle. His head turns my way, and his face pales when he sees me. "Yeah, you. Hands off," I repeat. He drops Willow immediately, making her stumble and glare at him.

"Honey, calm down," Sophie says, pulling on my back pocket.

"Calm down?" I glare at her. "This is your fault. Seriously, babe. Those skirts with your genes?" I shake my head. "Fuck no, I can't calm down."

"So your daughters can't talk to boys, but your son can do that?" She nods to where my seventeen-year-old son, Bax, has his mouth on some girl.

"I never claimed to be fair, babe, but the shit with your daughters is getting ridiculous."

"They're going to college at the end of summer, and as much as you want to, you can't keep them locked up forever." She shakes her head at me.

"They're not going away for college," I tell her.

"Whatever. Can you please sit down so we can watch the rest of the game in peace without you freaking out and scaring everyone?"

"You need to tell the girls that flirting shit isn't going to fly," I growl.

"Honey." Sophie leans into me, her mouth getting close to my ear. Her breath hitting my skin makes me instantly hard for her. Even now, almost nineteen years later, I can't get enough of my wife. "If you calm down, I will do whatever you want when we get home."

"You trying to bribe me with sex?" I ask, turning my face to look at her.

"It's not a bribe."

"What do you call it?"

"A promise." She winks.

"I can get you to do whatever I want without taking you up on that offer," I tell her with a smirk.

"True." She smiles.

"You are so beautiful, baby." I run my fingers down her cheek. "All that beauty… You gave all that shit to our girls, and now I'm paying for it."

"We have good girls." She pats my thigh.

She's right; I know she's right. Both my girls are straight-A students. Actually, all my kids are good kids. Willow and Harmony are getting ready to graduate and Bax is a year behind them. Then there's Talon, who's in junior high, and our adopted twins—our son, Sage, and daughter, Nalia—just turned six. Sophie got her dream—her large house in the country that we filled with kids. If she hadn't gotten sick after having Talon, forcing her to get her tubes tied, she would probably still be popping my babies out.

"Daddy, can I be a cheerleader when I get big?" Nalia asks, making me grit my teeth.

"You can be whatever you want when you get big, honey," Sophie tells my beautiful little girl, making me cringe.

"Do Daddy a favor, baby, and don't be a cheerleader." I pull her from the seat below me into my arms.

There is nothing greater than being a father, but it's also difficult watching your kids grow up. Having girls only makes it that much harder. Boys can look out for themselves, but girls need someone there to watch out for them.

Sophie

"GRANDPA!" NALIA YELLS, running across the backyard.

I lift my head from Nico's shoulder to watch my dad pick up Nalia and swing her around. My dad got out of prison and moved to Tennessee a few years ago. I love having him around. He has become good friends with Nico's dad, and he even started working for Nico's brothers doing construction. Before he got out of prison, we wrote letters back and forth. I think it was easier to talk to him through letters. I knew that I could say whatever it was I needed to say, and he could reply with whatever it was he needed to get off his chest.

It helped that I was never alone when I got a letter; Nico and I would sit outside or in bed and read them together. I knew he would be there to hold me when it was all done, and that was all I would ever need. After a while, I started sending my dad pictures of the kids and opened up to him about my family and everyday life. He told me about himself and what he was doing each day. It was difficult to talk about the past, but we did. And we each shared some of our favorite memories of my mom. I loved that we could share that.

He even sent me a key for a storage unit in Seattle that held things from my childhood home. I hated going through the stuff that had been stored there. Having to relive some painful things from my past was hard, but in the end, I was able to have pictures of my parents along with mementos and things I had left behind when I moved out.

"How's Grandpa's angel?" my dad asks Nalia, who's holding his face in her small little hands.

"So happy! I have a new boyfriend at school." She laughs, smiling at her grandpa, who, up until that moment, was smiling at her.

"What the fuck?" Nico whispers, looking over at me. I bite my bottom lip to keep from laughing.

"You're not allowed to have boyfriends, beautiful girl," my dad tells her, kissing her forehead.

"But he brought me chocolate," she tells him like that's the most important quality in a boyfriend.

"Me, Grandpa James, your daddy, or any of your uncles will give you whatever chocolate you want, angel."

"Really?" she asks, smiling.

"Really." He grins back before setting her on the ground.

As soon as she's free, she runs inside yelling to anyone who will listen that she's going to get chocolate. By that point, Nico is muttering under his breath about how this is all my fault and that I need to teach our daughter that boys are gross.

"I'm gonna go inside and see what the kids are up to," I tell him, getting off the overstuffed bed/chair that sits on our back patio.

"Don't think that we're not gonna talk about that shit tonight, baby." He kisses my temple before smacking me on my ass once I start to walk away. I look over my shoulder at him and laugh at the look on his face.

"Love you, Dad," I say, kissing my dad's cheek before walking into the house. I love my family.

Nico

"PLEASE STOP TEASING!" Sophie cries, trying to lift her hips higher into my mouth. I'm not having it; I press her hips down into the bed, keeping her just like I want her.

"Take it, Sophie," I growl against her.

"I can't! I want to come… Let me come!" she cries, trying to push me away.

I grab both of her hands, holding them against her hips as I bury my face in her pussy. Once she's dripping wet, I flip her onto her stomach, pulling her hips up high before slamming into her. I watch her hair fly back, her head drop forward, and her ass lift higher, meeting me thrust for thrust.

"That's it, baby. Fuck yourself." I still my movements so I can watch her taking my cock, fucking herself hard.

"Nico?" she whimpers.

"What, baby?" I ask, not even looking at her, my eyes glued to our connection.

"Fuck me," she moans.

I look up to see that her eyes are locked on me over her shoulder. I put my hand under her arms, lifting her up until she's sitting on my cock, and I do what she wants—I fuck her hard and fast. I feel my balls draw up as she begins to clamp down around me. My hand goes to her hair, pulling her head to the side so I can take her mouth in a deep kiss.

"Hell yes." I growl my orgasm down her throat as she whimpers hers into my mouth. "I can never get enough of you, sweet Sophie." I pull out of her, lying down on my back before pulling her on top of me.

That's the truth. It's going to be nineteen years since we first got together, and most days, it feels like the first. I'm still as anxious now as I was then to get home to her. She's not only my wife, but my best friend.

"I love you." She cuddles deeper into me.

I run my hand down her back, loving the smoothness of her skin. "Love you too, baby, but you need to get a handle on your daughters." I feel her cheek move against my chest and know she's smiling. "I'm serious," I tell her.

"I know you are, honey." She doesn't say anything else, and I know I'm fucked and there's not a damn thing I can do about it.

"WHY DO I have to be here when I have heard this story a million times?" Jax asks, looking annoyed. I watch my oldest nephew grab a beer before sitting down on the couch.

"I agree with Jax. I've heard all this before—the Mayson curse…blah blah blah," Cobi says, leaning against the wall.

"Can you hurry? I have a date," Bax says, looking smug before getting a pound from Jax.

I look at Asher and shake my head. My sons and nephews are a fucking handful. I thought my brothers and I were bad growing up, but hell no! We're looking more and more like choir boys compared to them.

"The younger boys have never heard about it, so shut up and sit down," Asher says, and all the boys automatically sit down and shut up. Once Asher finishes telling them about the curse and the history of it, they all look at each other and laugh.

"You, Uncle Cash, Uncle Trevor, and Uncle Asher are all just crazy. I don't care what any of you say. The Mayson curse isn't real. It's just something Great-Grandpa and Grandpa Mayson made up to make you guys worry or something." Bax shrugs, walking over to sit down next to me.

"I never believed it either," I tell them, and Asher, Trevor, and Cash nod in agreement. "Then I saw Sophie, and boom! It was like my soul knew hers, and I needed her to breathe. One day, boys, you're going to know what I'm talking about," I tell my sons and nephews. Just like me, they don't believe, and just like my dad, and his dad before him, they have been warned.

What none of us know was that we should've been sharing this same story with our daughters, for unbeknownst to any of us, the Mayson curse doesn't affect only the men in the Mayson family.

Assumption

The Underground Kings series
Kenton
Aurora Rose Reynolds

Prologue

I SEE YOU judging me. I know what you're thinking. She has to be a slut; she works at a strip club and takes off her clothes for money. Yes! I work at a strip club, and you may think I'm a whore for showing off my body, but this is a talent that has been forced down my throat since I was a young child. Look pretty and smile. I put on a show for those who choose to watch. However long I'm on stage, I'm not even me. It's what I imagine an out-of-body experience would be like—a performance, nothing more, nothing less. The people watching make assumptions about who they think I am or cook up a story in their heads of whom they want me to be. I'm just another beautiful face.

Beautiful. I hate that fucking word. Who gives a crap if someone is attractive on the outside if they are dying inside? My whole life has been about what I look like. I swear, the only reason my mother kept me was to have a real-life, living, breathing doll she could dress up and control, which is the exact reason why, as soon as I became eighteen, I got as far away from her special brand of crazy as I could. That's also why I don't date. The first thing guys do is look at me and see a pretty face, a nice body, and an empty space where my brain's supposed to be. They have no interest in getting to know the person I am on the inside. They don't care that I volunteer my spare time, and they couldn't care less that I'm going to school to be an RN. They don't ask about my hopes, my dreams, or where I see my life in twenty years. They don't care about me at all.

They just want someone pretty to follow them around and tell them how handsome they are, how special they are, while agreeing with everything they say. Fuck that! I did that for too many years. That's why I live inside books. At least there I can choose where I want to be—from the highlands of Scotland to a king's bed in a faraway land. And even if it's pretend, sometimes that's a lot better than reality.

Chapter 1

I LOOK OUT the plane window, my finger going to the glass, feeling the cold on my fingertips as I look out at the land moving quickly below me. It's funny how, from up here, everything looks so small. I've never traveled in a plane before today. Just the idea of being trapped inside a tin can while flying at six hundred miles an hour never appealed to me. I take a breath and look at the TV monitor that's in the seat in front of me. The small, animated plane on the screen shows that we're over halfway to Tennessee.

"Are you traveling for business or pleasure?"

I turn my head and look at the guy sitting next to me. He's slightly overweight and balding, but he also has wrinkles around his eyes, giving him the appearance of someone who smiles often.

I debate with myself on whether or not to answer before replying, "Business."

His eyes drop to my mouth then to my chest as I fight the urge to punch him in the throat. I hate when men go from nice to creepy.

I shake my head, turning away from him. I don't know why I even try. I feel a hand on my bare leg, and my head swings around quickly.

"Touch me again and I will rip off your balls and feed them to you," I tell him in a soft tone, trying not to bring attention to us.

He quickly removes his hand before swallowing hard. "I…I'm sorry."

I shake my head before turning my body away from his. I feel tears sting my nose, but I fight them back. No way am I going to cry now—not when, just six hours ago, my whole world exploded and I didn't shed one single tear. I lay my forehead to the glass, closing my eyes. I still can't believe how fast my life changed…

225

Yesterday

I GOT UP that morning and went to the hospital like I always do. I work at one of the busiest ERs in Vegas. I've been working there since I finished school and was required to get my clinical hours for my RN. As soon as I walked into the building, I was loaded down with work. Weekends are always crazy in Sin City, but yesterday seemed worse than normal—two drug overdoses, three stomach pumps, and one gunshot victim. Later, I was leaving the hospital exhausted, only to head to my real job. Well, the one that pays me the money I need to live.

"Hey, Angel."

"Hey, Sid." I gave him a half smile as I walked into The Lion's Den, the gentlemen's club I work at.

Do I like to strip? No. Does it pay my bills? Yes. The second I get on stage, I'm no longer me; my brain shuts off and my body takes over, the same way it used to when I was growing up and my mom forced me into pageants. I'm accustomed to being on display and used for my appearance. I wish life was different, but it is what it is. Some people complain about being overweight or having acne; for me, I hate being beautiful. I know it sounds stupid; I mean, why would anyone complain about being attractive, right?

Here's why: men see me as an object, and women see me as competition. No one is ever willing to give me a chance. They all judge me by what's on the outside, never taking a second to find out even the smallest detail about who I am. I know I'm a walking cliché. I hate being beautiful, yet I work in a business where I put myself front and center to be viewed and judged.

The difference? For the first time in my life, when I get on stage, it's my choice; no one is forcing me to do it. I get up there to earn the money so I can change my life in a way that will make it so I never have to be objectified again.

"Tired?" Sid questioned, following me. I have worked for Sid for the last three years. He is a friend of sorts; he's also my boss.

"Yeah. I can't wait until my clinical hours are over and I can start working at the hospital full time instead of having two jobs."

"I don't like that I won't see your face all the time, but I know you need to move on," he conceded.

"Some other girl will come in and you will forget all about me."

"Never, Angel." His eyes moved over my face and he shook his head. "You're working VIP tonight." He followed me down the hall towards the dressing rooms.

"Sure," I agreed, already exhausted. I needed a shower and a bed but knew I was going to be there for at least eight hours, so I might as well suck it up.

"The guys coming in are important, so you need to make sure they're happy the whole time they're here."

"I have done this before," I reminded him, stopping outside the dressing room door to frown at him.

"Normally, I wouldn't say anything—you know that—but I gotta go get on a plane, so I won't be here to check on them."

"I'll make sure they're taken care of," I assured him.

"Thanks, Angel." He kissed my forehead like he often did before walking away. I watched him go for a second before pulling myself together.

"Oh! Look who's here," Tessa said as soon as I entered the dressing room.

I ignored her and tossed my bag into my locker before pulling my scrubs off. Tessa is a bitch; she is just like the girls I used to compete against in pageants. To her, life is a competition, and she is determined to come out the winner, even if she has to throw everyone else under the bus on her way to the top.

"Mick said I could work VIP tonight," she said to one of the other girls in the room.

I ignored her, knowing better than to tell her that it wasn't happening. I was sure Mick did tell her that...after she took him in the backroom and gave him something to convince him. "Pixie said the guys coming in are some big-time land developers, so you know the tips are going to be outrageous. Thank God, because I need to have my tits redone, and that shit is not cheap."

I rolled my eyes and headed for the shower room. I had met a couple of nice girls during my time here, but most were just like Tessa—a whole lot of hair, tits, ass, and not much else.

I stood in front of the mirror and put on a coat of red lipstick before standing back, looking myself over. The VIP dress code is different than the rest of the club. The required outfit consists of a sheer, black overlay bra, black silk panties, a black garter belt with sheer hose, and black heels. My long, naturally red hair was pulled back on one side by a large flower; the rest was loose and wavy, flowing down my back and one shoulder. My creamy white skin, red lips, and smoky eyes made me look almost like a sexy vamp.

"You ready, Angel?" Sid asked, pounding on the door.

"Showtime," I whispered before opening the door.

"You look beautiful; I'm going to take you in there and introduce you before heading out."

"Sure." I followed him down the hall to the club.

The Lion's Den is well known in the area for its exclusivity. The walls are painted a dark brown, and the booths are designed into the walls, making the space feel intimate. The stage is in the center of the room, a single spotlight shining down on it. Every booth has a girl assigned to it, and VIP has two girls. We aren't allowed to interact with the customers without being asked directly to do so.

The club is less of a strip club and more of a place for men to hang out and drink while having beautiful women tend to them. If they choose to, they can watch the girl in the center of the room put on a show. I have been on stage several times in the three years I've worked here. I've never told Sid that I didn't like it up there, but he normally put me in VIP or assigned me to a booth for the night.

"Why are you so worried about these guys?"

"They're thinking about opening up a Lion's Den in one of the new casinos they're building."

"That's huge! Congrats, honey." I squeezed his bicep and gave him a smile.

"One day, Angel, I'm gonna take you away from this place and show you happiness. I wanna see that smile every day."

My heart did a little thud. Sid is a very attractive man, but he's not for me. I don't want or need a man. They get you all discombobulated, filling your head with a bunch of lies then expect you to follow them around. I did that once. I thought a man was going to save me from the hell I was living in. I gave him my virginity and my heart, and he gave me a child I wasn't allowed to keep and a heart so broken that nothing or no one can ever put it back together again.

I looked through the two-way mirror at the men around the table in the VIP room.

"All right," Sid says from beside me, "the man in the center at the table is John Barbato. He is the owner of three of the largest clubs in the city. The guy there on his left is Steven Creo. He's some bigwig on Wall Street and has backed more than half the new clubs and casinos opening on The Strip. The guy to the right of John has a location they're interested in purchasing."

"Got it. Who's working with me?" I asked him.

"Tessa. Mick said she would be the best out of the girls we've got on the schedule tonight."

"I'm sure he did," I mumbled, looking back into the room. "What other bouncers are on tonight?" I hated when Mick and Craig worked together. They were both more concerned about hooking up with the girls than what was going on out on the floor.

"Link's here now."

"Good." Link was a good guy and a close friend. He also took his job seriously.

"All right, let me introduce you quickly before I head out."

"Sure." I followed him into the room; the men's smiling faces turned in our direction.

"Guys, I want you to meet Autumn. She's gonna be your girl for the night. You need anything, you ask her and she will make sure you're taken care of," Sid tells them, gesturing to me.

"Nice to meet you," one of the men said, smiling, while the others nodded.

"Nice to meet you." I smiled back.

"Autumn will be right back. Give me a minute, guys."

"Sure," the one that had spoken before said.

As Sid and I stepped away, I heard from behind me, "Do you think the curtains match the drapes?" and they all laughed. I hated that saying, and I swore, once I was free of this lifestyle, I would kick the next man who said it in the nuts.

"Okay, I gotta head out. I won't be back for two weeks," Sid said once we were standing in the hall.

"Have a safe trip."

His eyes searched my face. His mouth opened and closed like he was going to say something, but instead, he shook his head, kissed my cheek, and walked off down the hall, muttering something under his breath.

Tessa came around the corner a couple of seconds later with a smug smile on her face. I hate to admit it, but she is beautiful. Her skin has a natural glow that makes her look healthy and youthful. Her hair is black and thick, reaching the top of her ass. Her eyes curve out at the corners, showing off her Asian-American heritage. "You ready?" she asked, looking at me from head to toe.

I avoided rolling my eyes at her before stepping into the room behind her.

After we took the first orders, we stood back while the men talked. I learned a long time ago to zone myself out. We were there as eye candy and nothing else.

There was a knock on the door, and I knew the drinks had arrived. Tessa answered it, opening the door wide, and the man who brought the tray in was someone I had never seen before. He looked to be mid-thirties and had long, shaggy black hair and brown eyes. When he set the

230

tray down on the table in the corner, he turned and did something odd that had me watching him more closely. His hand went to his back as he looked over at the men who were still busy talking. When his eyes came to me, he smiled before walking out of the room. I looked at Tessa to see if she had noticed anything strange, but she was busy handing out the drinks and flirting with the men at the table.

We stood to the side again once the men had their drinks. Every once in a while, they would ask me a question about the club, and I told them what I knew. About thirty minutes after they'd had their first drinks, I called and had more ordered. This time, when the guy came in, he did the same thing—hand at his back, looking at the table. I had no idea who he was, but I planned to find out as soon as the men left. One of the men received a phone call and stepped out of the room, and when he returned, he had another man with him. They all sat down, and this time when they called me over, they wanted a bottle of Chives Regal Royal Salute Scotch. One glass of the stuff cost close to six hundred dollars, making it over ten thousand dollars for a bottle. I placed the order and waited for it to be delivered. When the knock sounded on the door, I opened it up, and the same man from earlier came in and set the tray down. I watched to see if he would do the same thing he had done the previous times.

Sure enough, his head turned towards the table and his hand lifted behind his back, but this time, he lifted his jacket, pulling out something black. It took a second for me to realize what it was, and by that time, it was too late. He let off four rounds in rapid succession then turned and fired a round, hitting Tessa. I screamed as he turned the gun on me, and before I could think, I ducked down and ran as fast as I could out of the room. I felt a bullet whiz past me as I turned the corner and another as I entered the main part of the club.

I spotted Mick. Right away, his eyes got wide, and I yelled at the top of my lungs, "HE HAS A GUN!"

Everyone started screaming and running in every direction. I ran into a solid wall, and when I looked up to see it was Link, he wrapped an arm around my waist, turned, and pushed me behind the bar. I stumbled in my heels, falling to my knees and hitting the ground hard. I crawled under the counter and curled myself into a ball, shaking out of fear for my life. I listened as people screamed, but I didn't hear any more gunshots. I don't know how long I stayed like that, but it felt like forever until I heard police sirens.

"Autumn," Link called. I peeked out from behind my hands as he crouched down in front of me.

"Did you get him?"

He shook his head, putting out his hand for me to take. I shook my head no—I was safe. I didn't want to move from that spot.

"Come on, Angel. He's gone." I shook my head again. "Nothing is going to happen to you. I promise you're safe." I swallowed against the lump in my throat, squeezing my eyes closed.

"Tessa?" I asked him. His eyes closed and his head dropped forward. "No," I whispered, shaking my head. "No."

"Sorry, Angel," he said quietly.

"Why?"

"Not sure, but the cops are here. I need you to come out of there so you can talk to them," he told me gently, holding out his hand again.

I nodded, reluctantly taking it. Even though I didn't like Tessa, she didn't deserve what had happened to her. None of the people in the room deserved what had happened to them.

"I should have tried to help her."

"Nothing you could have done," Link said, and my eyes went from the floor to his. He shook his head, wrapped his beefy arm around my shoulders, and walked me over to a barstool. I sat there until the cops came up a few minutes later and told me that they needed to talk to me at the station.

"Can she get some clothes on?" Link—who had given me the shirt off his back and hadn't left my side—asked one of the detectives.

"Sure," the guy mumbled.

I slid off the barstool and dazedly walked to the dressing room.

When I walked in, all the girls were there, huddled together and crying. I didn't know what to say to them; most of them had been friends with Tessa. I felt horrible that they had lost their friend, but I was unsure if they would want me to express my condolences.

I walked to my locker and started to pull off my stockings when one of the girls came up to me, wrapping her arms around me. Shocked, I hugged her back, and more of the girls gathered around me. We all silently stood there for a few minutes. Most of the girls were crying while a couple mumbled about how everything would be okay. I wasn't sure anything would ever be okay again; I'd just watched five people die and was lucky to still be alive.

"I have to go with the police," I told the girls when it didn't seem like they were going to let me go. After a second, they all started breaking away from me one by one, giving me reassuring hugs.

"Call me if you want to talk," one of the girls, Elsa, said, handing me a business card with her personal information on it. I looked at it for a long second before nodding. I had never really been friends with any of them. Maybe that needed to change.

I went to my locker, pulling off my clothes before slipping on a pair of jean shorts, a black tank top, a large, oversized grey sweater, and a pair of black flip-flops. I grabbed my bag, shoved everything from my locker into it, and left the room without a backwards glance.

Link was waiting for me outside the dressing room door, his back against the wall, his head tilted back, looking at the ceiling. I had known Link since I'd started working at The Lion's Den. He was a nice guy—blond hair cut low to his head, tan skin, blue eyes, and a Southern drawl that made women fall to their knees. He used to flirt with me when I first started, but when I didn't return any of the banter, he laid off and became a friend. He's one of the only people who knows about my past and the things I've gone through.

"You didn't have to wait for me," I told him, pulling my bag across my body.

"I'm not letting you go through this alone." He pulled me into his side.

I could feel tears sting my eyes, and I fought them back. I wasn't going to cry until this was all over, when I could do it alone, hiding under my covers with my face stuffed into a pillow…like I always did.

"Thank you."

He gave me a squeeze, and I felt his lips at the top of my head.

"I DON'T UNDERSTAND why I have to leave the state," I told Link, putting another pair of shoes in my bag. I had no idea how long I would be gone, and Link made it sound like I wouldn't be able to come back to Vegas for a long while.

"Angel, I hate to remind you, but you're the only witness, and from what the cops said, the guy is a killer paid by the Mob to do hits on people."

I sighed, looking around my house. I hated that I was leaving, but I knew it was for the best. I'd been at the police station for over eight hours going over what had happened then sitting with a sketch artist. Somehow, the guy who had shot Tessa and those men had avoided every camera in the club. The cops had informed me that I needed to be extra cautious. I am the only witness, and they are concerned he might come after me. When Link found out what they'd said, he'd made a call to one of his friends from back home in Tennessee and asked if he would be willing to let me stay with him until the police caught the guy. The man, Kenton, had agreed, telling Link that I would be safe. I hate that I am leaving my home, but if my only options are either death or moving, the choice is begrudgingly clear.

"I hope they get the guy fast," I mumbled.

"Me too, but until then, you will be far away from here, where you're safe."

"Are you sure it's a good idea to have me stay with this guy? I mean, how well do you really know him?"

"We were best friends growing up. He's a good guy. You'll be safe with him."

I bit the inside of my cheek and nodded before going into the closet to get another suitcase. Might as well pack enough stuff to last me. Once I was all packed and ready to go, we got into Link's SUV and headed for the airport. I was nervous the whole way, feeling like something crazy was about to happen…

Today

"LADIES AND GENTLEMEN, we're about twenty minutes out from our arrival destination. The weather in Nashville is mostly clear and sunny. The temperature is eighty-five degrees. The pilot has now turned on the 'fasten seatbelt' sign. Flight crew, please prepare for landing," I hear through my sleep-ridden state and lift my head from the wall where I had rested it.

I wipe my mouth with the sleeve of my sweater before looking around to see that everyone is putting their belongings away. I make sure my seatbelt is secure before sitting back. My leg starts quickly bouncing up and down, and I rub the tattoo behind my ear, trying to think about something other than the plane landing.

Once we are on the ground, I wait until everyone is off the plane to make my way out into the terminal. I go to baggage claim and look around, but I have no clue what this guy looks like. All I know is that his name is Kenton and he is supposed to be picking me up.

I don't see anyone who looks like they're searching for someone, so I go to the conveyer belt and spot one of my bags as soon as I get there. I pull it off, stumbling back slightly from the weight as every guy here just watches me without offering to help. I look around again, wondering if I'm supposed to call someone to tell them that I landed. I pull my phone out, click it off airplane mode, and send a text to Link letting him know I have arrived. He sends me a message back letting me know that Kenton called and told him that he couldn't make it to pick me up and I should just catch a cab to his house. The door would be unlocked.

I shake my head, cursing under my breath, and almost miss one of my other bags going around the belt. Luckily, I catch it at the last second. I carry it over to my other bag and turn around just in time to see my last bag about to go through the tunnel. I run as fast as I can in my flip-flops and land partially on the conveyor belt, my bottom half being dragged along the floor as I grab the handle of my bag. I pull it back so hard that it flies over my head, causing me to land on my back with my hands over my head.

"You must be Autumn," I hear rumbled from above me.

I tilt my head back and look up at the man standing over me. He's upside down, but even from my awkward position, he is good-looking. His chuckle makes me grit my teeth though, and I stand up, putting my bag on its wheels before turning back to face him.

"You are?"

He raises a brow to me, shaking his head, looking me over from head to toe. My body heats immediately under his gaze. I take my sweater off, wrapping it around my waist and clearing my throat.

"You are?" I ask him again, getting annoyed that he's obviously finding this so funny if the smirk on his face is anything to go by.

"Kenton." He smiles. "Those bags yours?" He nods towards my other two bags.

"Yes." I blow some hair out of my face, looking into his blue eyes and wondering why the hell I feel so hot all of a sudden.

He looks away, going over to my bags while I take the time to look him over. He's tall—much taller than my five foot five. His hair touches the edge of the black T-shirt he has on. He needed a cut a while ago, but judging by the dark scruff along his jaw, I can tell that he doesn't care much about grooming. His shoulders are broad, tapering down to a lean waist. His thighs are thick, encased in a pair of dark jeans that have shredded around the bottom by his heels, and his wallet is imprinted in the back pocket like he wears them often.

I look at his ass as he leans over. I can't believe I'm checking a man out; I'm not one to be the slightest bit sexually interested in anyone. My eyes travel lower, looking at his feet, which are enclosed in a very large pair of black boots. I wonder absently if what they say is true about shoe size. I shake my head at my thoughts, dragging my bag with me towards him.

"I thought you couldn't make it," I tell him when I reach his side. My head tilts back to look up into his eyes.

"Yeah, change of plans," he mutters, looking at me.

I wait to see if he's going to say anything else. Apparently, he isn't going to, so I shake my head again and lower my face towards the ground.

"You tired?" His voice is dark and rich, and it does something crazy to my insides. I nod, lifting my head. "Let's roll. You can sleep when we reach the house."

I don't say anything else. Something is wrong with me; maybe I'm getting sick. I follow him out of the terminal into the car park. When we reach the parking lot, he stops and pulls a set of keys from his pocket. I hear the beep and look around, expecting him to be driving a large truck, a Hummer, or maybe even a tank. I never expected him to be driving a Dodge Viper, the black-on-black of the car only making it look hotter. I look at my bags, wondering how we will get them in the car.

"It'll be tight, but they'll fit," he mumbles, pulling my other two bags with him.

I can't help noticing the flex of his muscles as he gets my bags into the car or the fact even his fingers are attractive. It takes some maneuvering, but he does get my bags to fit. I sigh, sitting down on the warm leather once we're done.

"I'm just gonna drop you off at the house. I gotta head out for a bit, but you have free rein. Just make yourself at home. There's food in the fridge and fresh sheets on the bed in the guestroom."

"Thank you for doing this," I tell him, looking at his profile.

He is seriously good-looking, and the butterflies in my stomach are making me feel anxious about staying with him.

Acknowledgements

First, I want to thank God. My husband and sister lavish me with support and for that I cannot express my deep gratitude. I need to thank my fans, the love that you have for the men in my head is astounding. I can honestly say they would not come alive without the support that you provide throughout the writing process. To my family, both real and adopted – I love you all – thank you for supporting me. Hot Tree Editing, you have been amazing to work with. A special thank you to Kayla Robichaux: the men in my head will talk to you when they won't talk to me. To each and every blogger, reader and reviewer, I wouldn't be anything with out you, so thank you for taking a chance on an unknown author. TRSOR, you hard work on this blog tour has been incredible and completely successful. Jessica, Carrie, and Marta, you have been with me from the beginning, the advice and wholehearted dedication to my work is breathe-taking. Midian, the support and encouragement you provide in invaluable to me. To Natasha, your motivation is extraordinary. FBGM girls, our group of authors has become a second family, the ambition and determination that you show for all of your projects as well as mine is phenomenal – I love you, guys. To all of those that I didn't mention: don't think you are forgotten. You have a special place in my heart and know that I love you.

I love you all and cannot say thank you enough. So, thank you, one last time.

About the Author

Aurora Rose Reynolds is a navy brat whose husband served in the United States Navy. She has lived all over the country but now resides in New York City with her husband and pet fish. She's married to an alpha male that loves her as much as the men in her books love their women. He gives her over the top inspiration every day. In her free time, she reads, writes and enjoys going to the movies with her husband and cookie. She also enjoys taking mini weekend vacations to nowhere, or spends time at home with friends and family. Last but not least, she appreciates every day and admires its beauty.

For more information on books that are in the works or just to say hello, follow me on Facebook:
https://www.facebook.com/pages/Aurora-Rose-Reynolds/474845965932269

Or Goodreads
http://www.goodreads.com/author/show/7215619.Aurora_Rose_Reynolds

Or Twitter
@Auroraroser